how MAY I PLEASE *You*

BESTSELLING AUTHOR
WS GREER

First edition published by Kindle Direct Publishing 2024

Cover design by Isabel Lucero.

Interior Design and Formatting by Isabel Lucero.

author's note

Hi there! As the author of this book, I'd like to be the first to welcome you to *How May I Please You (The Darkest Kink #2)*. Before you turn the page, I want you to know how much I love the two characters you met in *The Darkest Kink*. Evan and Journey became my favorite characters to date while I was writing this book, and if you loved them in book one, you are going to fall even further in book two. The passion and insanity climb to new heights within these pages. Journey shocked the world with how she ended book one, and the shocks do not stop in this book.

Thank you so much for choosing to continue the story I started in November of 2023. This is the kind of ride you need to be strapped in for, so make sure you're prepared for what you're about to read. My author's note for *The Darkest Kink* said that it was the darkest book I'd ever written. *How May I Please You* is just as dark, but the twisted romance Evan and Journey share makes this book my best to date—in my opinion, of course. I truly hope you enjoy what you're about to read, and am eternally grateful for your support. But I do have to reiterate that you need to be prepared for the words following this note.

To my fellow kinksters who are also in the BDSM lifestyle in real life. I love and appreciate you all, and I'm so glad that you find comfort in my writing and trust me to represent the lifestyle accurately. However, I must emphasize the fact that the D/s dynamic in this novel is fictional. How Evan and Journey interact within the limits and rules of their dynamic is meant for them and them only. Just like in real life, every dynamic is different, and the rules in your dynamic will not be the same for Evan and Journey. For the sake of the story, they are an imperfect representation of the lifestyle. This is by design. Please keep this in mind when gauging their interactions.

While all characters and situations are completely fictional, some scenes may imitate reality and be harmful to those who have experienced violence, assault, or traumatic events. This is your warning. This novel contains depictions of knife play, bondage, impact play, breath play (choking/strangulation), stalking, murder, and blood play. It is intended for mature audiences only. Now turn the page ... and embrace your kinks.

you

one
~ journey ~

"DON'T MOVE. Not a single inch, Little Devil. Do you understand?"

"Yes, Sir," I reply, but it's not enough. You take a step back and lower your head until your eyes are level with mine. Your beautiful blue gaze makes my insides shiver with lust and love.

"Say it, Journey," you command.

"I won't move," I reply. "Not a single inch."

"Good girl."

Fuck. Hearing you call me your good girl—knowing that I've satisfied you is all I live for. I want nothing more than to make you proud, to make you love me, and I'll do whatever it takes. I always have. More than you know.

I watch you without a single muscle in my body twitching in the slightest. You step closer to me, so close that your musk swirls into my nose—your natural body odor mixed with masculine deodorant under your arms and cologne on your neck send me reeling. While I watch you, you focus on the task of securing my wrists to the Saint Andrew's Cross. My ankles are already bound to the large X, and now that you've attached my wrists, I couldn't move if I wanted to. My body is completely naked and exposed for you, open to your every desire and sadistic thought, and knowing your mind is swirling with ideas on how you want to use me makes me quiver. I've given you total control over me, Evan. You have my consent, and every second that passes feels like an eternity as I wait to see what you'll do with it.

You once told me that with my consent you would destroy me. Do it. Destroy me. Ravage me. Tear me into a million unrecognizable pieces and put me back together again. Only you know how. That's why I'll kill for you.

I submit to you. I belong to you. So whip me. Flog me. Break me. And I'll erupt, scream, and murder for you. I am yours, Evan. Full of love, lust, and lies. I'll do anything to keep you. Just tell me who. Tell me what. Your every wish is my command.

"Open your mouth," you demand.

I do not hesitate.

The moment my jaw drops open, you push a ball gag between my teeth and secure the straps behind my head. When you step back this time, I take time to marvel at your body. Your shirtless torso is a work of art as your stomach flexes with each breath. The beard on your razor-sharp jawline is well-maintained, as is your wavy brown hair. You stand a full six inches taller than me at six-foot-two, every bit the wide-shouldered monster I've been in love with for so long. You make me feel small, powerful, and protected at the same time, and the sight of you makes me weak in the knees and wet between my thighs.

I am bound to the cross with my mouth agape as

you stand before me, inspecting me from head to toe. I can see your arousal through your dark gray sweatpants and can't wait for the moment you unleash it for me. But our form of intimacy doesn't move that fast. This isn't just sex. This is a scene featuring the two of us, and I know you'll take your time on me. So I'm not surprised when you turn around to open the doors to the wooden wall locker next to you. You reach inside, ignoring a plethora of other toys to grab a red and black flogger—your second favorite toy. Your most cherished toy only comes out on special occasions, so tonight you'll work your magic with this one, and I wait with bated breath for you to begin.

"Do you remember the non-verbal cue in lieu of your safe word?" you ask, standing before me with the flogger dangling at your side, a thick vein running down your forearm before plunging beneath your index finger.

Unable to speak due to the ball gag, I nod. The non-verbal safe word is simple. I snap my fingers three times in succession and everything comes to a stop. It's easy, but I will never forget the safe word you gave me before we did our first scene together. You said it was fitting considering how we met, not to mention that I was and still am a detective with the Philadelphia Police Department. My safe word is arrest. Back then, you probably thought I would arrest you because of the body you buried behind your house, but I never would. I would also never think to use my safe word. Not only do I trust you, I want you to push my limits. I want you to hurt me. I may scream, but I would never blare a word to make you stop. We don't stop.

Just as a string of drool drops from my mouth, you step forward and cup it in your hand, catching my spit as you clutch my chin and press your mouth against the other side of the ball gag, kissing it gently. My desire to kiss you roars to life, but the gag is between us and it sets me on fire with want. How is it possible for you to be so impeccable? You are my perfect Dom, engulfing me entirely and consuming me completely.

You step away and I yearn for you to stay close, but you have work to do. Determination shines in your gorgeous eyes as you look at me. You're nearly in Dom Space already, and I'll help you get there. I am ready for you to begin. Paint your canvas, Sir.

"Take a deep breath, Little One," you command.

I inhale, and the *whack* of the flogger stings the flesh on my stomach like a lightning strike. I look down at my belly and find red already blooming just beneath my breasts. The pain whirls to life like a mini tornado atop my skin, but I embrace it. I fucking love it. I love you.

I can't explain the bliss I feel when the tails of the flogger crash against me again and again. Each strike jolts my body as you mark my flesh, sweat beading on your forehead quickly from the exertion. Every time you hit me, my stress melts away.

Smack.

I am no longer concerned about my job.

Smack.

I'm not thinking about money.

Smack.

I am no longer bogged down by everyday frustrations.

Smack.

The pain of my past shatters into a million translucent pieces.

Every bruise you leave behind makes me more whole. I am set free by giving myself over to you, allowing you to take the weight of my life into your hands and lighten the load with BDSM. This is why the lifestyle isn't for everyone. It takes a level of understanding that not everyone has, and it's so much deeper than most people know.

By the time you're finished, my entire torso is covered in red and pink streaks. A normal person would look at me and think I've been tortured. They would wonder how I could endure pain on this level, but they wouldn't know any better. We are not normal. We are elevated above those who think of sex and life one dimensionally. To us, this is perfection. This is bliss, and the soreness I feel tomorrow will put a smile on my face every time I move. I am a masochist, and the pain you inflict equals pleasure in so many more ways than one.

Panting, you drop the flogger and stand face to face with me, your breath hot against my mouth.

"You're so perfect, Little Devil," you tell me, rubbing my cheek with your knuckle while stroking your cock through your pants with your free hand. "How did I ever get so lucky to have you?"

You aren't the lucky one, Evan. I am.

You remove your hand from my face and place it against the newly damaged flesh on my stomach, making me suck in a breath.

"Does it hurt?" you ask.

I nod.

"Good. I love hurting you. It gives me everything I need in this life. To inflict pain on you is my greatest pleasure, Little Devil. The way you take it makes me so proud."

Tears fill my eyes knowing I've made you proud of me. You ... my Sir.

"Look how hard you've made me," you say, still

stroking your erection through your pants. "Look at my cock."

I look down just as you push the waistband of your sweats down to your thighs, revealing your cock in all its thick, veiny perfection. It throbs in your hand as you stroke it, and my heart flutters with need as you stop to catch my falling drool in the palm of your hand once again. This time, you use it to coat your dick, lubing it up until it shines with my saliva before stepping forward and positioning the tip at my entrance.

"I'm going to fuck you until I come inside you," you inform me, nearly growling with anticipation. "You've not missed your birth control, right?"

I shake my head.

"Good girl, because I'm about to fill you with so much cum it'll be dripping out of you for hours. Are you ready to be fucked into oblivion, Journey?"

I nod, more ready for your cock than I've ever been.

You don't waste another second. I feel your thickness stretch me out and fill me up and it takes my breath away. You move without thinking about it—like we were made for each other, existing within me thoughtlessly because I am where home is.

I stare into your eyes while you fuck me just the way you said you would. Each stroke is long, and every thrust is powerful. You become a god inside me, gripping my hips so hard I expect you to break the skin while you pound into me. All I can do is moan behind the ball gag, drool cascading out of my mouth and splashing onto your body.

My mind goes numb when you break me. I don't think about anything at all. I am free in this moment, and it all peaks in the blissful instant that you erupt inside of me. Your head goes back until you're looking up at the ceiling, and you let out an animalistic growl that echoes throughout the basement we've turned into our BDSM dungeon. Your muscles vibrate as your orgasm has its way with you, and when you've regained your composure, you pull out and step back, breathing hard.

I feel your cum begin to drip out of me as you rub my face again, locking eyes with me.

"You're so perfect," you remind me. "God, I'm so proud to own you, Little Devil. You make me so fucking proud."

While I pant like a dog, you pull your pants up and turn on your heel. I watch with my arms and legs still bound to the Saint Andrew's Cross as you walk to the corner of the basement and sit down in a leather, black armchair. That's where you stay while I am still bound, and I will wait patiently for you. Just because you've finished doesn't mean that our scene is over. Eventually, you'll come back and untie me, and we'll engage in whatever aftercare I choose. You'll rub my feet while we drink wine together, and I may even have you give me a shoulder massage or play with my hair while I relax. We'll get to all of that, but for now, I wait for you.

This is what we do. This is our dynamic. This is our way of life. We are dark and twisted, and if anyone ever tries to take this away from me, I will burn their entire life to the fucking ground.

I belong to you, Evan.

You ... my Sir.

chapter
two

WAKING up with the birds chirping outside, the sun squeezing its way through the closed blinds, and Journey at my side has become a routine part of my day that I can't function without. Especially the part where she is lying next to me, her head on my shoulder with her leg draped across mine. The warmth of her body comforts me more than any blanket ever could, and I can never help the smirk on my face as I look down at her and run the tip of my finger across her beautiful cheek. My Little Devil.

To say that Journey and I have grown together over the last six months would be an understatement. We're inseparable now. After everything we've been through, how could we not be? I met and fell in love with her just under a year ago, and in the beginning our life was a rollercoaster. She showed up on my doorstep looking for someone ... someone who was buried in my back-yard. Every cell in my body believed that Journey would be the end of me, but the tables somehow turned and she ended up being my true beginning.

Before Journey, I was an introvert who held everything in. I never said what I really wanted to, even when the voice in my head was screaming for me to lash out. After a life of keeping that beast caged, Journey was the one who unlocked the door and freed it. After I first met her, the voice went silent in my head because it was constantly spewing from my mouth. Journey unleashed my beast and allowed it to walk around freely, hunting who it despised all that time I kept it shackled. Now that some time has gone by, the voice returns in situations where I have to keep myself together. Not everyone is allowed to see me at my most depraved. Nonetheless, I no longer run from the beast. We are one.

Letting my true self takeover caused some issues for people who tried to ruin my life and derail my relationship with Journey. Those people—Detective Sam Winter and Cain Adams—are no longer among the living. It's their own fault, really. Regular people should know better than to fuck with people like Journey and I. Sometimes they have to learn the hard way. Too bad. So sad.

The investigations into those dead idiots ended six months ago. Journey and I have since moved in together, abandoning my little house in Strawberry Mansion so we could be under one roof in Elmwood. I didn't sell my old place. I couldn't. I grew up in that house, plus there is still something buried in the backyard. A trophy, of sorts. But leaving it to move in with Journey was still the right move. It's an upgrade for me, and it allows Journey and I to live the lifestyle both of us have always dreamed of. We get to immerse ourselves in our dynamic twenty-four-seven. While I still have my job with Lane Contracting, and Journey is still at the Seventh Precinct, when we come home I am her beast and she is my Little Devil. The tension of the past has died down, and now we get to just be ourselves in our dark and twisted world.

Without having to worry about what the police will find in my backyard, I no longer have to run off of job sites, which has led to a great relationship between myself and my boss, Trey Greene. He's the project manager of the concrete warehouse we're currently constructing, and as I climb out of bed and get dressed, I know he'll be happy to see me show up on time again. I've been stringing along multiple great weeks in a row, and my mood is immediately jovial once I'm cleaned up and standing in front of the coffee maker.

"Hi," Journey says as she enters the kitchen. Her black hair hangs down past her shoulders and sways as she walks with her head down, clipping her badge to her belt.

I place my new cup of coffee on the counter and face her. "Hey."

As soon as her badge is in place, Journey focuses solely on me and slides her hands under my arms to pull me into a tight hug. I can hear her breathing me in as I wrap my arms over her shoulders and squeeze. I breathe her in, too, sucking the smell of her hair into my nostrils and letting it fill me with ecstasy. This woman is my devil at night and my angel in the morning, and I love having her in my arms.

"How did you sleep?" I ask, knowing we don't have much time before both of us walk out the door to our respective jobs.

Journey flashes a smile that has the devil hidden behind it.

"So good," she says. "After a scene like that, I knew

I'd be out cold, especially once you started massaging my head. You know how that makes me feel."

Now I smile. "Either horny or sleepy."

She laughs as she says, "Well you'd already fucked the horny out of me, so sleepy was the only option left. It was totally worth it, though. As usual, you were perfect last night, Sir."

"It wasn't me who was perfect," I reply.

I kiss her on the forehead and take a step back to grab my coffee while Journey goes to the fridge for orange juice. She pours a glass and places the container back on the shelf before turning to face me. I take a moment to admire how beautiful she is with those dark brown eyes and that cute little chin dimple. The gaze in her eyes is still as intense as ever, but I love it. She's an intense person, someone not to be tamed by just anybody, and she's all mine.

"So, how are things going at the job site?" she asks before sipping her juice.

I lean back against the counter as steam rises from the coffee cup in my hand. "It's going well. This warehouse is massive and made entirely out of concrete, so we're doing tons of pouring here soon, but there's going to be some teaching today. Trey told me we're getting a couple of new people added to the crew."

"Oh, yeah? Do you know them or did they just get hired?"

"Trey knows them but I don't. They're from the Dover branch, but I guess they both moved and are transferring over. They're even still living out of hotels. Some guy named Stanley and a girl named Robin."

Journey drinks her orange juice down in big gulps, emptying the cup like she was dehydrated before placing it in the sink.

"That's cool," she says, nodding her head and staring into the living room as if someone is in there. "Awesome."

"You good?" I ask, following her gaze and finding nothing worth gawking at.

She whirls around with a wide smile. "Of course."

"Oh, okay. How about you? How's the new partner working out?"

"Ah, Detective Martin Summers. Ugh. He's fine, I guess. If I'm being honest, the guy is a little lazy."

"Yeah?"

"Absolutely," she replies, smiling despite her frustration with the new guy. "As much as I hate to say it, he's trash compared to Sam."

"Well, Sam was a go-getter who was looking to make big arrests, right?"

"I guess you could say something like that. He was definitely like that before ... he killed himself."

A smirk threatens to take control of my face, but I push it away and stare into the dark abyss of my coffee.

"Yeah," I say before clearing my throat. "Still such a tragic ending. Well, hopefully the new guy gets his shit together. You guys working on anything interesting?"

"Not really. Captain Saunders keeps throwing us little shit to look into, but it's never anything serious or time consuming."

"Well, hopefully something big comes along soon. You deserve it after everything you've been through."

"I agree." Journey looks down at her watch. "I should go. I don't need Saunders on my ass for being late."

I finish my coffee and set the cup on the counter so I can close the distance between Journey and me. We hug again and I kiss the top of her head.

"Have a good day, Little One. Make sure you text me later."

"Yes, Sir," she replies before pulling away. "Hopefully the day goes by fast because I desperately want a repeat of last night down in the basement."

I smile. "I can definitely arrange something ... if you're a good girl."

"I will be," she answers, grinning from ear to ear.

The next few minutes are spent grabbing things we both need to perform our jobs and heading to the garage together. We kiss while standing between my truck and her car, and then press the button to raise the door and bring in the sunlight. I let her pull out of the driveway first before backing out myself, and we drive away in two different directions. As much as I hate being apart from her, I know what the night holds for us, and I can't wait to come back to our dark and twisted world.

chapter
three

AS I DRIVE onto the job site, I immediately spot everyone in our crew gathered in the center of the massive concrete pad we poured last week. Trey is already standing in the middle wearing blue jeans, a green and white flannel, and brown overalls over his lanky frame. The usual suspects are mingling near him, and just as I pull up the parking brake on my truck, I notice two new people huddled off to the side the way people do when they're the only ones unfamiliar with everyone else.

"There he is, the man himself," Trey says as I approach the crew with a smile on my face. "Nice of you to join us, Mr. Godric. Right on time, as usual. Now that you're here, we can go ahead and get started."

I take a minute to greet the guys before falling into position next to the other craft leads on the project. We stand to the side of Trey as he begins to give our typical morning briefing to the rest of the crew.

"Alright, everybody, listen up," he begins, rubbing the hair on his chin. "Most of you have been on this warehouse project from the very beginning, so I shouldn't have to go over every little safety aspect of this job site. Clearly we're in phase one of construction. The pad we're standing on right now came out perfectly thanks to Mr. George Moore and his crew finishing it with the power trowels. Now we're onto the next task, which will be our biggest and probably the most important. Can anybody tell me what that is?"

"The walls," Larry says from amongst the crew, his large arms folded across his chest.

"Exactly. Thank you, Larry," Trey replies, nodding. "These are not your typical walls, folks. These walls are made of concrete, and they will have a ton of rebar in them—and no, I don't mean that literally, but there will be enough sticks in the grid to make your forearms massive from laying them down. There are fourteen walls that have to be poured—four on each side and three on each end. It's going to be time-consuming. It's going to be hot. It's going to be laborious, but we're being paid handsomely and I'd like to keep this project on schedule, so you're allowed to complain as long as you do it while you're working. George, you and your crew are on rebar. Jimmy, your guys have stub-ups, and Evan, you've got forms.

"Now, before we get to it, I'd like to introduce the two newest members of our illustrious crew. Everyone, this is Stanley Ronan and Robin Heart. Stanley is a heavy equipment operator, and Miss Heart is a carpenter. The two of them transferred from the Dover branch and were assigned to the best construction team in PA. Everybody be sure to welcome them to the team as we get going. Stanley, you're with George. Robin, you're with Evan's crew. Alright, people. Let's work."

The group disassembles, breaking up into our respective crafts, and I take the opportunity to approach the new woman on the crew. She forces a nervous smile as I extend my hand.

"Good morning, Robin. I'm Evan," I say, shaking her hand before leading her and the rest of the crew toward a large stack of uncut plyform. "Welcome to Philly. Looks like we'll be working together. I take it you've built forms before?"

Robin, a short redhead with barely-there freckles scattered across her nose, nods her head.

"Absolutely. I just need to get a look at the drawings," she says. "Or you can just tell me what to cut or put together. I'm flexible."

Flexible enough to fit inside a footlocker? Or would I need to break your bones to make you fit? Ah, good times.

"That's good to hear," I reply, ignoring the inner dialogue of my true nature. "I'm going to put you with Shawn. He's forming up the pieces we cut yesterday to get a head start, and then they'll be placing and staking them. You get that, Shawn?"

Shawn looks over from the corner of the pad where we'll lay the first set of forms. "All good, Evan."

"Cool. So, just get with Shawn and you'll be all set," I say to Robin. "Let me know if you have any questions."

"Awesome. Thanks, Evan," Robin replies before shaking my hand again and sauntering away to link up with Shawn's three-man team.

Is she swaying her ass when she walks? Maybe she wants a dance with the devil, but something tells me she wouldn't be prepared to bleed for me. Only my Little Devil has what it takes.

I smile to myself as Robin walks away, and I pull my phone from my pocket. Thoughts of Journey fill me with a need to talk to her before starting work.

. . .

Hey, Little One. Just wanted you to know I'm about to get started with work. I hope your day goes well. I love and miss you.

IT ONLY TAKES Journey a few seconds to reply.

I hope your day goes well, too, Sir. Have you met the new people yet?

Yeah. Stanley and Robin. They're quiet so far but we'll see how things go.

Cool. Either of them on your crew?

Yeah, Robin's with us. I put her with Shawn. I hope she knows her shit.

I'm sure she does. Okay, I have to go. Duty calls. Have a great day, Sir. Never forget that I love you.

I love you, Little Devil. Call me later.

Absolutely. Can't wait.

four
~ journey ~

I'M sure this is a bad idea, and I expect you'd probably be upset with me for it, but when I set my phone down after texting you, it's not on my desk at the precinct, it's in the cupholder of my car. I haven't gone to work yet because ever since you told me you had a new woman joining your crew for this project, I haven't stopped thinking about it. As a result, instead of heading into the office, I followed you to your job site and parked in the back corner of an adjacent lot. I'm sorry, Sir, but I had to see, and now that I have, I have no regrets.

Things between you and I have been so great that I'd be a fool to sit back and let another woman smile in your face and shake your hand. Especially one with red hair and a little button nose. I could tell when you approached her that she wanted you. I could see it in her eyes through my binoculars—it was like she was meeting her favorite rock star. Her demeanor lit up, and the moment her hand reached out to take yours she practically melted in your grasp. You may not have seen it, Evan, but I did. I'm a woman, and women always know. Our intuition is never wrong.

I know you're just doing your job, Sir. I don't blame you. I blame her. You simply wanted to be the best craft lead that Lane Contracting of PA has ever seen, and here comes this little bitch from Lane Contracting of Delaware to try and seduce you. The fucking audacity she must have to touch your skin before sashaying away like that, shaking her ass in the hope that you would watch her go. You didn't, which made me so fucking happy, but the fact that she tried it is enough for me. It's the principle, Sir.

Even now, as she squats next to your coworker Shawn, she keeps glancing over at you. Shawn is trying to get her to help them set those forms, but she is too busy looking at you. She wants you. She craves what is mine, but you and I are meant to be together. We belong together—I to you and you to me—and I won't fucking stand for this. I refuse to allow disrespect of our union. No fucking way.

Don't worry, Sir, I won't do anything to jeopardize your career. It's not your fault that your new worker is an ugly fucking slut, and I don't mean a slut in the same way that I'm a slut. The contrast is that she's just a slut, and I am *your* slut. Big difference. I belong to you and she belongs to no one.

So, she can go on about her day, stealing glances at you every free second she gets, and I'll wait patiently. I know how long the day will be for you and your crew, my beloved, and I think I'll have a little introductory meeting of my own. You won't have to worry about teaching anyone anything, or stress about how well she gets along with the guys you've been working with for years. I'll relieve you of that burden.

Don't worry about a thing, Sir, I'll take care of this for you. I'll make you proud and no one will ever suspect you at all. I'll take the weight off your shoulders and place it squarely on mine. For us. Today is little Robin's first day ... and her last.

sir

chapter
five

Hey, I'm home. You on your way?

WHEN I SIT down on the couch after a long day of overseeing the cutting of forms and staking them in the dirt, I'm relieved that I don't smell like ass and sweat anymore. I'm hot from the shower I just took, but I feel so much better. The beer in my hand is cold and already starting to sweat, but the first sip tastes like heaven on my lips. I sip it again before lifting my phone to check for a response from Journey, but there is none. It's not uncommon for her to leave the precinct late, but it is uncommon for her to not let me know something has come up and that she'll be home later than usual.

It's a dangerous game to play with me, Little One. If I have to track you down, there will be severe consequences both for you and the person who kept you from me.

With a frown, I push my frustration into the pit of my stomach and take another sip of beer, but a sip becomes a gulp, and the gulps occur enough times to finish off two bottles before I hear the sound of keys rattling at the front door. I set my second empty bottle down just as Journey pushes the door open and steps inside.

"Hey," I say, trying to avoid a bad mood after not getting a response over an hour ago.

Journey closes the door behind her and walks over to me, her arms immediately pulling me in close. As much as I want to shake her until she tells me what took so long, the feeling of her body close to mine takes over, easing away the stress I felt before she arrived. I guess that's what love does. Even when I want to be mad at her, love makes me relieved that she's safe and back in my arms where she belongs.

I take my time breathing in her scent. The skin on her forehead is hot when I kiss it and damp from sweat like she has been running. When I pull away to get a good look at her, I can tell her makeup is a little off as well. It's not smudged, but it has barely visible streaks in it.

"Are you okay?" I ask, curiosity and concern joining forces in my gut.

"I'm fine," Journey answers, running a finger across her forehead that I notice is slick with sweat when she puts her hand down at her side. "Just had a really long day. Work got tricky there at the end."

"Clearly," I reply. "I texted you over an hour ago and you didn't respond."

Journey exhales loudly as she untucks her shirt from her pants and starts to unfasten the buttons, revealing the white under-shirt underneath. She pulls it off her shoulders and tosses it onto the couch. The second it hits the cushion, I notice a red stain just under the armpit.

"Is that blood on your shirt?" I ask.

Journey's head snaps over, surprise taking hold of the expression on her face.

"What's going on, Journey?" I inquire, hoping to get answers before my temper flares up.

"Oh, it was no big deal," she says, regaining control of her face and erasing any trace of concern. "Summers and I got called in to assist with an arrest and it got a little ugly. The guy kept resisting and we ended up having to restrain him. I guess a little of his blood got on me."

My eyebrows raise. "Oh. So it was *that* kind of restraint."

Journey smiles when she replies, "Well, he may have kicked me by accident while he was fighting us, and I *may* have hit him back. Come on, you know you would've done the same thing."

I smirk as I pull her in for another hug. "My Little Devil. Why am I not even surprised?"

After everything Journey and I have been through, it doesn't shock me that she took out her anger on some asshole resisting arrest. She and I have literally murdered people together, even staging one to look like a suicide. Violence doesn't make me uncomfortable, but the fact that she didn't respond to me does.

"Listen," I begin as I take a step back and lock eyes with her so she knows I'm serious. "I understand that your work can get in the way of you coming home. I'm not upset about you being later than usual, Little One, but when I text you, you respond. When you don't, I get worried, and worry mixed with alcohol can combine to make a very combustible cocktail for me, one that could see me running out of this house ready to set the globe ablaze to find you. Don't tempt me to burn the world down, Little Devil, because I will gladly torch it all for you. You belong to me, and when I text, you answer. This is a rule from now on. No exceptions. Do you understand?"

Journey stares at me for a moment, a thousand words playing in her mind I'm sure. Her brown eyes lock on me as she grins and places a hand on the waist-band of my pants.

"I apologize, Sir," she says. "You're right. You texted as things were heating up at work and by the time it was all over, I didn't even realize that I'd forgotten to reply to you. I made a mistake and I'm sorry. I won't let it happen again."

With a loud exhale to calm myself down, I nod. "Good. Now go get cleaned up so we can have dinner."

"Yes, Sir," she says before picking up the shirt from the couch and walking down the hall toward the bedroom.

Over the next half-hour, I make sure to unwind. I slowly drink another beer and watch some TV while the sound of splashing water acts as background noise. I hear Journey get out of the shower and walk around before getting a text from her. When I look at my phone, a wicked grin takes over my entire face.

I'm so sorry for what happened earlier, Sir. It kills me to know I've upset you. Can you please allow me to make it up to you?

. . .

I LICK my lips as I type out my response and press send.

> We hadn't established it as a rule, Little One, so there's no cause for punishment. However, what did you have in mind?

JOURNEY RESPONDS IMMEDIATELY.

> Sir, please come to the basement.

GRINNING, I bite my bottom lip as I get up from my chair and make my way down the hall. Knowing Journey the way I do, I'm sure she has something exquisite planned. Plus, she's in the basement, which we filled with BDSM toys and furniture for us to use together. She wouldn't be down there without wanting to go all-out.

Just as I reach the bottom of the stairs, the sight of Journey begins to come into view with each descending step. First I see her knees, then her bellybutton, then her perfect, bare breasts, and finally her flawless face. Her hair is tied into a ponytail that hangs behind her back, and her palms are on her knees as she kneels for me, eyes locked on mine. Journey is completely naked without a hint of a smile on her face.

I come to a stop directly in front of her, and she licks her lips as she looks up at me.

"Sir," she says in a sexy tone that floods my cock with blood. "How may I please you?"

chapter
six

I BITE my lip so hard I expect the taste of blood, and it wouldn't even matter. All I care about right now is the sight of the gorgeous woman below me, kneeling in anticipation of how I'll dominate her. She's a vision, a delectable, perfect, seductive vision that I can't wait to get my hands on.

When Journey asks how she can please me, my mind explodes with vivid, devious answers. Thoughts of all the tortuous ways I can satisfy both of us make my knees tremble. Even after irking my nerves earlier, I want this woman more than I can put into words, and it's so much deeper than just wanting to fuck her. I want to torment her with foreplay before driving her to the brink of insanity with toys. I want her rabid for me. By the time I'm ready to fuck her, she has to feel more than just desire for my cock. She has to need it, to crave it, to be consumed entirely by her desperation to have me inside of her. I want her to choose death rather than accept going without me stretching her insides. That's the answer to how she can please me. Her craving is what I desire most.

"Look at you," I finally say once I'm grounded again, my depravity stepping to the forefront of my mind and making me feel like a god. "You're my perfect little slut, aren't you?"

Journey's teeth scrape against her bottom lip as she nods. "Yes, Sir."

"You know you upset me earlier, and now you want to make it up to me by submitting," I state.

She nods again. "More than anything."

"So you'd really be upset if I denied you, wouldn't you?"

Journey's eyes widen. "Yes, Sir," she answers, and I can already hear the agony in her voice.

Perfect.

"Is that what you think I should do after you didn't respond to me today? Should I not respond to you now?"

The lustful look on Journey's face starts to slowly melt like ice on the hot concrete.

"Sir, please forgive me," she pleads.

I inhale deeply, my cock throbbing from the sound of her voice. "Fuck, I love it when you beg me. Do it again."

She licks her lips. "Please. *Please* forgive me. I will do anything for you. Just name it, Sir, and it is yours. I am yours. Please let me make it up to you."

"No," I snip, falling deeper and deeper into my dominance. "Not until you prove your commitment to me. I'm going to take full control of you, Journey. You will do exactly as I say when I say it. You will prove that you can follow my instructions, and if you miss a single step, I'll tie you up and leave you a soaking wet mess alone in the dark. I don't care if your pussy leaves a river on the floor. I won't fuck you until you've proven yourself to me. Do you understand?"

She exhales without even taking a deep breath, her eagerness showing itself. "Yes, Sir. I'm yours to do as you please. Use me however you see fit. You have my consent, Sir. Always. Forever."

"You're fucking right you're mine, now stop talking and don't move," I growl before walking over to the bed on the far wall and picking up the leash and collar draped across the end of it.

When I return to Journey, who hasn't budged, I place the collar around her neck as tightly as I can without cutting off her air supply before grabbing the end of the leash and giving it a tug. Journey's body shifts a bit, but I can tell she's breathing fine.

"Now, crawl for me, Little Devil. Follow your leader," I command as I turn around and begin taking slow steps back to the bed.

Journey turns herself around without standing and follows me on all fours. She crawls silently like a good girl is supposed to before stopping at the foot of the bed and returning to a kneeling position to await my next instructions.

When she looks up at me, I take a moment to let it all sink in. I know how much it must take for anyone to trust another person with this much responsibility. Being a submissive is so much harder than being a Dom because allowing someone to take this level of control over your most sensitive parts has to be terrifying. Knowing that she trusts me to own her and give her everything she craves in this room is the thing that gives me the most pride. Her trust and consent is the greatest gift she could ever give me, and I will not squander it. I will be every bit as brutal as she needs me to be.

While she kneels, I squat down until we're eye level, choking up on the leash until her face leans toward mine. "Are you ready to prove yourself to me, Little Devil?"

She nods, struggling to swallow with the leash tight around her neck. "Yes, Sir."

"Good. We're going to test your limits today. What is your safe word?"

"Arrest."

"Good girl. Now climb onto the bed and stay on all fours."

I take a step back to allow Journey the room she needs to get on the bed, but I keep the leash tight in my grip. Once she's in position, I walk to the back of the bed and tie it around one of the four bed posts, leaving barely enough slack for her to move at all. She can shift her body backwards, but if she moves forward—away from me—her restraint will keep her in place, choking her until she comes back to me.

The sight of Journey on all fours sends a tsunami of blood roaring to my cock. My erection makes itself known through my pants as I pull off my shirt and stand behind her, the man in me ready to fuck, the Dom in me ready to own her. Instead of grabbing my cock and pushing it inside, I drop to my knees and engulf Journey with my mouth. She squeals on the bed as my tongue glides across her ass before dropping down to her pussy and getting to work. She tastes so fucking good I never want to eat food again. I only want this taste on my tongue for the rest of my life, and I lick her pussy so that she knows it. I eat her disrespectfully, like she's not the woman I love but a woman I've only felt hot, soul-consuming lust for. My tongue becomes a machine that can't stop until she's teetering on the edge of an orgasm, then I back away and smack her ass once for good measure.

"You are not allowed to come," I tell her, squeezing her ass but keeping my hands away from her pussy so that she doesn't fall over the edge by accident. Once the threat of orgasm has receded, I run my fingers between her wet pussy lips, coating them. "My god, you're such a slut for me aren't you? We both know you are, but being soaking wet for me isn't enough to prove your commitment. No, tonight we're going a step further. I highly suggest you don't let your brain go numb to the point that you forget your safe word. Tonight, you just might need it. Now, keep that ass up in the air for me."

Journey scoots back to relieve tension on the leash before poking her ass up higher. I smack it hard and spit on her, my saliva landing perfectly between her cheeks.

"Good girl. Higher," I demand, and my cock throbs with desire when I am obeyed. "That's it, Little Devil. Stay just like that."

As my spit begins to slowly slide down Journey's ass, I step away just long enough to open a drawer in the center of the room and grab a small butt plug with a metal loop on the end, and a bottle of lube. I know that anal is one of Journey's soft limits, and I intend to push her to it. As a soft limit, she has identified this as something she's interested in but unsure of, and this is why we have safe words. If she doesn't like it, she can use her safe word and I won't hesitate to stop with no questions asked. Her soft limit will become her hard limit, and we will never go near it again. If she doesn't say her word, tonight will be the first time she uses a plug for me.

I return to the bed and set the lube next to her. "Keep that ass up, Journey. I won't repeat myself."

Journey lifts her ass as much as she can just as I spit

on her once again. As I grab the lube and begin slathering it on the plug, I make sure to tell Journey what I'm about to do. When trying something new, I don't want to catch her off guard.

"Do you trust me, Journey?" I ask

"Yes, Sir," she replies. "With my life."

"Good. I want your trust to be bigger than your fear. You have to trust that I would never hurt you more than you desire, and that I will always stop if you demand it. You are in control, Little Devil. I'm about to push you to your soft limit by inserting a butt plug. When I say, I want you to take a deep breath, and when you do it, I need your trust to overcome your anxiety— trust that I won't hurt you, and trust that I will stop for you. Do you understand?"

Journey doesn't hesitate. "Yes, Sir. I'm ready."

"Good girl. Now, take a deep breath."

When I hear her suck in air, I slowly push the lubed butt plug inside of her. It's a tight fit for sure, but I've lubed the toy and her hole so much that it slides in without much of a fight. I watch in satisfaction as the toy settles inside of her, fitting snugly just as it should.

"You're such a fucking good girl, Little Devil," I say, smiling like a kid with a new toy. "Look at you. Fuck, I love you so much. You make me so goddamn proud. Tell me how it feels to have a plug in your ass."

"It's ... new. It's tight, but ... I'm good, Sir. I ... think I like it."

"I knew you would, Baby Girl. I'm so proud of you ... but that's not all. I need you to scoot back all the way to the edge of the bed to relieve the tension on the leash, and put your face down on the mattress with your hands behind your back. Do it now."

Journey does as she's told while I go back to the

drawer and grab a pair of handcuffs with a small chain attached to each one. I reposition myself behind Journey, and connect the ends of each chain to the loop on the butt plug, then secure the cuffs around Journey's wrists. If she moves her hands at all, it will tug the plug, and just seeing her in this compromising position sends me into a frenzy. I can barely wait another second to be inside of her.

"Oh my god," she says to herself, arching her back to get more comfortable.

"You're doing so good, Little One," I say as I step away one last time. "Now for the grand finale."

I pull a magic wand vibrator from the drawer and use it to give Journey immediate relief from the new sensation in her ass. Flicking the switch, the vibrator hums to life and I press it against her clit.

"Holy shit," she exclaims, and I know from the sound that she isn't in pain. Journey is experiencing nothing but bliss and I fucking love it.

"Yeah? Tell me how it feels," I say as I push my pants down and step out of them using my free hand.

"Fuck, Sir, it's so good," she answers.

"Good. Now tell me how *this* feels." I step forward until my shins are against the mattress and push my cock all the way into Journey's dripping pussy.

She sucks in a deep breath and tries to move forward, but the leash snags around her neck. She can't run from me now. She has no choice but to take what I'm giving her. If she doesn't like it, she can say the safe word. Otherwise, I will fuck her into submission so that she never forgets to obey me again.

"You can't scoot away," I say as I slowly begin fucking her with the vibrator pressed against her clit. "You can't use your hands to climb off the bed." My strokes are long, going from the tip of my cock until I'm balls deep, giving her every single inch. "All you can do is take it, Little Devil. Your only option is to give in to me, belong to me, submit to me. I own you, don't I?"

I speed up my strokes.

"Oh my fucking god," Journey says, unable to control her words. "Fuck ... yes ... you own me, Sir ... fuck."

"That's my good girl. Take it."

I begin pounding Journey with my cock relentlessly. She has had time to get used to the plug, so I won't hold back any longer. I can't. My cock aches for a release and I have to keep going until I have nothing left to give. I fuck her like a complete savage, pounding her pussy violently and making the entire bed rock against the concrete walls. Her screams only urge me on, telling me that this is what she needs. She doesn't need to be coddled or made love to. My Little Devil needs to be fucked hard, she needs my dick to put her in her place and I will not fail. This won't end until she knows who she belongs to.

Sweat beads on my forehead and runs down my face as I keep going, my breathing labored. I slap Journey on the ass and revel in the sound of her scream, but I don't slow down. An orgasm slowly works its way up my body, starting in my feet before it reaches my torso and threatens to ignite like dynamite, but before I come, I need Journey to.

Without skipping a beat, I remove the vibrator from Journey's pussy and turn it down to the lowest setting, then I place it against the loop on the butt plug.

"Oh fuck!" Journey shrieks, but she can't move. She presses her face against the mattress while I keep the wand in place, vibrating the plug and filling her body and mind with all new sensations. Her voice is muffled by the bed when she yells, "My god! Oh my fucking god. What the ... fuck ... fuck ... fuck, I'm going to come!"

"Yes," I bark as my own orgasm is finally allowed its freedom.

I let go and stroke hard and deep until my orgasm detonates at the same time as Journey's. The two of us shatter into a million pieces, our bodies convulsing and folding us in half as we are wrecked with pleasure. I come so hard that stars take shape in the corner of my vision and I have no choice but to stop moving and let it have its way with me.

Journey, on the other hand, goes limp until her body slides downward, unable to control herself any longer. I have to move out of the way and let her body slide off the bed and stop at my feet, barely able to keep herself upright as she quivers. She leans against the bed with her face glued to the covers while I lower myself onto the floor so that I don't collapse from over-exertion.

That's how we stay. Me, on the floor, panting up to the ceiling with my eyes closed—Journey, sitting limp against the bed with her hands cuffed behind her back and a plug in her ass. Neither of us move. Neither of us can. Neither of us want to.

Exactly as it should be.

chapter
seven

"HERE YOU GO," I say, bringing the wine glass to Journey's lips. When she tries to take the glass from me, I pull it away. "No, it's okay. You don't have to do anything, baby. I got you."

Journey takes a sip of the red wine and nods when she's done, signaling for me to place the glass back on the end table until she's ready to use it again. Once both of my hands are free, I place them on her shoulders and go back to massaging her. This is how the rest of the night will go because my Little Devil deserves it. After allowing me to explore her soft limit and push her through it, I know how dedicated she is to me—not that her being late coming home from work would *actually* make me question her loyalty. I know better than to think that this woman is anything other than one hundred percent mine.

And if I find out otherwise, someone will bleed.

After the scene we had tonight, both of us were exhausted. We laid on the floor next to each other for a few minutes, letting out heaving breaths until I was finally strong enough to lift myself up and take care of my submissive. I helped Journey to her feet and removed the cuffs from both her hands and the plug she was still wearing, before having her bend over the bed and slowly pulling out the plug. I made sure to take my time because anyone who has experienced anal penetration knows that the exit is just as painful as the entrance. I saw the relief on her face once she was free of the toy, and it made me so proud to know that she went through it to push herself, but also for my satisfaction.

Once we got ourselves cleaned up with a joint shower, where I washed her body with her loofa and made sure every inch of her was clean before cleaning myself, we got out together and I applied her lotion for her. I covered each of her limbs with the smell of lavender and vanilla, and brushed her hair while she sipped red wine in front of me, then we moved to the bed, where I sat with my back against the headboard and pulled Journey between my legs to start her massage. She's my perfect submissive, and she deserves the absolute best from me.

"How do you feel?" I ask, pressing my fingers into her neck. Her head falls forward as she lets out a beautiful little moan.

"I'm ... perfect," she replies before moaning again.

I chuckle. "I don't mean the massage. I mean your body. You pushed yourself tonight. I just want to make sure you're good, Little One."

Journey takes a moment to enjoy my fingers climbing up the back of her neck before saying, "I'm okay. A little sore, but that's to be expected after the first time, right?"

"Yeah, that's probably true for most things in this lifestyle, whether it's the first time or not. I probably should've started with just my fingers, but the beast in me wanted to push you, and you did so great. You made me so proud. And if all you feel is a little soreness, then I think we did it right."

"Thank you, Sir," you reply gleefully. "You most definitely did it right. You do everything right."

"I don't know about all of that, but when it comes to *this*, I hope I'm always doing it right. Nothing matters to me more than caring for you. You belong to me. It's my job to take care of what I own."

"I *absolutely* belong to you, Sir. I wouldn't have it any other way."

"Me either, Little Devil. Me either."

As the wine bottle empties and the night comes to a close, I slide my hands down Journey's arms until I come to a stop at her knuckles. I rub her hands gently while kissing the back of her neck, trying my best to make her feel good in more places than one. When I squeeze one of her hands, she winces quietly and pulls her hand away before she can stop herself.

"Oh," I say, realizing I've hurt her, the complete opposite of what I'm trying to do. "I'm sorry. Are you okay?"

I feel the moment Journey's body tenses. After being relaxed for a while, it's pretty obvious when her muscles tighten and her neck goes rigid. Even from behind I can tell she's worried about something.

She clears her throat and nods, but doesn't turn around to face me.

"Yeah, my hand is just a little dinged up," she replies.

I frown as my chest fills with concern and all of my attention goes to her hand, lifting it up to do my own inspection. With a closer look, I can see the beginning stages of bruising on the knuckles of her right hand.

When I lift the left hand, there are scratches on it like she encountered a cat who wasn't in the mood for company.

"This is from the scene? There's no way this is from tonight, right?" I ask, truly baffled by the sight of the marks and bruises on her skin. My eyes widen as I realize the scratches aren't confined to one hand, and they don't stop at her wrist. Journey has barely-visible scratches running all the way up both arms.

She clears her throat again. "No, it's not from the scene. It's from ... work."

"From work?" I say. "The guy you had to apprehend?"

"Yeah, that's right," she answers quickly like the memory just came back to her. "Yeah, that guy was really giving us problems. I didn't even realize he'd done all of this."

"Yeah, I didn't realize it was that bad when you described it earlier. Your knuckles are bruised, babe. How many times did you have to punch the guy?"

"Umm, a few," she says with a playful laugh. "I may have lost my cool a little bit, but he eventually got the message and stopped fighting me ... I mean us. Once he realized there was nothing he could do about it, he stopped resisting and we got him cuffed. Some people resist, but it never matters. In the end, I get what I want."

"Yeah, I'd say you do," I joke, but I still feel a tingle of apprehension under my skin. "Did anybody else get hurt?"

"The arresting officer got a few bumps and bruises from the scuffle they had before we joined in. Detective Summers got a little messy, too, but I'm sure he'll be in the office tomorrow being annoying like he always is.

Overall, everyone was fine, including the perp who was still able to walk when it was all said and done. I'm fine, Sir. No need to worry."

"Are you sure?" I ask, my concern slowly contorting into anger. Someone put these marks on my property, and if that person ever steps into the sunlight again, I will be there to knock them into permanent darkness.

"I'm sure," Journey assures me, finally turning to face me. She shifts her body completely until we're chest to chest and places a bruised hand on my cheek. "I know what you're thinking, and you don't have to. It has been handled. The guy is behind bars and it's over. No need to dwell on it or make any plans to visit anyone's house in the middle of the night. It's over, Sir, and I'm fine. I don't want to upset you, so just let this one go. Okay?"

No, it's not fucking okay. Someone deserves to die for this. Violently. Gruesomely. Painfully. Slowly.

Thoughts of running down an unknown man with my truck as he exits the precinct play in my mind like a daydream.

After I run him over, I'll tie his feet to the back of my truck and drive down the fucking highway with my foot stomping the gas, until there is nothing left but bits and pieces.

I want to lash out. I want to go fucking hunting, but to appease Journey, I do as she asks and let it go.

"Okay, Little One," I say, grinding my teeth.

"Thank you," she says before pulling me into a kiss. "Now let's get some rest and hope that I don't have to put my hands on anybody tomorrow."

I smile when she does because my love has somehow become a mirror. When she smiles, I smile. When she hurts, I hurt. When she hates someone, I want them dead. The love we share has us connected emotionally, and while it's completely new to me, I'm obsessed with it.

She is every dark and disturbed thing I never knew I always wanted, and when we lay down, I wrap my arm around her and pull her close to me. Even though the drama of her day has already happened, I feel better knowing I'm shielding her with my body and protecting her now. I can't be with her twenty-four-seven, and I know she can handle herself, but the next time I hear that someone has put their hands on her, the strongest bars in the world won't be able to protect them from me.

chapter
eight

"GOOD MORNING, LITTLE ONE."

"Good morning, Sir," Journey replies as she steps into the kitchen with her nose in the air, making a show out of sniffing while wearing a cute little grin on her face. "Something smells good in here."

"I made you breakfast," I say at the exact moment that I spin around and show her the plate of food in my hand containing bacon, eggs, avocado toast, and hashbrown.

"Aww, Evan you didn't have to," she tells me, but I can see the gratitude etched in her face.

"Right, but I wanted to. You made me so proud last night. I just wanted to do a little something for you. No big deal. Come on, it's already getting late so let's hurry up and eat before we have to go."

Journey finishes the final buttons on her shirt before leaning in to kiss me and taking the plate. As she goes into the dining area to sit down, I grab my plate and two cups of orange juice for us and follow her lead.

We eat without saying much. Admittedly, my mind

is on how fucking perfect last night was. Memories of how incredible Journey looked with her ass in the air and her handcuffs chained to her butt plug pop in and out of my mind in vivid, graphic detail, and I can barely think of anything else. After work tonight, I wouldn't mind seeing what other boundaries I can push her to.

By the time I'm almost finished scarfing down my food, I find myself glancing at her hands as she lifts the fork to her mouth. Her arms are covered by the sleeves of her shirt, but I can still see the scratches and bruises on both of her hands. My body warms with the thought of what she must have gone through to get those marks on her and it makes me furious. I don't let it show on my face, but I have half a mind to make a call to the precinct and get info on the guy she arrested last night. I wonder if he's getting out on bail. If so, when? I told Journey I would let it go, but that's the last thing I want to do. I don't want to let go. I want to grab on tight enough to cut off the oxygen to his brain for what he did to my Journey.

How easy it would be to bury another body beside Sierra.

As much as it pains me, I push my boiling hot anger down into my stomach as we finish eating and start to get up from the table. I take both plates to the kitchen so that Journey doesn't have to lift a finger, and wash them off followed by the cups. I place everything in the dishwasher and start a pot of coffee we can both pour from before we head out, and just as the coffee finishes brewing, my phone rings in my pocket.

I frown at my screen as I see Trey's name written across it, because I'm about to be on my way to the job site and I'll actually show up ten or fifteen minutes early rather than late. So why would he be calling me right before we go in?

I place the phone on speaker and set it down on the counter so I can pour Journey's coffee for her before pouring my own. I grab her travel mug just before I say, "Hey, what's up, Trey? Not used to hearing from you this early. You calling in sick?"

Trey chuckles, and even from just that short sound I can tell something is wrong.

"I wish I was calling in sick, but something just came up that has me confused," he says, his voice quickly turning serious.

"Yeah? What's up?" I ask as I hand Journey her travel mug and grab mine.

"Umm ... how did things go yesterday with the new girl?" Trey asks.

I shrug even though he can't see me. "It was fine, I guess. Nothing spectacular and nothing detrimental to the crew. Why?"

"Well, the reason I ask is because ... she just quit."

My eyes widen. I turn to Journey, expecting her to be just as surprised as I am, but she has her back to me as she puts the top onto her travel mug.

"She quit? When?" I inquire.

"Just now," Trey answers. "I'm up here at the main office getting ready to head to the job site, and Robin comes in wearing a big ass hat and oversized sunglasses like a fucking movie star diva who doesn't want the paparazzi snapping her pictures."

"What the fuck?"

"I know, right? But it gets weirder. She comes in and tells me she has to quit, and when I ask why, she says things just aren't going to work out. Something about a toxic environment."

"A toxic environment? Are you fucking kidding me?"

She has no idea how toxic it could've been. What would be more toxic than being strangled to death?

"That's what I wanted to say, because I didn't see anything going on yesterday that I thought would be a cause for concern. So I asked her to provide me with some details so I could figure out what to do and how we could resolve the issue, and she started stuttering and not saying anything that made sense. She couldn't come up with anything at all, so I told her I couldn't do anything to fix it if she wouldn't tell me what happened. She replies, 'You're right, there's nothing you can do to fix this. I just have to leave. I'm sorry, Trey,' and starts to walk out.

"So I stop her at the door and ask if it had anything to do with you, since you were her craft lead. Bro, I swear to God, she runs her finger under her glasses to wipe away what look like falling tears, and I swear she has one eye that's completely black, and the other is all swollen. I don't say anything at first, but then I start to look closer and I can see these dark red marks on her neck like somebody tried to choke her out. The girl looks like she got jumped last night, but right as I'm about to ask her what the hell happened to her, she goes, 'This has *nothing* to do with Evan, and *please don't* say anything to him about this. *Please*. I don't want ... fuck, I have to go.' Then she jets out the door like I was chasing her with a fucking chainsaw. Can you believe that?"

"No, I can't ... at all," I say, frowning so hard that it hurts my face. "I don't understand, man. I barely spoke to her, so I don't know why she'd get all weird when you mention my name. Dude, I swear nothing happened between her and me. I can ask Shawn if something happened with him since she was on his crew, but I was next to them virtually the entire shift and didn't see anything go down. At the end of the day, she said bye to us and said she'd see us tomorrow, so I don't know where this is coming from."

"I don't know either, bro," Trey says. "Anyway, I know we're getting ready to be at the site, but after it happened I was so confused that I needed to call and see if you knew anything. I didn't know if something took place that I didn't see, or if I needed to worry about her trying to pursue a lawsuit or something."

"No way, man. I have no idea what she's talking about."

"Okay, I figured that much. Alright, no worries, bro. I'll see you here in a bit."

"Yeah, I'll see you soon."

The call ends and I place my hands on the counter, leaning against it for support with a frown on my face as Journey approaches me from behind. When I spin around to hug her, she doesn't look the least bit surprised by the conversation.

"Did you hear that?" I ask, still bewildered.

"Yeah ... that's crazy," she answers nonchalantly. "I don't know what may have gotten into her, but you're probably better off without her. It'll all work out and be for the best, I'm sure. Anyway, I have to get going."

She lifts herself up on the tips of her toes to kiss me quickly before spinning on her heel and heading for the garage. I stay stuck in a cloud of confusion as I force myself to pour my coffee, and just before she walks out of the door, Journey turns around.

"Hey," she says. "Never forget that I love you."

I force myself to smirk as I reply, "I know, Baby Girl. I love you, too."

Journey grins, pausing to stare at me for a moment before turning around and walking out the door.

.

det. summers

nine
~journey~

BY THE TIME I reach the Seventh Precinct, I'm still reeling from the conversation I overheard at home. While I knew you would eventually find out about Robin, I didn't expect Trey to call and tell you while I was still standing there. I hadn't planned on putting on a performance for you, and it kills me to admit that I had to because I don't like lying to you, Evan. Nonetheless, I did this for us. Robin had to go, and that's all there is to it. I couldn't let her stay and disrespect what we have. I could never do that, so I have no regrets about what happened. Like so many other times in my life, I did what needed to be done. Honestly, the fucking bitch is lucky I let her live.

Getting out of my car now is a lot like it was when I did it yesterday. I acted as if it was a normal day— just a regular girl getting out of her car at the same time as another woman who just happened to be entering the hotel at that exact moment. It was purely luck that it was rush hour and all of the parking spaces at Robin's hotel were taken, forcing her to pick a spot far from the entrance. There were only a few spaces left, making it look like I had no choice but to park close to her.

We got out at the same time, greeting each other with polite, dismissive smiles as we exited our respective vehicles and headed toward the entrance together. She was only a few paces ahead of me as we went, but don't worry, Sir, I made sure to check for cameras as we approached the door. You would've been proud of me, because just as we turned the corner to go inside, I noticed a camera facing the entrance, and I knew I couldn't be seen walking in with her, so the camera ended up being my cue.

Before we could turn the corner, I gripped Robin's hair in my fist and yanked back as hard as I could, snatching her head backward and keeping her out of view of the camera's lens. I knew I didn't have much time. Like I said, it was rush hour and people were bound to be coming to this same hotel at any moment. I had to move fast.

The look on her face when she realized I was attacking her was priceless. It's not the type of thing you forget, and I've always rather enjoyed it. I remember when you and I had some fun a few months back because people didn't know how to mind their own business, and you loved that look, too. You were so proud to let your beast take over and wreak the havoc it desperately craved, and I was honored to be by your side during those thrilling moments. Honestly, I sort of miss the way you were then, but I digress. Luckily for me, I was able to see the terrified expression on Robin's face last night, and it was a dream come true.

The first thing I did was slam her frail, little body behind the bushes running alongside the building. Once we were back there, I felt a little better knowing we were out of view, but I still knew better than to move slowly. The second her body hit the ground, I began punching her in the face. While I'm not the biggest person in the world, I could tell she felt it when my blows landed. Plus, being caught off guard makes everything worse. Her senses were discombobulated the way anybody else's would be in the same situation.

I hit her over and over again, causing her face to quickly swell. Oh my god, I wish you could've seen it, Sir. Her head was like a red balloon with two tiny black dots for eyes. It was hilarious and I hated that I couldn't take my time and laugh at her. Cars were driving by and I had to get out of there to make sure this wouldn't come back to you. Once she was subdued, I wrapped my hands around her throat and started to squeeze with all of my might.

"I don't have time, so I'll be brief," I said to her while she gasped for air like a fish out of water, clawing at my arms. "You will not work at Lane Contracting in Pennsylvania again. You started today and you will quit tomorrow. If you don't, I will come back and slit your throat from ear to ear, and while your mouth frowns from the pain, your neck will smile while you bleed out. When you speak to Trey, you will not mention what's happening to you now, and you will not mention Evan. You will not think of Evan. You won't even dream of Evan when you move back to fucking Delaware. If I find out otherwise, it's all over for you, and after you're gone I'll find members of your family and make their necks gush red just out of spite. Now, you look like you're turning blue and might pass out in another second or two, so nod that you understand before I accidentally send you to the morgue."

She nodded, and out of the kindness of my heart, I

let her go and returned to my car without looking back. You see, Sir, I know that you and I are in a happy place and don't *need* to kill anybody, so I chose to let her go. Even though I can't tell you about this, I think you would've been proud. Now you don't have a new person slowing down production at your job, and I don't have some redheaded whore bopping around in front of my Sir, smiling hard and batting her fucking eyelashes. I killed two birds with one stone without even having to actually murder her. Yay me. You don't have to worry about a thing, Sir. It's taken care of. She won't be back.

As I enter the precinct, I do the thing I've always done so well—push my devilish thoughts to the back of my mind. There is no place for them here, and the last thing I need is my new partner, Detective Martin Summers, thinking I have something to hide. I went through enough of that with Sam Winter—may he rest in piss.

"Good morning, Detective Monroe," Martin says as I approach my desk and sit down.

You have no idea, Sir, how much I wish I didn't have to have a partner at all. It kills me to have this guy smiling at me at the start of every morning.

"Morning, Martin," I reply. "How many times do I have to tell you to just call me Journey?"

"And how many times do I have to tell you to call me Marty?" he quips, his mouth holding his usual smile that I would waste a wish from a genie to get rid of.

Marty Summers is a little shorter than you, Sir, at about six-foot. He's not completely hideous, but in the rare moments that he's not smiling, he has the look of a man whose tank of patience emptied years ago. His hazel eyes are the kind that linger, as if everything he's looking at has a hidden meaning that he must decipher in the moment. He has a long face that I'm sure you'd make fun of, with an angular jaw that's always wearing a five o'clock shadow. Honestly, his presence isn't completely unbearable, but the only man I ever want to talk to is you, so I have days where I struggle to hide the fact that I don't want him around. I think he notices it sometimes, but to my dismay, he handles it with grace.

"What's the matter, *Journey*, you look like you're having a rough morning," he says.

I boot up my computer and get ready to click through emails that contain a lot of words but don't say anything.

"Do I?" I ask him, hoping my surprise from this morning isn't showing on my face.

"Yeah, a little."

"Well, if I do, it probably has something to do with home and is nothing for you to worry about."

Summers puts his hands in the air and rolls his chair back. "Oh, shit. Don't shoot me, Detective. I was just wondering how your morning was going. My mistake. Don't ask about anything that occurs before work—note taken."

I frown before plastering a disarming smirk on my face. "I'm sorry. I don't mean to be snippy. It doesn't bother me to talk about personal stuff. It's just that you and I are still getting to know each other."

Summers nods. "I understand. How long were you and your last partner together before you felt comfortable with him?"

I freeze, because questions about Sam always hit me like a gunshot to the gut. I know we got away with it, and it's totally different when we talk about it amongst ourselves, but when someone else does it out of the blue, panic strikes like a snake bite. It takes focus to keep myself together.

I look over my shoulder at Summers and reply, "Sam and I weren't partners for very long before ... yeah."

I almost want to applaud myself for making it seem like I really care about what happened to my dead partner.

"Oh. I apologize. I didn't mean to upset you," Summers says with genuine guilt in his throat.

"It's fine. I just don't like talking about it," I reply.

"I totally understand. Even though you didn't know him long, I can only imagine how hard it must've been to go through that. Especially being the one that found him. Fuck. I'm sorry. For what it's worth, if you ever want to talk about it, I'm here for you. I mean, we are partners after all."

I nod, swallowing a fake lump in my throat as if I could actually cry over that fucking asshole that was secretly in love with me—that piece of shit who went and got a warrant to search your property and caught us as we were moving Sierra Cross's body out of your back-yard. You had to strangle that prick to death just to get him off of me. I will never feel anything but hatred for that man, but that isn't anything fucking *Marty* Summers needs to know.

"Yeah, thanks," I reply before shifting my eyes to my computer. If there is one thing I will not be talking about to anyone, it's Sam's unfortunate suicide. "Anyway, Marty, what do you say we get to work?"

Summers, picking up on the clue I'm putting down, nods while pressing his lips together.

"Okay, Journey," he says, and we get our day started.

chapter
ten

"GREAT JOB THIS MORNING. I mean it, you guys have been kicking ass. Everybody, take two hours for lunch today, alright? We'll get back on it at one o'clock."

Trey's announcement sends a jolt of energy through the entire crew, giddiness spreading like fire catching. Faces light up with excitement for the unexpected change as everyone thanks him and quickly disperses like he might change his mind. Car doors fly open and tires peel out of the gravel parking lot before I can even get to my truck.

As I reach for my door, I feel a tap on my shoulder and find Trey standing behind me, his dark skin covered in beads of sweat from the morning's hard work.

"Hey, Evan," he says. "I don't mean to hold you up, but I wanted to just check with you one more time about the situation yesterday. I wasn't sure if you'd had time to think about it after we talked on the phone this morning; but you're sure nothing happened that might give this girl cause to drop a lawsuit?"

My forehead immediately wrinkles with a frown the

way it did this morning when I first got the call from Trey.

"Bro, I'm telling you, if something would've happened," I answer, making sure I look Trey in the eye, "I would've told you about it. I wouldn't keep a secret that I know could put you in hot water. You're my guy, I wouldn't do you like that."

You're literally the only person I'd think twice about before killing. As long as you don't push it, of course.

Trey nods, but I can still see the outline of anxiety on his face. "I know, I know. I just don't understand. I couldn't care less about her quitting. She was only here for a day, so it's not like we need her, but I just don't get it. It's my job site to supervise and I feel like I should've caught it."

"Dude, this isn't on you. There was nothing to catch," I reply, tapping him on the shoulder gently. "Whatever happened with Robin is her own thing. I asked Shawn about it, too, and he said the same thing we're saying. Nobody saw anything happen with her. Sometimes shit just doesn't work out. It's all good, man. We had a productive morning without her. We're good to go."

"I feel you, but what about the bruising on her face and neck? The roughest sleeper in the world isn't waking up with all of that."

I shrug, ready to move past the topic. "I don't know how she got that, but I know none of us did it, and that's all that matters. Trust me, Trey, it's cool to just let this go. Go enjoy the long lunch you just gave yourself, and let me get in my truck so I can, too."

Both of us laugh as I open my door.

"You're right," Trey replies. "Don't let me hold up,

bro. Go enjoy your extra time. What are you gonna do with it? Go home and take a nap?"

"That's tempting," I reply as I hop into the driver's seat. "But I think I'm going to go surprise my girl and take her out to lunch."

━━

IT'S rare that Journey and I get to see each other during our work days because we're usually so busy. As a detective, Journey has to eat whenever she can find time between whatever investigation she's working on, and my lunch is usually only an hour that can quickly be reduced by half if the project is behind schedule. So with an hour and a half left on today's lunch break, I pull into the parking lot of the Seventh Precinct and park directly next to Journey's car.

I've never done this before. In fact, Journey and I have always made sure that we *don't* do this. Up to this point, I'm not sure anyone in her department knows that she and I are together. After the Sierra Cross investigation, we decided it was smarter to avoid being seen together by other officers of the law. We weren't sure how many of her colleagues saw my face when Winter labeled me a suspect. So to be safe, I've avoided doing what I'm about to do. The way I see it, enough time has passed for us to be in the clear. Plus, all I want to do is stick my head in the door and surprise her, not announce that I'm Evan Godric, former suspect in a missing persons case.

When I get out and begin to make way inside, I get uneasy about being surrounded by cops. Technically, Journey is one, but her badge is as black as my heart, so I don't have to worry about her slapping cuffs on me for the things I've done. No, she'd much rather wear the cuffs herself and have me slap her.

As I turn the corner to go into the building, I'm relieved of having to go inside and stand amongst a bunch of people who would love to arrest me if they found what I left in the backyard of my house in Strawberry Mansion. Journey nearly slams into me as she rounds the side of the building with her partner following closely behind her.

"Fuck," she exclaims before realizing it's me. "Evan? Hey. Uhh, what are you doing here?"

She pulls me into a hug, but it's a nervous one. Even with her body pressed against mine, I can feel her head on a swivel, wondering who is around to see me.

"Hi," I greet her, squeezing her tight. "I got an extended lunch today and thought I'd come take you out. Are you free to leave or do you have somewhere you need to be?"

"No, I'm free to leave," she says, then she swings around and looks at her partner who's grinning like he has been let in on a secret. "But I did just promise Summers ... Marty, that I would treat him to lunch."

Journey's partner shakes his head enthusiastically.

"Oh, don't worry about me. I can find my own lunch."

Seeing as how I've never officially met Journey's new partner, I take this as an opportunity to introduce myself to the man who spends half his day with my woman. It's a risk introducing myself to a detective, but from what Journey tells me, this guy is new and harmless. I extend my hand for him to shake and he immediately latches on.

"It's nice to meet you, man," I say. "I'm Evan."

"Detective Marty Summers. Journey has mentioned

you before, but she hasn't said much. It's very nice to meet you, Evan."

"No surprise there. My Little One likes to keep me all to herself," I say playfully, smiling as we end the handshake. "I hope whatever she has said has been all good things."

"Of course. Anyway, don't let me intrude on your plans. You two go ahead and have fun together."

"No, it's really okay. You're more than welcome to join us," I interject. "In fact, I'll join you wherever you were planning to go, if you don't mind."

Journey frowns for a second before giving in with a head nod. "Of course not." She grabs my hand and begins leading me through the parking lot. I can feel her staring at the side of my face as we go, and I smile to try to ease her tension. By the time we reach her car, I can sense her accepting that we're doing this. "I'll drive. You have to sit in the back now, Marty."

"Totally fine with me," Marty says, smiling.

Journey and I walk in front of him, but as we get in the car and make our way out of the lot, I swear I can feel his eyes still on me. Even as Journey drives down the street and pulls into a small restaurant with outdoor seating, I can feel her partner's gaze on me like the sun beaming through a magnifying glass and burning a hole into my skin. When I look at him as we walk inside, he just smiles at me and nods.

Hmm. All it took was a short drive for this prick to start annoying me. If he keeps it up, he'll have to figure out how to stare with his eyes gouged out.

The young hostess brings us to our seats and we quickly order from the lunch menu before being brought coffee and water. There's a brief silence that makes the table feel awkward, but it's Marty who breaks through the silence.

"So, what is it that you do, Evan?" he asks.

I clear my throat and sip my coffee before answering, "I work construction for Lane Contracting. I'm a carpenter by trade."

"A carpenter? Wow, that's awesome," he replies. "So you could build me some furniture in my shitty apartment."

We all share a stiff laugh.

Fake laughing for the sake of this asshole? Fucking stop it.

"I suppose I could," I reply. "But my skill set is pretty much put to use building frames for walls and forms for concrete. Not a whole lot of finish work besides chair rail and crown molding, and even that is sporadic."

"Well, if you ever need a job to put your finer skills to use, just let me know," Marty says.

The waiter arrives with our food and places it in front of us accordingly, and we all dig in. A minute or two filled with the sound of chewing and gulping passes before another word is spoken.

"So what about you?" I start this time. "You're my girl's partner now, so we should probably get to know each other better. Where are you originally from?"

"Right here in Philly, baby," he answers proudly, still beaming the way he has been since we met in front of the precinct. "That's right, I was born and raised in Washington Square West. Went to college at the University of Pennsylvania and became a detective to better serve my city."

Serve your city? You've got to be fucking kidding me.

I glance over at Journey who looks just as disgusted

as I feel. It's not that Detective Summers is a bad guy. It's just that he's so different from us. His upbringing in Washington Square West was lightyears ahead of where Journey and I were raised. He attended a nice college and chose to become a detective out of a long list of options while Journey and I had no choice but to do what we had to or die in the streets of our neighborhoods. I know it's not his fault. He didn't choose to be born and raised where he was, but it still makes me sick to my fucking stomach to know he had a life that was so much easier than ours.

"How about you, Evan," Marty goes on, still chomping down on his BLT sandwich like it's the best thing he has ever put in his mouth. "Are you from Philly, too, or did you move here as a kid?"

I try to stay in a jovial, pleasant mood for this little lunch date, but my face hardens as I answer. "I'm from Strawberry Mansion."

Marty's eyes raise as he swallows. "Oh, wow. I bet you're glad to have made it out of there, huh?"

Made it out of there? What if you don't make it out of here? I think there has been enough fucking holding back.

I feel it when it happens—the moment the dam breaks and the harsh feelings I've been able to maturely scoot past in my mind come stalking back to the forefront. I've been so content with life and where Journey and I are that I haven't thought about hurting anyone in a long time. The kinky scenes we play out in our basement feed my hunger to inflict pain, and with Cain out of my life, there haven't been very many triggers for my aggression. Until now.

Who does this motherfucker think he is? The only people who are allowed to talk negatively about a bad neighborhood are the people who are from that neighbor-hood. That's something that should be taught to everyone in fucking high school. It's the same when discussing an abusive parent. I can say whatever I want about how shitty my mother was, but if anyone else does, they're signing their fucking death warrant.

"I stayed in Strawberry Mansion, in the same house I grew up in, up until a few months ago when I moved in with Journey in Elmwood," I inform the fucking prick. Journey places a hand on my knee beneath the table, but I continue. "I've never been ashamed of where I'm from, nor am I ashamed of where we live now. Some of us didn't have the luxury of growing up with a silver fucking spoon in our mouths in fucking Washington Square West."

Every ounce of calm drains out of Summers' face, and it is quickly refilled with terrified regret. "Whoah, I apologize. I certainly didn't mean anything offensive by that. My mistake. I just thought that ... Strawberry Mansion just has a bit of a reputation, that's all. I wasn't trying to talk down on where you grew up or say that being from there is something to be ashamed of. I'm truly sorry if I offended you."

I should stab him in his fucking hand with my fork. Then he'd be really sorry.

But I can't. Instead, I look at Journey and see the pleading in her eyes. This is her new partner, someone she has to work with every day, and it would be awfully suspicious if *this* partner killed himself, too.

"It's cool," I reply, doing my best to not say the things I desperately want to. *Like how I would love to watch blood spill from a gaping wound in your fucking neck.* "I didn't mean to ... I get a little carried away when talking about my past. My mother is from there. That's where she died so I get a little sensitive."

"I understand," Marty says. "That's why you didn't want to leave the area—it's where all of your memories are."

"I didn't even leave the house," I inform him, suddenly emotional and feeling the need to rein myself in.

"You stayed in the same house all of that time until recently. Wow. I get it, man. I really do. Again, I apologize for being offensive. No harm intended."

"It's fine," I answer, trying to move on, but we spend the next fifteen minutes in silence as we finish our food and head out.

Once we're back at the precinct, Marty shakes my hand and apologizes one final time before leaving Journey and I to talk without him. We stand in front of my truck, both us with the same exasperated look on our faces.

"Well, that was a fucking nightmare," Journey says. "This is why we said we wouldn't be seen together around my job. I thought we were going to have to hide another body for a minute there, which wouldn't have bothered me."

"Wouldn't have bothered you?" I snip, still feeling tight about the conversation. "All I wanted to do was surprise you for lunch, but if another one of your partners dies, you're definitely going to be the main suspect."

"Yeah, you're probably right ... but I'm still glad you came. It was great to have lunch with you, Sir. Don't worry about Summers. He's an idiot who doesn't know any better. I told you he was annoying."

"That you did, and somehow it was still an understatement. But I don't want to do anything that could cause problems for you at work, so I hope everything is cool."

"He'll be fine," Journey says. "All that guy does is smile all day. I'm the one who has to plaster on a happy face while that fucker annoys me from the start of the day to the finish."

"I'm sure that's hard as hell."

"You have no fucking idea."

"Well, how about this?" I say, reaching out and taking her soft hand in mine. The touch of her skin instantly makes me feel better. "It's Friday, which means we're both off tomorrow. How about we go out and have some fun to make up for how fucked up lunch was?"

"Ooh, you have my attention," Journey says. "It's going to take something incredible to scrub this near disaster from my memory. So, what did you have in mind?"

I smile as I hear the words in my head first, then say them out loud. "I'm thinking we go back to where it all started for us. Let's go to The Black Collar."

chapter
eleven

WALKING across the street toward The Black Collar feels like approaching a family reunion. Giddiness rises up in my chest and I smile involuntarily. To people like Journey and me, this place is nirvana; a judgment-free zone where like-minded people gather to be who they truly are. There is no need to wear a mask once you're within these walls, and outside of my own home, I've never felt more comfortable than what I do when I'm here. It has been far too long, and my body vibrates with delight the closer I get to the building.

As usual, the line to get inside is long and filled with people who probably won't get in for one reason or another. Most of them haven't filled out the online questionnaire that is required, or they've been banned for being creepy assholes but they think enough time has gone by that their transgression has been forgotten. It hasn't, but most of them won't know that until they reach the front of the line.

My beloved Little Devil is shrouded in all-black tonight—a black dress that hugs her curves enough to make me jealous of the fabric, with black heels that make her ass even more mouth-watering. Her hair is in tight curls that bounce behind her back as she walks, and her makeup is flawless as usual. The woman is a walking wet dream I never want to wake from, and all I can do is try to look halfway decent while walking next to her. I stride over the pavement in dark gray slacks and a black button-up with silver buttons and matching cufflinks. We're a combination of sexy and sultry as we step onto the curb and cut in front of the line to approach the bouncer.

"Evan Godric and Journey Monroe," I say to him while interlocking my fingers with Journey's.

The oversized bouncer looks down at the tablet in his large hands and enters our names, glancing over the top of it while he awaits the results. As soon as he sees what he needs to, he nods and grabs the thick black rope in front of us, granting us access.

"You guys are good to go," he says, placing red wristbands on us both before stepping to the side. "Welcome back."

Journey and I grin as we step past the rope, but before we can make it through the door, we hear commotion behind us that grabs our attention.

"Hey, what the fuck? Why are you letting *them* in and not me?" A random guy asks the bouncer with much more attitude than he should have when speaking to a man that size.

The bouncer glares at the guy, who's dressed in blue jeans and a white Polo shirt. "Look, bro, you're not on the list. It's not my fault you didn't fill out the form online and your friends did."

"I forgot!" the guy barks. "You can't just make me stand out here while you let these assholes in, and my friends are already inside having a good time. This is bullshit."

I suppose there are too many witnesses to beat a man until his face caves in.

Shaking my head, I chuckle as I grip Journey's hand tighter and lead her through the doors.

The inside of The Black Collar makes my chest fill with glee. The slow, sexy music sways the room to its hypnotic beat, pounding the black walls with each kick of the heavy drums. Flashing strobe lights illuminate the sea of scantily clad people living their best lives as we walk down the hall toward the bar, passing rooms filled with the sounds of cracking whips, slapping paddles, and tantalizing moans of agony and pleasure.

"Fuck," Journey says, her face lighting up like the strobes above us. "God I missed this place."

"You and me both, Baby Girl," I agree. "We definitely have to start coming here more often. It's been way too long."

"No question," she replies, her eyes glued to a scene in a nearby room with three people locked in pillories while being tormented with very large pinwheels.

"Come on. We're going to the Main Stage," I tell her before tugging her hand and continuing down the hall.

There's an entire forest of people for us to push through, but we manage to make it to the open section of the club, where the space expands into a dance floor and bar. The massive square on the right is sardine tight, filled with people high on their favorite substance or drunk from a special concoction made at the bar on the left. Speakers that look more like cannons are mounted in each corner of the room, filling the area with enough bass to burst an eardrum, while three cages dangle above the crowd, each occupied by a sexy someone in tight leather, dancing erotically. It would take a hand grenade to wipe the smile from my face as Journey and I pause long enough to take it all in before continuing on our path behind the bar to reach our destination; the VIP area.

A bouncer checks our wristbands before holding the curtain open for us to enter the Main Stage. Excitement blooms in my stomach as we walk hand in hand and make our way toward the front of the seating area, where we're pleasantly surprised to find two open seats at the end of the third row, in perfect view of the stage. We sit down just as the lights dim and the audience around us begins to cheer as a man and woman enter the stage. We recognize them immediately to be the owners of the club, Nolan Carter and his wife Bree.

These two are legends in this club. Nolan has been the owner since its conception, putting shows on the Main Stage as a direct example of what the BDSM lifestyle is supposed to look like to people who don't know better—the judgmental people who hear the word *kinky* and think it means vile devil worshiper. Every time he walked on stage he was a representative for what this lifestyle is supposed to be like, and women were begging to be his partner, practically throwing themselves at his feet for a chance at being restrained and fed to a sadist with a hefty appetite.

Nolan put this club on the map, so much so that it attracted the attention of the Philadelphia Inquirer, who sent a vanilla journalist over to interview him. The two of them went on a wild ride together, one that was full of pleasure and pain, but also danger and violence.

By the time it was all over, every member of The Black Collar was reading the Pulitzer Prize winning article that Bree published, titled *Interview with a Sadist*, and learning all about how the two of them met and fell in love. Now that they're married, they run the club jointly, and the shows they put on have become fabled to the point of disbelief. Journey and I smirk like kids coming down the stairs on Christmas morning in anticipation for what they'll have for us today.

Nolan walks to the center first, wearing black pants and no shirt, showing off his glistening caramel skin. When he glances at the audience, we can see the blue in his eyes from here, making him look majestic as he takes center stage and grabs a rope from the small bed placed there. He ties the rope into an intricate knot and glares offstage. Without Nolan saying a word, his wife walks over in a beautiful red lingerie set that makes every man in the audience rearrange themselves in their seats. Bree is a vision, with dark brown hair tied into a ponytail putting her porcelain face on display and highlighting her own blue eyes.

"It's no wonder these two got married recently," I lean over and whisper to Journey.

"Seriously," she agrees, shaking her head in awe. "They're both fucking beautiful."

Bree struts onto the stage, never looking anywhere except at Nolan who keeps his eyes on her as she walks in and climbs onto the bed. She rests on both of her knees, waiting patiently and silently as Nolan wraps the rope around her, creating gorgeous designs that are so intricate they look as though he went to college just to learn how to make them.

"Oh shit," Journey mumbles quietly. "He's doing Shibari."

I fix my gaze on the stage and watch as Nolan puts on a display of geometric rope work that looks more like art than kink. He ties a rope around each of Bree's legs, the fabric climbing up each limb like living vines that know exactly where they are supposed to go. He ties another over his wife's arms, securing them behind her back in a move the police would be jealous of. The man is a master at work, and I even find myself envious of him.

By the time the club owner is finished, Bree is dangling from a rope that hangs from the top of the stage, gently swaying over the bed like a swing in the breeze. If she's in any pain, she doesn't show it. She's still just as effortlessly beautiful as she was when she walked in.

"That's so fucking hot," Journey whispers again, making me wonder if she's talking to me, or if what she has witnessed is so incredible to her that she just has to say it out loud.

As Bree sways on stage, Nolan stalks around her, watching the product of his work like an artist admiring what he has created for the world. While he watches Bree, I keep my eyes on Journey. I see the admiration in her eyes. She loves what she has seen, and she doesn't have to tell me with words that this is what she wants to experience. Sometimes, being a partner means paying enough attention to pick up on signs that are left behind, even if they're unintentional. Unfortunately, I have no idea how to do Shibari. However, I do know my Little Devil, and my love is enough to make me try what I think she'll love. An idea sparks in my mind and sets my imagination ablaze with devious plans that I can't wait to carry out. I'm so ready to do this that I don't even look at the stage anymore. All I can see is Journey and the things I want to do to her.

"What?" she asks when she catches me staring.

I shake my head, a smile still tugging my lips. "Nothing. I just have an idea."

"Yeah? What kind of an idea?"

"One that requires us to go home, and for you to give yourself to me."

"Oh? Then what are we waiting for?"

"The end of the show."

"Sir, I'd much rather put on a show with you than sit here and watch one. Can we leave? Right now?"

I lick my lips as the smile takes control of my face. "Absolutely."

Journey and I quietly get out of our seats, doing our best not to disrupt the pure artistry on stage, and make our way out. I take my girl by the hand and guide her through the crowd outside the VIP area. We weave around bodies, pushing some aside because now that I can picture what I want to do to Journey, I refuse to let anything stand in the way.

We eventually burst through the door and step into the night air where the line of people trying to get in is still long and energetic. The bouncer nods at us as we walk by, but he doesn't look happy about standing in front of a bunch of people who are pissed that they can't get into the club. Even the asshole who was complaining about his friends leaving him behind is still there, glaring at us as we walk out.

"Wow, you let them in and they didn't even stay that long," he says to the bouncer, but his gaze stays on us. "Fucking piece of shit and his whore get in before me? This club is a joke."

I feel it when it happens—the moment the beast in me wakes up from a peaceful slumber and takes full control. There are certain lines that can never be crossed without consequences. Journey is at the absolute top of that list, and the anger that awakens in me is unlike any I've ever felt before.

"What did you say?" I growl, stopping at the curb instead of crossing the street.

The guy who just ruined his life turns to me with a confident expression.

"You heard me," he replies. "What? You got a fucking problem?"

The bouncer quickly steps from his position in front of the door and stomps up to the asshole. "Hey, you get the fuck outta here. I've been putting up with your shit all night, and now you're antagonizing VIP members. You're banned from The Black Collar. Now go, and don't ever come back."

"Banned? Are you fucking kidding me?" he blares, throwing his hands up in the air. "Fine. Fuck this place and fuck your VIP members—a bunch of fucking freaks who pay monthly to come be degenerates. You all fucking disgust me. I'm outta here."

"Yeah, whatever. Just fucking go," the bouncer replies.

The man from the line takes a second to stare down the bouncer, but eventually walks away just as Journey and I start across the street. I keep my eyes on him even as we reach my truck, and I see it when he slips into the darkness of a nearby alley, probably using it as a shortcut to get to the parking lot on the other side of the club.

This is it. Get him now or forever hold your peace. Defend Journey or be a little bitch in her eyes until the end of time.

Once I realize what he's doing, I jump in the car and start the engine in a hurry, pressing on the gas and speeding out of the lot the second Journey gets her door closed.

"Where are you going so fast, Sir?" Journey asks.

When I look over at her, she's smiling a wicked grin. I see the devil in her eyes and she sees the beast in mine, and we both know the answer to her question.

chapter
twelve

RAGE SCORCHES my veins as I try to push the gas pedal through the floorboard of my truck. The engine roars like a lion on four wheels, catapulting us forward as we hit the street and swerve around the corner. I run a red light, seeing nothing but my destination as I go, and Journey sits beside me silently. The two of us are a match made in hell because we feed off one another. Knowing she won't reach over and grab the steering wheel to try to stop me only makes me want to defend her more. Nobody else could be this perfect for me. No one else could sit next to a madman breaking traffic law after traffic law and love every second of it, especially knowing the way this will end. When I get to where I'm going, we both know it won't be anything pretty.

I swear it's going to be fucking hideous.

I reach the other side of The Black Collar in what feels like only a few seconds of driving, and bring the truck to a stop at the end of the alley. There are barely any lights on my end, and even less in the alley itself, so I open my door knowing there's almost no chance of cameras being in this area. Music beats against the walls loud enough for us to hear it, so I know the noise we make will be drowned out. Good.

What I'm about to do will be in the dark, so the only thing I need to be concerned with is witnesses walking past the alley on either end. Fuck it. If they see something they're not supposed to, I have Journey to cover me. She's a fucking detective. We can get to anybody if we really need to. Witnesses are only witnesses if they can speak.

Journey and I get out of the car together, holding hands as we stalk down the obsidian alley. In the darkness, the asshole from the club comes into view just before the halfway point, and when he recognizes us, he chuckles to himself.

"Oh, what is this shit? You bring your whore to protect you while you try to confront me in the fucking alley?" he blares, raising his arms as if challenging me.

He's unafraid, which I commend him for. The only problem is that the lack of fear has nothing to do with the outcome. Plenty of people have gone into battle fearlessly and died horrendous deaths.

I let go of Journey's hand so that mine can curl into a fist as I keep walking, not saying a word. Nothing I want to say requires me to speak. When I don't respond to him, the unnamed asshole fills the silence with his own words.

"You really wanna do this?" he asks, this time with a little quiver in his voice. Maybe his bravery is a front after all, but it's too late now. Dread will neither protect nor save him.

As we finally come together, my heart pounds in my chest, rattling all of my organs as aggression brings my blood to a boil. I lock eyes with him one last time, just before I take off in a full sprint that brings our bodies colliding together. I lower my shoulder and slam it into his gut, lifting him entirely off the ground in a tackle that would make any linebacker proud. We hit the ground with a thunderous *thud* that bounces his head on the concrete like a basketball.

"Fuck!" he screams, trying to get me off by flailing his arms.

You would think that someone talking so much shit to a bouncer would know how to fight. To my surprise, this prick is just like any other asshole looking to bully strangers on the street. He's arrogant and used to getting his way—used to talking shit to people and being ignored. His parents probably let him cry his way out of everything when he was a kid, so now he's a fucking asshole as an adult. Well mommy and daddy can't save him now. No one can.

Instead of swinging my arms like an insufferable jackass, I swing once, curling my hand into a fist and bringing it crashing down on his face like an anvil. His head bounces against the ground again as blood splashes from his nose like a water balloon bursting. His hands suddenly stop flailing and slam against his face, his eyes cinching closed in agony as he screams.

"Shut the fuck up," I yell, before lowering my mouth to his ear and whispering. "Stop screaming, or I promise I'll get the knife from my truck and cut your fucking tongue out."

"You broke my fucking nose," he bellows in response, still holding his face and writhing beneath me.

I turn to Journey and don't even have to say it. My Little Devil grins and turns on her heel, speed walking to the truck. As she goes, I turn my attention back to the man still struggling under my weight.

"You called my Little Devil a whore," I say as I

wrench his hands away from his face and bring my forehead down, slamming it against his nose in a vicious headbutt.

He screams again just as Journey returns holding a switchblade from the glove compartment of my truck. She forces it into my hand while simultaneously replacing my hand with hers to hold the guy's arm down.

"No! Get the fuck off me!" he screams at the top of his lungs when he realizes what is about to happen. It's too late now. He should've realized I wasn't kidding when I warned him before.

"I told you," I growl as I position myself higher so I can hold his other arm with my knee instead of my hand. "I said to stop screaming, but you refuse to listen ... and you called her a fucking whore, you motherfucker."

"Oh, god! No. Please stop!"

"Oh, I will. As soon as I'm done keeping my promise. Say ahh."

The unknown man screams one last time, just before I wrap my fist around the handle of the knife and use it to beat him over the face. I hit him once, twice, three times before he finally stops squirming. His eyes close as the muscles in his neck go limp, his head slumping to the side.

"Oh my god," Journey says, looking down on him with a smile on her lips and joy dancing in her eyes. "I thought he would never shut up."

Finally, with no concern for being bitten, I pull the guy's bottom jaw down and grab hold of his tongue between two fingers.

"He's going to shut up," I reply. "For good."

Holding his tongue in one hand and the switchblade in the other, I slash the blade across his tongue, severing it nearly in half. One half slithers back into his mouth while the other falls by his ear. Blood shoots from the wound and I have to clamp his mouth back shut to keep it from getting on me. He may choke to death on the liquid, but I'm much more worried about my outfit being ruined than I am about his chances of survival. If he does live, he'll remember not to talk shit to strangers, because talking will be much, much harder for him from now on.

I wipe the blade of my knife off on his clothes before tucking it away in my pocket as I stand up. Journey gets to her feet and looks down on the unconscious body that now has a steady stream of blood coming from the side of his mouth.

"I thought you were going to kill him," Journey says.

"Nah. I'm not in the mood to hide a corpse or worry about it being found."

"And what if he calls the cops? He could ID us."

"I thought *you* were the cops," I answer with a smirk. There are perks to dating a detective, and when Journey understands what I'm saying, she grins, too.

Journey lets out a sigh. "Okay. Then put it in his hand," she says, still looking down.

"What?"

"His tongue. Put it in his hand so that when he wakes up it's there to answer the question of why his mouth is in so much pain."

I grin. "Oh, you're just downright diabolical, aren't you?"

"Just following your lead, Sir."

"I fucking love it."

As my Baby Girl suggested, I take the severed

tongue and place it in his palm for him to discover when he wakes up. He'll be in for quite the surprise, and I wish I could be here to see it.

When I stand up, I look at Journey and find her eyes fixated on me.

"You're un-fucking-believable," she tells me. "You did all of this for me?"

"Of course I did. You know I would never allow someone to disrespect you. You are mine, Little One. What kind of Dom would I be if I let some fucking prick standing outside of a club talk down to you? Never, Journey. I would *never* let that happen. Plus, it feels good to let it out from time to time. It feels phenomenal to act on how I feel."

"I fucking love you so much," she says, stepping forward to place her hands on my belt. "And now I want to act on how I feel."

"Yeah? Tell me what you want to do."

"I want you in my mouth, Sir. Right here, right now. Can I please you?"

I turn my head, glancing at both ends of the alley to make sure we're still in the clear.

"Do it," I reply. "Let me in that fucking mouth. Show me how happy you are that you belong to me."

"Mmm, yes Sir."

I bite my lip as I watch the love of my life drop to her knees in a skin-tight dress without caring for it at all. She is unbothered by her discomfort because pleasing me is what matters to her most. Fuck, I'm a lucky man.

Journey fiddles with my belt, unfastening it quickly and making her way through my zipper in a hurry. My stiff erection drops out of the opening like it was fighting for air, and the second it shows itself, Journey plunges forward, taking me all the way to the back of her throat.

I throw my head back. "Fuck."

Journey moans as she sucks me, the sound of her making me even harder. I close my eyes at first, falling into the bliss of her tongue working its way up my shaft before blanketing my head. But when I open my eyes, I get to watch her do it. I see when she pulls me out of her mouth, looking up at me as she runs her tongue up the underside until it comes to a stop at my slit. Her eyes bore into mine and it sends a pulse of pleasure up my spine that makes me have to grip a nearby dumpster.

"Your fucking mouth feels so good," I tell her. "Keep it up and I'm going to explode in it."

"Yeah? Do it then," she commands, suddenly taking control over me. "Detonate in my fucking mouth. Make me swallow it right here in the alley. Right next to the man you beat half to death for me. Give me your cum. I want it now."

Journey shoves my cock back in her mouth and begins a lethal combination of sucking the head and twisting both of her hands in opposite directions on my shaft. The sensation hits me like an arrow to the stomach, nearly folding me in half. I hunch over, my mouth gaped open wide enough to suck up all the oxygen in the alley as I gasp like I'm dying.

"Jesus fucking Christ," I exclaim, gripping the dumpster hard enough to bend the metal. "I'm about to come down your fucking throat, Little Devil. Oh fuck. You're going to make me fucking come."

Journey doesn't slow down or let up for a single second. She keeps going, sucking and twisting, stealing my soul from my body with her perfection, and I absolutely unload. I ignite and erupt like a fucking volcano, my cum exploding out of me so hard I can barely stand. I buckle forward and have to grip her head just to keep myself upright.

Once she's satisfied that I'm completely drained, Journey stands up, licking her lips and sucking her fingers clean like the goddess of sex. She's so seductive it makes my heart rumble. I grab her by the shoulders and pull her into a passionate kiss that borders on painful. Our tongues collide and commence a dance that sends blood rushing through my body. Even after an earth-shattering orgasm, she has me ready for so much more.

"We have to go," I tell her as I force myself to push her away and re-secure my pants. I look down at the asshole who is still unconscious from our little run-in and then back up to Journey. "As much as I'd love to see the look on his face when he wakes up, I think it's better that we're not here. Plus, I absolutely am not done with you, Little Devil. Let's get out of here."

Journey smiles and licks her lips, taking in the last bit of my cum as I take her by the hand once again, and lead us both away from the scene of the crime.

chapter
thirteen

MY ADRENALINE STAYS on full blast, pumping through my veins at a million miles per second as we pull into the garage of our shared home and close it behind us. The second we are shielded from the outside world, I reach across the truck and grab Journey by the throat.

How badly I want her can't be put into words. Tonight was like dropping gasoline on a forest fire, and I am hotter than ever. It started with the scene on the stage of The Black Collar. Seeing the way Journey responded to Nolan and Bree's exhibition sent a hot spike of desire through my body. Her eyes were alight with want, and seeing her that way made me desire nothing more than to give it to her. I knew at that moment that I had no choice but to bring my Little Devil home and reenact what made her blaze with anticipation. I rushed my needy little whore out of there only to be confronted by some lame piece of shit who just didn't know how to keep his mouth shut long enough for us to cross the street and be out of earshot. Luckily, my violent interaction with him only made me hotter for Journey.

The way she hurried back to the truck to retrieve my knife and handed it to me mid-fight was the ultimate aphrodisiac. She's the Harley Quinn to my Joker, a deviant in need of the darkest love. Mine just happens to be pitch black, and I will shroud her in it.

When my hand slams against her skin, Journey lets out a lustful moan. The sound of her reacting to me makes me quiver. It doesn't matter that I came already. My cock is throbbing for round two, and I can't impale her fast enough.

"Fuck, I want you so much," I growl into her mouth as I pull her face close to mine. "Get the fuck over here right now. I don't care if you break every window in the truck. Get on top of me."

Journey flashes a grin before yanking off her seatbelt and obeying my command, kicking the glove compartment and slamming another foot against the shifter to get to me. I help her by using both hands to grab her neck, squeezing as she comes to me. I can hear her wheezing as I apply pressure to her windpipe, but she doesn't complain or tap out. My Little Devil can handle it all and wants more. She slams herself down on top of me, banging against the steering wheel without a care in the world for the destruction we cause.

When our mouths come together, fireworks ignite. Heat envelopes both of us, fogging the windows in five seconds flat as we try to tear each other apart. I yank at her clothes, enjoying the sound of the fabric tearing as I snatch it upward. I need access to her skin. I need to touch it. I have to have my hands all over her right now and time is moving too slowly for me to be satisfied. I rip a long line up the dress, tearing it until her legs have enough freedom to spread wide for me and I can slip my hands between her thighs. I jerk her panties to the side and slide two fingers into her wet pussy, adoring how she is already drenched for me.

"Yes," she whispers into my mouth, her words slithering down my throat and engulfing my insides with hot lust.

"Grind for me," I tell her, pulling her head back with a fistful of her hair. "Ride my fingers like you do my cock."

"Fuck. Yes, Sir," she replies, wasting no time to do as she's told.

Journey begins grinding her pussy against my hand, her clit rubbing against my palm, so I curl my hand upward to increase the friction. This wasn't part of my plan, but I need her too much to stop now. She made me come already anyway. It's only right that I return the favor before we get to the real scene I have in store for her.

"Keep going, Baby Girl. Don't stop," I demand.

Journey continues, breathing heavily against my neck as her clit gets the attention it needs while her pussy is filled with my fingers. As I expected and craved, it doesn't take long before her breathing becomes rhythmic and her luscious skin starts to light up, pink blush slowly cascading from her neck to her chest.

"Oh god," she says, still grinding. "Sir, am I allowed to come?"

"If you don't, I will punish you severely. I want you to come on my fingers the way my whore is supposed to. Soak me. If I don't need a towel when you're done, I won't be satisfied. Now give it all to me. Unload all over me, baby."

"God ... yes!" she bellows just as every cell in her

body evaporates. She ruptures, her ability to maintain control shattering against her will and sending her body into violent convulsions. Pain grips me by the neck as she squeezes me hard, grunting in my ear as the orgasm ruins her.

"That's my girl," I whisper as she finally starts to come back down to Earth. "You're such a good girl for me, baby—the perfect dirty slut. My god I'm in love with you."

Journey practically collapses on top of me. Fatigue has taken over her limbs and left her with no more strength to move. It's fine. Her work is done. Now it's my turn to work for her.

With Journey still panting in my ear, I pop open my door and struggle to climb out with her still in my lap. She tries to stand as we exit, but I wasn't kidding when I said her work was done. I won't even allow her to walk. I lift my woman off the ground and she wraps her legs around my waist, allowing me to carry her inside and through the house. When we reach the stairs to the basement, I don't put her down. I fight through the growing exhaustion and continue down the stairs with her legs clenching my waist and her arms draped around my neck.

When we reach the bottom, I walk over to the bed and finally put her down. She lies on her back and spreads her legs for me, showing me just how much she came with glistening wetness still coating her pussy. She's a fucking sight to behold. I bite my lip and shake my head just looking down at her, truly in awe of her exquisiteness.

"Do you know how perfect you are?" I whisper, my heart pounding from how excited just looking at her makes me.

"Thank you, Sir," she replies, beaming.

"Don't thank me yet. I'm about to turn that pretty little face into a twisted mess of pleasure and pain. Tonight, you're forbidden from doing anything other than allowing me access to you. All of you. I want to use every inch, no restrictions whatsoever."

"Of course," she says. "What do you have in mind, Sir?"

"I'm no Shibari expert, but tonight I'm going to improvise. Crouch in front of the bed with your knees at your chest and your arms behind your back. Stay that way and don't move."

Journey takes a deep breath, preparing for another scene with the beast in me before sliding off the bed and standing in front of me. I remove her dress and try my best not to give into my desire to bend her over and push myself inside. I battle back and forth with the urge until she's naked, then I force her down and into position.

Once she's set, I walk to the back corner by the stairs and grab a long rope hanging from the wall. Usually, this is purely for the BDSM dungeon aesthetic. Tonight, it becomes a tool.

When I return to Journey, I begin wrapping the rope around her body. I'm not trained in Shibari the way the owner of The Black Collar is, but I manage, wrapping it around her torso and arms horizontally before doing it vertically over her shoulders to create a few squares down her sides. It's not beautiful or intricate, and the end of the rope dangles loosely like an untied shoe string, but it gets the job done. I'll definitely have to learn more in order to give my Little One exactly what she saw on stage. Even though I'm new at this, I love seeing her this way. Journey loves it too, because I can clearly see that she's ready for another orgasm as her pussy drips for me.

Now that she's ready, I lift her onto the bed and set her down on her side. Since she is naked in this position, I have total access and freedom. Her ass and pussy are completely uncovered and ready for me to use in any way I see fit. If I move to the other side of the bed, I can fuck her mouth with ease. All she can do is take it, and that fact makes me hungry to begin.

Before I start, I place a blindfold over Journey's eyes so that she can't see what's coming. I only want her to feel me, her senses heightened by removing her ability to move and see.

"Do you trust me, Little One?" I ask as I go back to the drawer and remove a small flogger with six-inch chain link tresses. If they were any bigger, they would cause too much damage, so the falls are made much smaller than usual. The feeling of being hit with this is different from a typical flogger with leather or hide. I'm going to give her something new to fall in love with.

Journey licks her lips. "Yes, Sir. You have all of my trust."

"Good. I guess it wouldn't matter now if you didn't. You've given yourself to me and allowed me to tie you up. You have no choice but to trust me. Luckily for you, I'm not a monster. I'm just your beast."

I let the chains of the flogger slide against Journey's leg, climbing her body like a tiny spider before reaching the thickness of her ass. There, on the meatiest part of her leg, I slap the flogger against her flesh. It lands with a short *thwack* that makes Journey jump, but the rope keeps her from getting too far.

"How did it feel?" I ask, stalking around her body until I end up near her head. Her mouth looks so wet and seductive I have half a mind to drop everything and fuck it until I come again.

"It's new. What is it?" she asks.

"A flogger, but with tiny chains as tresses."

"I thought so. It stings more but I love it. As long as you're the one wielding it, I will always love it. Please keep going, Sir. I can take it."

"Oh, I know you can, Little Devil." I flog her again, harder this time—enough to make her skin redden. "I know you will take the pain of a thousand deaths for me, and I will proudly inflict it on you. Take it, Journey. Take the pain for me."

I whip the flogger across Journey's exposed skin over and over again, marking her legs and ass. I whirl the flogger around with nothing more than a flick of the wrist, but the damage it leaves in its wake is beautiful. Such little effort required to mar her skin. Once I'm finished, all I want is to fuck her. My cock leaks with precum, and I'm finally ready to unleash it, so I strip out of all of my clothes and prepare the task at hand.

I drop the little flogger on the bed near the pillow and return to my tied up princess. I'm sure her limbs ache to be released from the grip of the rope, but I'm not finished just yet. I rub my palm over her body, assessing the damage I have created and reveling in it. When I reach her ass, I stop and insert a finger into her pussy.

"Just as I suspected—soaked for me," I acknowledge with a proud smile.

"Always, Sir," Journey replies.

"Good, because I'm ready to come inside you more than I have ever been. Are you ready to receive me, Little One?"

"Yes, Sir. Please fill me up."

I stand on the side of the bed and slide Journey over until her ass is nearly hanging off, giving me unobstructed access. I grip her ass and slide inside without having to use my hands as a guide. She's so wet my eyes widen.

"Goddamn, Journey. Your pussy is so needy."

"Only for you, Sir. Always for you."

I begin pounding her pussy with brutal strokes that echo around the basement and creep up the stairs. "That's right, Little Devil. Always and only for me."

I grip a length of the rope and use it as leverage, squeezing it tightly as I fuck Journey like she's my most hated enemy. I fuck her hard and without remorse as she screams beneath me, unable to move or fend for herself. She takes all of it, giving herself over to me while I absolutely fucking wreck her pussy until the moment I explode inside of her.

I grunt, scream, growl, and swear as the orgasm consumes me entirely. My muscles quiver until I pull out and rest my arms against the bed, bending in half as I lay my head on Journey's ass. Once I'm able to stand again, I untie Journey, remove the blindfold, and watch as she slowly stretches her limbs. I see the agony on her face from the soreness, but she doesn't complain. In fact, she looks happy, grinning as she stretches out and makes her body usable again.

When she's finished, I don't bother cleaning myself up when she gets up to go to the bathroom, walking across the basement naked before coming back to me in the bed. I reach out and pull her down, snatching the covers over us as we lay on our sides with my arms around her. We'll get to aftercare in a little while, but for now, I just want to hold the woman who would both die and kill for me. For her, I would knock a thousand men unconscious and slice through their tongues without thinking twice. This is what our love looks like, and nothing can stop it.

fourteen
~ journey ~

"HEY, ANGIE. IT'S DETECTIVE MONROE," I say into my cell as I sit in the living room with a glass of wine. The lights are out in the entire house, and you're asleep in the basement after our scene, but I'm restless.

I can't stop thinking about what happened at The Black Collar. You defended me in the most brutal, beautiful way, cutting that asshole's tongue out of his mouth for disrespecting me. It was almost surreal to watch you handle him so viciously, which is what led us to the basement tonight. You tried Shibari for me, and while your rope work was a little clunky, I'm simply grateful that you made the attempt for me. You didn't have to, but you're so thoughtful, Sir. You take care of me in the best ways, and now it's my turn to make sure you're taken care of.

"Detective Monroe? You're up late, aren't you?" Angie Lu, the department's clerk replies.

"Yes, I am, but tomorrow is my day off so it's okay," I reply.

"Oh, well then I understand. What can I do for you?" Angie asks.

"Well, I got a call from a friend tonight," I say, weaving a web in my mind that comes out of my mouth as quickly as it hits my brain. "She was extremely upset and claimed that her boyfriend got into an altercation while he was out at ... well, I don't want to put her personal business out there, but ... he was at a BDSM club. She said they were on the phone together while he was walking back to his car as he left, and she heard shouting and scuffling. Then the line went dead and she hasn't heard from him since. She knows I'm a detective so she called me to see if I'd heard anything, so I'm just calling to check if any calls have come in tonight about an assault at any clubs."

The sound of Angie clicking away at her computer lets me know she's looking, and after a short minute she has the answer I've been waiting for.

"Actually, yes," she says. "There was a 911 call made by a bouncer at a club called The Black Collar in Center City. The bouncer claimed a man was attacked in a nearby alley and had his tongue sliced in two. EMS responded, as did two officers. The victim, Jay Brock, was escorted via emergency transport to Thomas Jefferson University Hospital about an hour ago."

"Oh, wow," I exclaim, putting on my best performance. "I can't believe it. Yeah, Jay Brock. That's my friend's boyfriend. Okay, assign my name to that case, Angie, and I'll take it from here. Thanks so much for your help."

"You got it, Detective. Have a nice night."

"Oh, I definitely will."

I'M NOT sure it even registered with you when I left the house a little while ago. To your credit, you've had an exhausting evening. You fought for me in the middle of an alley. You took your first crack at Shibari, and then you fucked me senseless the way you know I love it. When I tapped you on the shoulder to tell you I needed to handle my newest case, you simply said you loved me before going back to sleep, snoring the second your eyes closed. I smiled at you and rubbed your cheek, knowing you wouldn't have to worry about anything by the time I returned to our bed.

It's a risk walking into Thomas Jefferson University Hospital. Jay Brock is the man you brutalized on my behalf tonight, and I don't know if he was found in the alley or if he cried to the bouncer for help, but somehow he had the police called for him. I was worried this could happen, but I have a plan that I think is foolproof, Sir. Time will tell. Unfortunately for Jay, I recognize the two officers sitting outside his hospital room as soon as I round the corner from the nurse's station. Apparently, his call went to the Seventh Precinct.

"Good evening, gentlemen," I greet them as I round the corner.

Officers Jenkins and Flannery both stand when they see me.

"Hey, Detective Monroe. How's it going?" Jenkins asks, shaking my hand.

"I'm good," I answer. "I hear we have a guy with a sliced tongue."

Flannery nods. "Yeah, it's gruesome. The bouncer who made the call says this guy was antagonizing patrons as they entered and exited the club, so it could've been anybody. But what's left of the victim's tongue is so swollen now that he can't even speak. We tried to take a statement but he was in a lot of pain. The doctor's sedated him and are preparing him for surgery to try and reattach his tongue, so we were planning on waiting until after he's in recovery to take his statement."

"They're going to try to reattach it?" I ask with raised brows.

"Yeah, that's the crazy part," says Jenkins. "The guy had the cut piece of his tongue in his hand when he approached the bouncer. The EMTs put it on ice in the ambulance before driving him here."

"Shit," I exclaim, fighting back a smile. "Okay, well luckily for you two, I'm assigned to this case, and if they're about to take him into surgery, I'm not waiting for him to recover before I get his statement. Is he awake right now?"

"I don't think so," Flannery answers. "They sedated and drugged him to try to bring down the swelling before the surgery."

I nod. "Interesting. Well, let's see if he's awake enough."

Without another word, I burst through the door and walk over to Jay Brock. He's asleep in his bed with a mound of cotton balls in his mouth. His face is bruised and battered from the damage you inflicted on him, and his nose is visibly crooked. This is what happens when you disrespect me. God, I fall more in love with you every day.

"Jenkins, wake him up for me please," I say to the uniformed officer closest to me.

"You got it."

Jenkins steps up to the bed and places a hand on Jay Brock's shoulder, shaking him gently as he says his name. It takes a moment for Jay to open his eyes and shake off the fog of the medicine coursing through his veins, but eventually he makes eye contact with Jenkins.

"Sorry to bother you, Mr. Brock," Jenkins says. "I know you're tired and have been through a lot, but it's imperative that we get your statement before you go into surgery. We don't want you to forget anything, and a detective has been assigned to your case. So, if you're up to it, we need to get this statement right now. Then you can go back to sleep. Sound good?"

Jay nods.

"Good," Jenkins continues. "Alright, this is Detective Monroe from the Seventh Precinct. She's a fantastic detective who will help you put all of this together and bring in the people who attacked you. Give her every detail you can by writing it down on this notepad."

Jenkins hands Jay a small pad and pen from his pocket, and Jay nods again. Then, Jenkins moves aside and I step forward. The second Jay sees my face, his eyes widen so much I think they'll fall out of his face and roll onto the floor. With Jenkins and Flannery behind me, I allow myself to smile at Jay while showing him my badge so that he knows just how fucked he is.

"Good evening, Mr. Brock," I say, still smiling as I sit on the edge of his bed. "As my friend, Officer Jenkins said, I'm Detective Monroe from the Seventh Precinct. I understand you were attacked tonight, is that correct?"

Jay stares at me, tears quickly filling his eyes.

"Aww, I know the memory of the attack is hard to relive," I go on. "But I need you to think about it ... keep thinking about exactly what happened to you in that alley, and try to remember who your attacker was. Picture their face in your mind. I'm going to ask you some questions, and you can either write the answers down or simply nod your head. Either way is fine with me. Can you do that for me?"

Jay nods slowly, fear entombing his body.

"Good, let's start with the basics. Your name is Jay Brock, and your address is listed as 2305 Fairway Terrace in Colonial Park on your driver's license. Is that correct?"

A single tear falls down Jay's cheek as he nods.

"Good. It's important that we get that right so that we know exactly where to find you if things don't go well ... I mean, if we need to ask you more questions. Now, were you attacked in the alley next to The Black Collar BDSM club tonight?"

He nods up and down.

"Okay," I reply, jotting the info down on my own notepad to make the show look real for everyone in the room. "How many people attacked you, Jay? Just nod when I say the right number. One? Two? Three?"

He nods.

"Oh, so *three* people attacked you. Interesting. Were they all male?"

Jay nods.

"Did you know these individuals?"

He shakes his head.

"Okay. You're doing great, Mr. Brock. Now, here's the most important question. Could you identify the people who attacked you? Do you remember their faces? Now, before you answer, just remember that my name is Detective Monroe, and I know where to find you ... if you're having trouble remembering the details. Now, could you identify the people who attacked you tonight?"

After a moment and more tears falling from his face, Jay shakes his head no.

I grin. "That's too bad. Even if you saw security footage of people entering and exiting the club, you still couldn't point them out?"

He shakes his head again.

I smile from ear to ear.

Good boy.

chapter
fifteen

"WELCOME TO ANDREA'S. My name is Chad and I'll be serving you today ... but do me a favor and sit tight for just a second. I'll be right back to take your order."

Journey and I frown as we look at each other before laughing.

"That was odd," she says.

"Yeah it was," I answer, shifting my body in the seat to make myself more comfortable.

I wonder at what point in time everyone in the world got so fucking annoying.

Journey sits across from me in a green top with white pants. Her hair is flowing today, washing over her shoulder and running down her chest in a dark waterfall. Her brown eyes stare back at me, making images of last night flash in my mind. I never knew something as simple as sitting across from someone in a diner could be so alluring. My need for this woman knows no bounds.

I clear my throat and momentarily break eye contact before saying, "Stop looking at me like that before I take you in the bathroom again. You know we've already christened one of the stalls here."

Journey's smile is diabolical. "Oh, that's right. We did, didn't we? Let me see. If I'm not mistaken, you went in the stall first while I was sitting out here with Summers. I gave you a minute to get situated before I went in and kneeled for you like your good girl. Then you fucked my mouth and left. Do I have it right, Sir?"

I swallow hard as my cheeks heat up from the memory. My entire body begins to warm from the thought of that day and I suddenly have to adjust in my seat again to hide my growing arousal.

"Yeah, I think that was how it happened. That was right after you met your new partner following Winter's death."

Journey says, "It was. He and I were barely talking then. The guy seemed so nervous. He was really on edge in the beginning, totally skittish around me like he'd never worked with anyone before. He's still annoying but I'm glad he got over that."

"I bet. Meanwhile, I have to get over how hard you just made me by mentioning how we used that stall the last time we were here."

"Oh, really? Is it fully hard? Can I put my foot on it under the table?"

I smile but speak firmly. "No. You've done too much already. Now be a good girl and behave so we can have lunch ... so I can take you home and make you my dessert."

"Mmm, yes Sir," Journey says, just as the sound of our waiter clearing his throat slices through our conversation.

"Yeah ... are you ready to order, or are you still

talking about having each other for dessert? Because I can circle back," the waiter interjects.

At first I think he's joking, but when I look up, there isn't a hint of a smile on his young face. Journey isn't smiling either, so I decide to let it go so that things don't get out of hand quickly. Because if my Little Devil snaps, I'm snapping, too, and nobody wants that. Hell, I still hear the sound of my knife cutting through the tongue of the last guy who didn't know how to be respectful.

What a beautiful fucking sound.

"We're ready to order," I reply, tapping Journey's hand so she stays calm with me. "I'll have the ham BLT with a water, please."

"Great," Chad says, turning to Journey with zero enthusiasm. "And for you?"

Journey glares at the young man who looks like he isn't even old enough to shave yet. His hairless face is devoid of happiness and full of attitude. I assume he's just a kid who doesn't want to be at work today, but the look on his face makes it feel like he hates us personally.

"Journey," I call to her to break the building tension that has quickly made our little piece of the diner sweltering hot. "It's fine."

My kinky detective clears her throat, obeying her Dom.

"Okay," she says, doing her best as she looks up at the kid. "I'll have the patty melt if that's okay with you."

"It's fine," Chad says, snatching up our menus like he's in a hurry and hightailing it to the back.

"What the fuck is his problem?" Journey asks, frowning hard.

"I couldn't tell you," I answer with a shrug. "But let's try not let it ruin our day off together, especially after last night: the club, the Shibari, the guy in the alley, and our night in the basement with our own Shibari show. My good mood is immovable."

Journey glances in the direction of the kitchen where Chad seems to have scurried off to, but she shakes away whatever thoughts are running through her head and smiles when she looks at me.

"Yeah, last night was incredible. Admittedly, I'm still a little sore, which I always love the day after we have a scene. That's how I know it was next level."

"What's still sore?" I inquire, hoping to obtain some new information to store in my memory. Knowing how my Little One feels both during the scene and after it are vital to my growth as a Dominant.

"My legs a little, but my arms and shoulders for sure," Journey answers.

She lifts her right arm in the air and rotates it, trying to stretch it out. She maneuvers her arm in a big circle just as Chad returns with a plate in each hand. Journey doesn't see him and accidentally knocks one of the plates out of his hand and onto the floor, where food skitters everywhere and the plate shatters with a loud crash. Everyone in the diner turns to us and Chad turns beet red, dropping the leftover plate on the table so hard that food falls off it.

"What the fuck?" he bellows, glaring at Journey like he could kill her. "Why are you spinning your damn arms around like this is a fucking Pilates class, lady?"

Journey snatches her arm back down, clearly sorry for the accident while being pissed off by how this kid is talking to her. She stands up, anger pouring from her eyes, and this time I don't try to calm her down.

"I didn't mean to do it," she says, clearly trying to keep her composure. "And I'll gladly pay for another one since it was my fault, but if you don't quit with the fucking attitude, you're going to cause a problem."

"Oh, you want a problem over the food *you* just knocked out of *my* hand? We can have a problem if you want one. I don't care if you're a girl or not. Don't get in my face after you just ruined the fucking meal."

Now it's my turn to stand.

I know he's just a kid, but my patience is running extremely fucking thin.

Chad looks right at me and raises his fists, squaring up like a boxer in the ring.

"You want to go, motherfucker? Fine, let's do it," he barks just as a very large man in a sky blue button-up comes rushing from the back.

"Whoah, just calm down," the guy says. "Go to the back, Chad. Let me handle this before you get yourself fired."

"Fired?" Chad screams, falling into a temper tantrum he can't seem to climb out of. "I'm not the one who knocked over the plate, Mr. Clark, and I already know you're going to take it out of my paycheck. It's fucking bullshit."

"I said that I would pay for it," Journey tries to chime in.

Chad isn't having any of it. "Fuck you," he snaps.

"Hey," I cut in, stepping forward to defend Journey but struggling with keeping my beast at bay. "You might want to watch it. You're on thin fucking ice, kid."

"Oh, now you're threatening me? Call the cops, Mr. Clark. I'm being threatened at my place of work."

"Chad, you have got to calm down," Mr. Clark says, placing a hand on Chad's shoulder to try and turn him away from us.

"Call the cops?" Journey adds, reaching into her

pocket and yanking out her detective badge. "I *am* the cops, you little shit."

Journey shoves the badge in Mr. Clark's face, and the diner goes silent. Journey glares at the kid and who I assume is the manager, waiting for them to say something now that they know she's a detective, but they have no fight in them now. The kid knows he fucked up and shakes his head before walking away.

"I fucking quit," he spits over his shoulder, then he walks out of the diner without another word.

"Damn it," Mr. Clark whispers to himself.

"Are you the manager?" Journey asks, using what she has described as her cop voice.

Mr. Clark turns around, frustration weighing heavily on his face. "Yeah, I am. I'm sorry about all of that. Chad has had it rough lately."

"Yeah? Well, he seems like a little asshole," Journey snips. "No worries, though. I'll pay for both the food and the plate that was broken."

"That's fine, but I just lost an employee when I really can't afford to. So ... it's fine."

Journey's eyebrows jump to the top of her head. "Wow. So you're blaming me for that little prick walking out on you?"

"Ma'am, I'm not blaming you for anything. It's a very frustrating situation."

"I'm sure it is," I interject. I pull a one hundred dollar bill out of my wallet and shove it into the manager's hand before placing an arm around Journey's waist and turning her toward the door. "Sorry for the inconvenience. That should cover everything. We're going to go before the situation gets any worse. Thanks for your help."

"His *help*?" Journey snips, but I pull her with me,

pushing through the exit and stepping out into the sunlight.

I keep my hand on the small of Journey's back as I guide us to the parking lot, passing a blue sedan with a man wearing a low hat, staring at us like even he knows we almost caused a riot inside. He is probably contemplating whether he should go in after seeing what was clearly visible through the windows. I ignore him and everyone else as I push us forward until we reach the truck. I open Journey's door for her and close it, finally able to breathe now that she is behind a closed door.

When I get in, I turn to Journey who is clearly fuming. "Well that wasn't what I had in mind for spending our day together."

We would've had a much better time smothering someone together like the good old days.

She exhales, but it does nothing to relieve the tension in her face. "Not exactly."

"It's okay," I say, placing a hand on her knee. "Don't let it get to you, Little One. It was just a kid with an attitude. We can let this one slide."

Journey's eyes snap over to me. "Can we? We didn't let it slide with the guy from the club. Why now?"

"Because he's just a kid," I answer. "Things have been going great with us, Journey. We're happy and not having to run from the police. We don't need to murder every person who rubs us the wrong way and put ourselves in their crosshairs. We've been fortunate thus far, but let's not push it over a kid working in a diner. Okay?"

Journey stares at me for a while, and I wish I could hear the thoughts in her head. I can tell she felt disrespected in there, but we've already left multiple bodies in our wake and I don't want it to start drawing attention.

I rub her cheek with my hand, doing everything I can to extinguish the fire I know is blazing in her right now. Luckily, I see when she sighs and lets it wash off of her.

"You're right," she says. "Let's not let it ruin our day off together."

"That's my girl," I reply, starting up the truck and driving away.

Journey keeps her head turned away from me, staring out the window as we leave the parking lot and drive past the diner. Her body is tight and I can see her biting her lip from here.

"You good?" I ask.

When she turns to me, she's no longer biting her lip. She's smiling from ear to ear like nothing ever happened.

"I'm good," she says, reaching over and taking my hand in hers. "Everything is perfect."

sixteen
~ journey ~

"I'M NOT SURE EXACTLY, but Captain Saunders called and said he wants me and Summers on it. Something about a robbery in Center City. We just need to go in and take another statement from the victim then we can really dive into it in the morning. I promise it'll be fairly quick."

When you turn to look at me, I'm relieved to not see suspicion in your gaze. I don't sense distrust in your facial expression as I climb off the bed and go into the closet to throw on something a bit more professional. I'm also glad that you can't see me getting dressed, because if you could you'd see the tightness in my body. There is no other investigation starting tonight. There is no robbery.

You know me so well, Sir, there's no way I could hide how I'm truly feeling from you for long. Unfortunately, I've been exerting myself all day trying to hide my feelings and can barely do it anymore. Then again, I know you just as much as you know me, and I think that if there ever is a day that you find out about this, you'll understand. You might be upset that I disobeyed you, but you'd get it. Of course you would, Evan. You're my Sir.

"Okay, so I'll see you in just a bit. I love you, Sir," I tell you, planting my knee on the mattress to lean over and kiss you, falling in love with the way your lips feel on mine like I do every time our mouths touch.

"I love you. Be careful, Little One. If anything happens to you, you know I would murder the entire population of Pennsylvania over it."

My heart hums at your words. I fucking love you so much, Evan. I'm sorry that sometimes I lie.

"I know you would," I tell you, kissing you again. "I'll be back soon."

I struggle to pull myself away simply because I don't like being apart from you, especially when I'm not required to for work, but this must be done. I stand up straight, holding your hand a second longer before letting go and closing the bedroom door behind me. In the garage, I quietly shuffle a couple of storage boxes around and find a little section where I stored barbeque utensils last summer. There, right next to the charcoal, I find a nearly full can of lighter fluid.

The streets are quiet on my drive—not many people out at this time of night. The sky above me is cloudless and black, sprinkled with a vast assortment of stars of different sizes and brightnesses. It's calm and peaceful, making me feel at ease as I press the gas after a stoplight, bringing my destination into view. I'm unanxious as I drive around the building in search of cameras on the outside. To my disbelief, I don't see any from here. I mean, it's 2024. Who the hell doesn't invest in some sort of security system for their business? The owner of Andrea's Diner will find that to be a critical mistake.

After surveilling the surrounding area, I park my car

at the entrance of the small alleyway between Andrea's and the clothing store next to it. It's unfortunate that the store may become an innocent victim in all of this, but sometimes there is collateral damage when dealing with assholes. It's not my intent to put the clothing store out of business, but if it happens, so be it. I hope they have insurance.

The last time I was in an alley, I was watching you cut a man's tongue in half for calling me a whore because he couldn't get into The Black Collar. You were so perfect, straddling that asshole with blood on your fist and controlled rage in your eyes. I was in awe of you, as I have always been, but seeing you do such damage for me was breathtaking in the best way. I couldn't help but suck your cock right there in the alley because you're just so good to me, Sir. Fuck, even thinking about it now makes me wet all over again, and now that I know that Jay Brock's attackers will ever be found, I'm on cloud nine.

I love this about us. I adore how abnormal we are at our hearts. Both of us are capable of walking around all day and acting like we aren't thinking about burning the world down over our inconveniences. I know you feel it just as much as I do—the desire and need to brutalize someone for being disrespectful. You've gotten pretty good at keeping your desires encaged. Of course you have, Sir. You're so incredible. It doesn't surprise me that you'd try to keep from hurting someone if you can. That's a good thing. You protect us both with your control over your emotions. What you said earlier today is true. We don't need investigations being opened up because we lost our cool.

But if a crime is committed within the jurisdiction of the Seventh Precinct, then the investigation will come to my office and I will have control over how it plays out. I get to pull all of the strings—the same way I was the puppeteer in the investigation of Sierra Cross's disappearance.

I don't like having so many secrets, Sir, but the things I keep close to my chest are there for a reason. I want you to know everything about me, but I can't let you know *everything about me*. The most important thing for you to know is that I love you more than I have ever loved anything. I would never let anyone hurt or disrespect you. I'd protect you the same way you'd protect me. I also have to protect and guard myself from disrespect, which is why I had to force the redhead from your job out of state. It is also the reason I'm approaching the back door of Andrea's Diner with the top popped on a can of lighter fluid and a box of matches.

It only takes a second to empty the can beneath the door of the diner. I have no idea what's on the other side. It could be an office, storage area, or the kitchen. Whatever it is, it will be where the heat begins before it spreads to everything else inside. Based on the dumpsters back here, I'd assume it's the kitchen. They probably use this door to throw out the trash and have their smoke breaks after they are rude to paying customers.

Sometimes valuable lessons have to be learned, Sir. You and I have taught plenty, sending a few of our students to an early grave. While you've honed your skills at straddling the line of murder without crossing it, I've gotten better as well. No one will die today. I didn't kill Robin either. You see? We're both becoming better people together. However, Robin, Chad, and Mr. Clark will all learn not to fuck around with me.

I'm back in my car before the fire shows any visible

signs on the outside of the diner, and by the time I hear sirens in the distance, I'm already near the highway. I drive the speed limit to get back home, making sure to not draw any unneeded attention on my way, and I smile at you when I re-enter our room and kiss your perfect lips again.

"That was quick," you say as I change back into my nightgown in the closet.

"I told you," I reply, flicking off the light and getting into bed next to you.

I push my ass against your cock as you grab me by the waist and pull me close. Your warmth feels so good, reminding me of the many reasons why I hate being away from you. I always want you near, Sir. You are my home. With your arms around me and your breath on my neck, all is perfect in the world. Nothing that I've done matters as long as I have you, and I smile knowing that you are mine ... and that Andrea's Diner is already a pile of ash on top of a blackened foundation.

det. monroe

seventeen
~ journey ~

THE PHONE HAS a habit of ringing first thing in the morning when we're in the kitchen together. Right when I walk in and try to spend a few minutes marveling at the way you look, taking in your masculinity and sex appeal that oozes off you without you even knowing it.

There are lots of conversations about the male versus female gaze, and you don't even know that you are the latter. You are effortless in your sex appeal, dominant without trying to be, smart without attempting to impress me with it, helpful, thoughtful, empathetic, and caring in every moment. It shows in how you look after me when we finish a scene, making sure we never skip aftercare. It's apparent in the way you hold me at night, tugging me in so close that I can't help but feel protected and loved. It's all on display now, as you cook breakfast for me again without me having to ask for it or complain about not feeling well. You don't do things just to make me feel better, you do them because you know I will like them, and you never take yourself too seriously ... until it's time to protect me. You are the female gaze, which is why I can never take my eyes off of you. It's also why I hate that my phone rings right as I'm breathing in the sight of you.

"Hey, good morning," you greet me as I enter, looking over your mountainous round shoulder as you scramble eggs in a skillet.

I wrap my arms around your waist and hug you from behind. "Hi, Sir," I reply before hoisting myself on top of the counter and answering my phone on speaker. The voice of Captain Eric Saunders booms into the kitchen like thunder.

"Good morning, Detective Monroe," he says.

"Morning, Captain," I answer. "I'm about to see you at the precinct here soon, aren't I?"

"Actually, no," he says. "I've got an assignment for you and Summers."

"Oh, what's up?" I ask, but a pang of nervousness blooms in the heart.

Last night, I told you that Captain Saunders had called and asked me to look into a robbery. If you weren't so caught up in dividing the eggs into equal portions for us, I'd be anxious. It's strange that the captain would call and put me on an assignment right after doing the same thing last night, especially without saying something about dropping the other case. Nonetheless, you don't even glance in my direction. I love the way you trust me.

"I need you and Summers to get down to Andrea's Diner, just a few blocks from the precinct," Saunders informs me. "There has been a fire over there—took out the entire diner—and the manager thinks it may have been arson. I need this to be a top priority, Monroe. The owner, who's out of town, is a friend of mine. I'd like to take care of this for her and get her some answers.

Go get with the manager—his name is Robert Clark—and find out what the hell happened to my favorite diner."

"Alright, Captain. We're on it. I'll talk to you later," I say, watching you from behind as you pour orange juice into two cups and walk them over to the table.

"Thanks, Monroe. Keep me updated."

"Will do. Alright. Bye."

I end the call and hop down to join you at the dinner table, where you sip from your cup while watching me take my seat. I don't look at you because I don't want the obvious to pour from my eyes. If I turn my head in your direction, my nervousness will become too glaring. I feel like it's too late. My anxiety crawls on my skin like spiders and gives me gooseflesh. Fucking Saunders just had to call and say this right now, and I just had to put the fucking phone on speaker.

"Did he say that Andrea's burned down?" you ask, making my skin feel like it's tightening around me.

I clear my throat and sip my orange juice to buy myself some time before answering, "Yeah. Can you believe that? We were just there."

You stare at me. I feel it on the side of my face like a hot beam of sunlight.

"Yes, we were," you say, your tone soaked in accusation. "It's pretty strange that the place would burn down right after we had an issue there."

"Yeah, and right after that little fucker quit. I'd bet my next paycheck that he had something to do with it."

"You think the kid burned it down?"

"If not him, probably someone close to him. You know how kids are these days. Anyway, as crazy as it is, I'll get to the bottom of it. In the meantime, I guess you and I are going to have to find another diner to frequent."

Your eyes never move away from my face. It's like you're trying to read me, but I'm written in a different language. I don't like it, Sir. I hate that you're looking at me the same way so many others have in my past, trying to get a bead on what makes me tick like a judgy therapist. My father looked at me the same way. I hated it then and the feeling hasn't changed over time. It's even more unbearable coming from you. Fuck.

"Okay, so I need to go get started on this," I blurt out, pushing my chair back from the table and standing up. I bend over and shove four quick forkfuls of food down my throat and chug the rest of my orange juice so that your cooking doesn't go to waste, then I lean in to kiss you on the cheek. "I hate to dine and dash, but Saunders said to make this a priority. I need to get with Summers and try to get to the bottom of this ASAP. I'll call you later, okay?"

"Alright," you reply, still looking at me with a tiny furrow in your brow.

"I love you," I say over my shoulder as I head for the garage.

"I love you too, Journey," you answer.

My stomach cramps at the fact that you didn't call me your Little Devil or any other pet name you have for me, but I don't say anything about it. I can't. I open the garage, climb in my car, and drive away wondering if you're inside questioning me.

⸺

"MORNING, DETECTIVE MONROE," Summers greets me as I approach the scene. He's dressed in tan pants with a white button-up, his brown hair neatly styled as usual.

"Marty," I say, stepping up onto the curb and getting a good look at what used to be Andrea's Diner.

The smile tugging at the side of my mouth is nearly impossible to keep at bay. I manage because I can feel Summers' eyes on me, but I'd give anything to be free to laugh out loud right now.

The diner is mostly gone. All that remains are charred seats and tables that are falling apart. The metal on the legs of the tables is melted like lava swallowed them, while the plastic tops are destroyed, dissolved and flaking away like dry skin under the sun. The bar counter has been reduced to a withered piece of wood not even a quarter of the size it once was, while all of the lights have been destroyed. The only part of the diner that looks like it survived is the kitchen, which is clearly visible now that the doors leading to it have been burned to a crisp. The metal stoves and ovens remain standing, but the black ash has consumed them, too, making it all look ghastly even from the sidewalk outside.

"Damn. It looks like nothing survived," Summers says, announcing the obvious.

"Looks that way," I reply, stepping forward to inspect closer. "Any idea where it may have started?"

"It's still early so it's hard to tell," he answers, following me up to the ruined entrance. "From the looks of it, it may have begun in the back of the building. The back door is completely gone, and the boxes that were stored back there were the perfect kindling. We'll have to collab with the crime scene analysts and FD on this, but the hottest spot seems to be in the back."

"Electrical fire?" I ask, just trying to give other reasons this may have happened other than the real one.

"Could be, but it doesn't look like it. The fire department thinks an accelerant may have been used, but they're just getting started looking into that. Could be a day or two before we know for sure, but there are no signs of a breaker malfunction. The fire chief has already confirmed that he suspects foul play."

"Any cameras in the area?"

"None that could see the restaurant," Summers replies. "The clothing store next door has cameras, but they're all pointed at their entrance so they didn't pick up anything of substance. That place is lucky it's even still standing."

Outstanding. You may not like that I did this, Sir, but you'd be proud of how I've made sure it doesn't blow back onto us. Always and forever, Evan, I have us covered.

"Damn, that sucks," I lie. "So, the fire chief suspects foul play?"

Summers stops directly in front of me and places his hands on his hips. "That's what he said."

"Okay, well here's the thing," I start, damn near giddy to plant this seed and watch it grow. "Evan and I actually ate here yesterday."

"Oh yeah? Wow."

"Yeah, we had lunch, and while we were here we had an issue with one of the waiters. This kid had an attitude the entire time he was serving us, but when I accidentally knocked a plate out of his hand, he lost it. He was cursing at us and having a fucking melt down like that plate falling was the straw that broke his camel's back. It got so bad that the manager had to come over just to try and calm the kid down."

"Mr. Robert Clark," Summers chimes in. "He's over with the fire chief right now."

"Yeah, that's him," I go on, fully invested in weaving this web. "He came over and tried to get the kid to relax, but it only made things worse. The kid, whose name was Chad, ended up getting fired on the spot and storming out. It was quite the scene."

Summers nods his head as his eyes hit the ground, and I can see that he's eating up what I'm feeding him. His mind goes to work, connecting my dots exactly how he's supposed to. I wish you could see the look on his face, Sir. I bet you'd get a kick out watching him slowly catch on. In just a few seconds he has put my puzzle together exactly how I wanted him to.

"You think it might be the kid who was fired?" he says, speaking of it as a statement instead of a question.

"I think it's a good place to start," I reply, feeling proud of myself. "Let's go talk to Mr. Clark and see if we can find out where the kid lives."

When we approach Mr. Clark, his face melts like his diner when he sees me. The only way it would be better is if you were here so that he could see you, too. I bet he'd piss himself. I can see it in his eyes that he now knows that we were not the customers to treat rudely. Too little, too late.

"Good morning, Mr. Clark," I say, staring sharpened daggers into him. "It's unfortunate that it's under these circumstances."

He swallows hard as his eyes bounce between Summers and me. "Yes, it is. Are you the detective tasked to find out what happened here?"

"Yes, I am," I reply. "And I'm going to do the best I can with no hard feelings about yesterday."

"I'd appreciate that."

"Mmhm. Now, considering what I saw with my own eyes, there's a bit of information that I need from you, Mr. Clark."

He sighs, almost like he knows exactly where this is going. "Right. What do you need to know?"

I pull out a small notepad and pen, making the show look as real as possible in front of Summers who listens intently.

"I meant what I said about there being no hard feelings," I say with a grin. "But we both know how this looks after everything that went down yesterday, which means I need you to tell me where I can find Chad."

eighteen
~journey~

THE TRIP to Fairmount is short, which is good for two reasons: I don't like being in the car with Detective Summers for too long if I can help it, and because I always want to stay as close to you as I can. Work is as important to us as it is to everyone else, so I know that I have to do what I have to do, but god I miss your body's scent. I crave the feel of your skin grazing across mine. Even as we pull into the parking lot of the two-story home of Chad Swanson and his family, I'm thinking of you, Sir. When this is all over, I'm going to run into your arms and throw my legs around you as we kiss. You are my daily fantasy, the dream that stays on my mind when I know I should be concentrating on the task at hand. Regardless of what I *should* be doing, I'm always thinking of you. My Sir.

"Journey ... you okay?" Summers' voice dissects my thoughts and snatches my attention over to him.

I smile with pinched lips. "Yeah, of course. You ready?"

His smile mirrors mine and I wonder if he's faking it, too. "I am. Let's do this."

We get out on our respective sides, looking up at the massive house with pink and white details. Pink siding butts up against tan stone, while white pillars hold up the large porch and overhang in front of the door. I can see the white fencing in the back from here, and a dark brown gazebo standing tall over it. I wonder what's back there. What does a family who clearly makes a ton of money have in its backyard? A pool? A giant shed with two riding lawn mowers inside? Maybe a basketball goal? My curiosity doesn't stop me from walking up to the door, but I wonder what people with too much money do with it. Even with our combined incomes, you and I don't have this kind of money, and it makes me hate this family before Summers can rap on the decorative white door and press the button on the Ring camera.

"Can we help you?" a woman's thin voice asks from the Ring.

"Hello," starts Summers. "My name is Detective Martin Summers and this is my partner, Detective Monroe. We're here to speak with Chad Swanson and his guardians."

A pause before a man takes over.

"What is this in regard to?" he inquires. It's a good question, but since I've already decided that I don't like anyone behind this door, I'm annoyed before the words can hit my lips.

"We're investigating a crime and have some questions for your son," I snip. "It'd be a lot easier to do this face to face instead of through the camera. We'd appreciate your cooperation."

I see Summers glance at me out of the corner of my eye, but I don't bother looking over. What the hell is he looking at anyway? I wanted to say so much worse.

Instead of getting a reply through the camera again, we hear the sound of footsteps followed by at least two deadbolts being turned on the other side of the door. Once the security measures have been removed, the door swings open and we're greeted by a tall, pasty man with pale skin and blond hair, wearing a pink Polo and tight jeans. Without asking a single question I already know this is Chad's father. He looks like his name is Bartholomew and he doesn't smile, but I don't blame him. I wouldn't smile either if I looked like that.

"Umm ... is there a problem?" Bartholomew asks. "Why are you here to question our son?"

As I fix my lips to answer, a long-haired blond woman approaches from the back in a tight white shirt and a pastel pink skirt. Maybe a tennis court is in the backyard.

"Yes, what's this about? It's not every day detectives come knocking on our door," she says.

Summers smiles like he wants to answer but I beat him to it.

"Well, it's not every day that a diner in Center City that employs your son gets burned down. As I stated earlier, we need to ask Chad some questions. Now, we don't have to do it here if you're unwilling to cooperate. We can simply detain Chad and ask him our questions down at the precinct, or you can summon the lawyer I'm sure you have on standby. Either way, our questions will be asked and Chad will answer them. Just let us know how you'd like to proceed."

Bartholomew, pastel lady, and Summers all gawk at me, so I force a toothless smile to try to ease their tension.

You should see the looks on their faces, Sir. You'd think they never encountered someone who is direct before. I imagine people like this are not used to speaking with anyone other than yes men. Regardless of what they're accustomed to, they've never met someone like me before.

"Uh, okay," Bartholomew says. "Come on in, I guess. We'll grab Chad and have a quick chat in the study. The conversation will let us know whether or not we need to summon the standby lawyer."

Sarcasm? Attitude? Is that what I'm sensing from Bartholomew? My eyes widen, but Summers taps me in the forearm as the homeowners step aside and let us in. I cut my eyes over to him and he shakes his head as if telling me to cut it out.

I'd give anything to have you here right now. With you around, Evan, no one would touch me. Even though you gave Chad a pass because he's young, I know you'd lose it over Summers making contact with my body. *Your* body. It belongs to you. An accidental brush against my skin is the same as having a death wish when you're around.

Barbie and Ken lead us into the house where we round a corner and step into a tidy study. The place is decked out in mahogany furniture and decorated with sculptures of animals on pedestals. An eagle flies in the far corner while a tiger roars in another. A statue of a brown bear that's nearly as tall as me intimidates the room from his spot next to the couch. I eye his teeth as I sit down and Summers squats next to me. Barbie and Ken sit across from us on a leather couch of their own, their expressions stone cold.

"Chad is on his way down," Bartholomew says first, a furrow in his brow. "I'm Stanley, by the way. Stanley Swanson, and this is my wife Annette."

"It's very nice to meet you both," Summers says

cheerfully.

"I wish I could say the same," Stanley—the father formerly known as Bartholomew—replies. "What exactly is going on and how does it involve our son?"

"Well, Mr. and Mrs. Swanson," Summers says quickly, working hard to stay ahead of me. "We were called in to investigate a fire that burned down Andrea's Diner last night. As it turns out, my partner here was at the diner with a companion when they encountered your son. He works there, correct?"

Why is he asking when we already know the answer? Ugh.

"Yes, he does. Well, he did," Stanley replies.

"Right. Well, Detective Monroe says she was witness to an incident that took place—one where your son dropped a plate after clearly having a bad day, and stormed out of the diner after being fired."

"Fired?" Annette jumps in with a puzzled look on her face. "Chad told us he quit."

"I did," a young voice cuts in from behind us.

Summers and I turn around to find Chad Swanson standing in the doorway, an oversized vintage Sublime T-shirt draped over his shoulders with baggy pants that look like they were pulled straight from the nineties. The adoring son doesn't look anything like the product of the country club mother and father seated across from us. He's clearly a problem child, which is perfect for me. I guarantee he has never heard a single song by Sublime, and I hate him even more for it.

Chad strides into the room with his eyes fixated on mine. From the moment he enters to the second he sits down, no one else is in the room but me. His glare isn't much different from the one he wielded at the diner the last time I saw him. He has the same narrow eyes, tight jaw, and evil glare as before, and I wish more than anything that he was in the diner when I struck the match.

Better yet, I wish you and I could get our hands on him together. What a mess we could make with this little brat. What a lesson we could teach before we snuff out his life.

"Chad," Annette says, guiding her son to the spot next to her on the couch as she looks at him lovingly. "These detectives are here to speak with you. They say there has been a fire at Andrea's, and that there was an issue yesterday while you were at work. Detective Monroe here claims that you stormed out of the restaurant after being *fired*. Is that true?"

Chad keeps his eyes on me like he's trying to make me spontaneously combust with his gaze. Little fucker.

"That is absolutely not true," he says, finally forcing his eyes over to his worried mother. "I mean, part of it is true. I did see her there, and maybe I was having a bad day, but *she* was the one who made it worse. She knocked a plate full of food out of my hands, which caused Mr. Clark to come in. I knew he would charge me for it, so I was upset."

"What did you say to get yourself fired?" Stanley cuts in. I can tell from the look on his face that he has dealt with one too many issues with Chad and he's tired of it.

"I wasn't fired," Chad barks back. "Mr. Clark was going to charge me for the plate I dropped. He has done it in the past, and not just with me. So I quit before he could even go there. I can find a better job. One that doesn't force me to deal with people like her."

"People like me?" I snip with a raised eyebrow when I see Chad gesture toward me.

He scoffs. "Yeah, cops who come into the place treating workers like crap, sitting at the table talking about sex loudly in front of the other customers. It was disgusting. I'm only seventeen, you know? I shouldn't have to stand there and listen to that when I'm just trying to do my job."

All eyes in the room slice over to me just as my jaw drops to the floor. Chad isn't just a young piece of shit. He's a smart, manipulative, young piece of shit.

What I wouldn't give to bury him next to Sierra Cross.

The look in Summers' eyes tells me that he's questioning me. Combine that with the fiery gaze of Chad's parents and I feel like I'm on the stand at my own trial, the judge and jury glaring at me with newfound hatred.

I wish you were here to defend me. You'd know what to say in the blink of an eye. You're so quick witted that an accusation like that wouldn't stand a chance. Nevertheless, I have to handle this without you, as much as it pains me.

"First of all," I begin with a pointed finger. "Whatever *private* conversation I may or may not have been having with my partner is none of your business. Secondly, you were clearly eavesdropping. You could have announced your presence as soon as you arrived at the table instead of standing there listening to what was being said. We would have stopped talking immediately if you would have just given us that respect. Lastly, you didn't know I was a detective until you became belligerent and I felt the need to show you and the manager my badge. If I didn't announce that I was law enforcement, who knows how much worse you would've gotten. Your attitude is the reason you were fired."

"I wasn't fucking fired!" Chad bellows. "Why are you lying about that? Mr. Clark didn't fire me. I quit."

"From where I was sitting, you were fired," I shoot back.

"Liar. You're trying to make it look like I went back to get revenge by setting the place on fire, aren't you? You're trying to set me up."

"Now why would I do that?" I ask with a scoff.

"You're clearly a terrible person," Chad snaps.

"Regardless of what you think of me, young man, I am the detective investigating a fire that took place at your former place of employment after you had a heated argument with both a customer and your manager. I have reason to be suspicious of your whereabouts after you left the diner."

"Wait, what time did this fire take place?" Stanley asks, his face contorted into what looks like a painful scowl.

"The call came in around four this morning," Summers answers. "Which means the fire could have been started anytime between then and three o'clock."

Stanley and Annette glance at each other, and I don't have to be a mind reader to understand their silent communication. Little Chad wasn't here at that time.

"I was with Paula," Chad immediately says with wide eyes. "I swear to God I was with Paula."

"With Paula, where?" Stanley interrogates, doing my job for me.

Chad hesitates and I raise my eyebrows. There's no way it's going to be this easy, right?

"We were just ... out," Chad says.

The muscles in my face nearly cramp from the effort required to keep from smiling.

"Out, *where*?" Stanley asks.

"We were just driving around. Nowhere in particular," Chad explains. "Paula and I just get bored at her house sometimes, so we go for a drive until we get tired. That's what we did last night. We drove through the city just talking before she brought me back home. I swear I didn't set the diner on fire. You have to believe me."

"Did you stop anywhere?" Annette asks.

"No ... well, we stopped once, but only to get gas."

"Where?" Summers cuts in, laser focused on everything Chad says.

"Umm ... I'm not sure," Chad answers, digging his hole even deeper with his bare hands.

"I need you to try and remember, Chad. It's very important that you do," says Summers.

"Umm ... I think it may have been a Shell station or something. Just outside Center City."

"Was it a Shell station or wasn't it?" I jump in, tightening the screws so the kid slips up.

Chad frowns as his eyes begin to mist. "I don't fucking know. I didn't expect to be grilled like this over hanging out with my girlfriend."

"Well, you may want to get your story straight, because all hell could break loose if you don't," I say, drawing the ire of both parents.

"Hey, do not talk to my son like that," Stanley chastises. "It is not your place to speak to our son that way. How about you stick to investigating and leave the parenting to us?"

"Maybe if you parented better I wouldn't be investigating," I fire back.

Summers leans forward with his hands raised, showing he's unarmed. "Whoa, whoa, whoa. There's no need to get hostile. He gave his alibi, now we just need to look into it. If it all checks out, everything is good to go."

"If it checks out?" Chad asks with a glower. "Wait, there's no way you're pulling Paula into this."

"Chad, we'll need her to corroborate your story," Summers informs the family.

"You leave my girlfriend out of this," Chad barks. "She doesn't need you breaking down her door, accusing her of shit in front of her parents the way you're doing me."

"Why don't you want us to ask her? Is it because you're lying?" I ask.

"What's your fucking problem, lady?" Chad exclaims.

"I don't like being lied to," I reply. "And I can spot a little troublemaker when I see one."

"Alright, we're out of here," Summers cuts in, standing up and moving in front of me so that I can't even be seen. "Mr. and Mrs. Swanson, thank you for your cooperation. We'll be in touch. I know it may be difficult after this, but try to have a nice day."

"How the hell are we supposed to do that?" Chad blares as he stands.

Summers motions for me to get up and I oblige, following him as he quickly walks out of the study, turns the corner, and snatches open the door. The family follows us out, hurling questions in our direction and becoming even more offended when they don't get an answer. Stanley and Chad team up and spit insults in our direction as we get back in the car, and we can hear them still pelting the outside of the vehicle as we drive away.

"What the hell was that about?" Summers asks once we've cleared the verbal field of fire.

"What?" I say, swerving onto the highway.

"You were too hot in there, Monroe," he says. "You were coming for that kid like you *wanted* him to be guilty. You can't have personal bias like that."

"It wasn't personal bias. I was just doing my job. You were being the good cop, so I played the bad one."

"Good cop, bad cop? Are you freaking serious? This isn't a TV show, Monroe. Is that how you used to do it with Detective Winter?"

I pause, taking my eyes off the road just long enough to look at him with the fury of a thousand gods in my eyes. "Jesus, why are you always bringing up Winter?"

He scoffs as if I've said something childish. "I'm not always bringing him up, but I am trying to understand you better. We're partners and I want to know who I'm working with. I need to be aware of the tactics you'll use when we're questioning someone together. That's all I'm saying."

I put my eyes on the road as I press the gas, but I have a strong desire to keep looking at him, assessing his intentions.

I don't like people, Sir. I don't trust them. People always have underlying motives and figuring out what they are is a challenge that annoys the shit out of me. The only person worthy of trust is you.

I used to only be annoyed by Summers. His constant smiling and asking questions about Sam have gotten on my nerves more times than I can count. I've been able to push it to the side and get my job done without it truly affecting me, but tonight I'm more than just annoyed. For the first time since he transferred from another division and became my partner, I feel something else for him.

Suspicion.

chapter
nineteen

I GET HOME from work before Journey does, which is typical. What isn't normal is the heavy feeling in my stomach. There is a weight inside of me, pulling me down into a place I don't think I've ever been when it comes to my Little Devil. The weight feels a lot like a giant seed of doubt that has sprouted and is growing up my throat, only inches away from spewing out my mouth and showing itself to Journey, and she is the one who placed it there.

I don't remember hearing the phone ring the night Captain Saunders called and told Journey to investigate a robbery. I was asleep, but I don't sleep heavily. Murdering people and burying bodies in your backyard tends to bring heightened anxiety and insomnia to your doorstep. In the past, I have woken up every time Journey has received a late call for her job. Her ringtone is one of the most annoying sounds I've ever heard in my life, but somehow my restless brain ignored it this time. All I know is that she told me she was leaving to investigate a robbery and that it wouldn't take long to get the victim's statement. Right then—the second she walked out the door—the seed of doubt was planted.

The morning after her robbery investigation, Journey gets a call that I do hear. I'm standing right next to her when Captain Saunders tells her about the fire set to Andrea's Diner, and I hear him assign her to it, even telling her to make it a priority. What do I not hear? Saunders telling her to drop the robbery investigation. He doesn't mention it at all. He never tells her to let it go and that it will be assigned to someone else. Nothing.

I love my Little Devil more than anything in this galaxy, but that doesn't make any sense. What the fuck are you up to, Beautiful?

I saw the way she hurried her way through breakfast: nearly spilling orange juice on herself as she tossed her head back to gulp it down, jamming the fork into her mouth to shove all of her food in before the previous forkful could fall out. She was all over the place —totally out of character and I don't know why.

I put someone beneath the dirt before I ever met Journey. I didn't do it on purpose. It was the beast in me that reached out and took what it wanted. It wasn't until I met Journey that I learned I am not the person running from the beast. I am him. Journey allowed me to be myself, and it resulted in putting a couple more people under the ground to protect us. To this day, I have no regrets about what happened to Winter or Cain. I would gladly do it again for my Little Devil, which is why I don't understand why there seems to be a veil of secrecy shrouding her actions now. She knows I would brutalize anyone for her. There isn't anything she couldn't tell me.

So why didn't I hear the phone ring?

Why didn't Saunders mention the robbery investigation?

Why did she sprint out of the house after choking herself on breakfast?

The garage door goes up just as I'm settling onto the couch with a cold beer. My scent is a combination of lavender and mint after a hot shower that relaxed every part of me except my overthinking brain. I pick up the remote and turn on the TV just as the door opens and Journey walks inside.

My heart hammers just from the sight of her. It's as if our time apart was eons instead of mere hours, and the Dom in me wants to hug her, kiss her, and force her to her knees all at once. But I know she's tired from work. I can see it on her face—the way her smile is weary from faking it all day. Her shoulders slump as she walks, and the light in her eyes is dim like a star so distant it is barely visible to the naked eye. My Little One is exhausted, so I choose not to bombard her with questions right now, because what she needs from me at this moment is love and affection after a hard day's work.

"Welcome home, Baby Girl," I greet her as she enters and puts away her keys.

Journey comes into the living room, places her gun and badge on the coffee table, and drops to her knees. She crawls over to me and places her head in my lap, closing her eyes as if she doesn't want to see anymore of the day. I sigh as I run my fingers through the hair of my perfect submissive—my one and only.

"Rough day?" I ask, ignoring the TV and seeing only her.

She lets out a long exhale before answering, "I wouldn't call it rough. Just long. I missed you."

I smirk, my heart reacting to her words. "I missed you, too, Little One."

"You smell good," she says, taking in a big breath.

"Just got out of the shower."

"I need one but I'm too exhausted to get up from this spot."

Chuckling, I reach down and take her by the hand as I stand. "Come with me."

I lead Journey into the bedroom, where I sit her down on the mattress to wait while I start the shower. As it heats up, I go back to her and begin unfastening her buttons, pulling off her shirt before dropping to my knees to remove her shoes, socks, and pants. My eyes instinctively glance at her pussy when I slide off her panties, but I maintain control over my urges like a good Dom should. Once she's undressed, I guide her to the shower, but before helping her inside, I remove my clothes, dropping them at my feet.

"I thought you said you just had a shower," Journey says.

"I did. I'm not washing myself. I'm washing you. Now get in."

With a quick bite of her lip that she tries to hide, Journey steps into the shower and plunges her head beneath the water. I follow her, and as she wets her face, I grab her loofah and drizzle it with body wash before placing it on her back. I slowly move the loofah around on her skin, licking my lips as I clean every crevice on her backside. When she turns to face me, I do the same thing, coating every inch of her with suds until she relaxes and steps back into the water, her stress spiraling down the drain with the soap.

Once she's all cleaned off, Journey glances down at my aroused cock and licks her lips. I'm not surprised.

There has never been a time where she and I could shower together and not play afterward, but when she reaches for me this time, I politely push her hand away.

"No. Not now," I tell her. "Just let me take care of you, Little One."

She nods as she says, "Yes, Sir," but her eyes stay glued to my cock.

I smile as I help her out of the shower and into the bedroom, where I wrap her in a towel while using another to dry her off. I go over each limb before repeating the process with her lotion, then I climb onto the bed behind her and pull us all the way back until we reach the headboard. With Journey comfortably between my legs, we lean back and I brush her hair for her.

"Why are you so good to me?" she asks.

"Because you're mine," I answer, continuing to run the brush through her wet hair.

I take my time, brushing slowly to give her enough time to unwind completely from her day. After a few moments of silence, I finally say what has been waiting impatiently in the background since the moment she walked in.

"Tell me about your day," I say. "How did the fire investigation go with Andrea's?"

Journey clears her throat and sits up straight, whatever she's about to say requiring a straight back and hardihood.

Almost as if it's rehearsed. I wear a mask every day, Little One. I can recognize the signs.

"Everything went fine," she begins. "Summers and I took a little trip to Chad Swanson's house in Fairmont and talked to him and his parents. The kid is definitely a little troublemaker."

I keep stroking her hair. "I'm sure he is. But did he start the fire?"

"It's hard to say right now. He has a weak alibi, so ... he'll be the one."

I pinch my lips together, taking a second to build up to it because I know there's a chance she'll be offended. But I have to ask her outright. Fuck all of this beating around the bush.

"Journey ... did you set the diner on fire?"

After being completely loose and relaxed, the muscles in her neck and shoulders turn to stone.

"What? Of course not," she answers quickly—confidently. "What would make you think that?"

I set the brush down on the nightstand and wrap my arms around her so that she knows I'm not judging her, but my brow furrows.

"I know that kid offended you," I respond. "I know you were pissed about the way he talked to you, and I know that if he were an adult, he'd either be missing body parts or face down somewhere secluded because I would've handled it. But he was a kid—a teenager that I chose not to hurt because he was having a rough day. It's okay if that bothers you. I just want you to know that you can tell me anything, Journey. I've always got your back. You and I have wreaked havoc before, and I would wreak it with you again, even if I disagree with your decision. You come first. You're above everybody on this god forsaken planet to me. So if you did it, just tell me and we'll deal with it together. Did you do it?"

Journey lets seconds that feel like hours pass by before finally replying, "Evan, I didn't burn down the diner."

She's fucking lying.

But she has no reason to lie. I've given her every out

I can, so when she says she didn't do it, I try to believe her. What other choice do I have? We stay in our cuddled position against the headboard for a while, my arms swaddling her as I nuzzle her neck and kiss her shoulders, the voice in my head telling me not to give in so easily. But it's Journey. I love her. I trust her. If I don't, then she's no different than the rest of the people in the world. People I would gladly gut for lying to me.

I try to drown the seed of doubt, dousing it with hope and trust, but even as we move from the bed into the kitchen for dinner, the voice is still there, louder than it has been in months.

She's lying to you. Do not take this lying down. She. Is. Lying.

I can't shake it even as we eat together, and it's with me when it's bedtime and we cuddle again to go to sleep.

I don't know why, but I feel like there is a hidden treasure chest inside of Journey that she hides from the entire world—including me—and inside is a trove of secrets.

twenty
~ journey ~

NO ONE KNOWS that I poisoned my father. He'd been an alcoholic for years, his liver shriveling and dying centimeter by centimeter with each sip from the bottle, so when it finally gave out after years of abuse, the doctors weren't surprised. We'd just come from an appointment regarding his failing health, and his care manager warned him that it could be too late even if he stopped drinking, which he used as an excuse to pile it on even heavier. In his drunken fits of rage, he always took out his emotions on me. I'd been abused by him in nearly every way imaginable, so when the doctor told him he could be near his end, I decided to speed up the process.

Antifreeze tastes sweet. At least that's what the internet told me when I looked it up after learning it had been used to kill people before. I also learned that once it enters the human body, the person who consumed it is practically doomed. The amount I put into my father's whiskey bottle wasn't enough to change the look of his favorite drink or alter its taste. He never even knew that with every sip, I was poisoning him. He must have liked the sweeter taste, because he downed that particular bottle faster than any I'd seen in the past, and that's really saying something. The doctor didn't even bother to examine his organs after he passed, because they already knew his history with alcohol, so I never got confirmation on whether or not it was me. I was also never charged with his murder. Sometimes not knowing is better. Nonetheless, I do know I put antifreeze in his whiskey and then he died, and I've kept that tidbit of information to myself since the moment it happened. Secrets are not new to me.

It is not my intention to hurt you, Sir. Of course not. I love you. You are the very essence of my dark and twisted existence, and I can't imagine my life without you. Keeping the information about Andrea's isn't about you, Evan. It is about me. I don't want to tell you, and it's not because I think you'll react in a way that will fracture our relationship. It's simply because *I don't want to tell you.*

This is who I am. There are things about me that I just don't tell anyone. No one knows about my dad the same way no one knows about the fire, the same way no one knows that I watched you bury Sierra Cross in your backyard. I don't know if you finding out this information would mean anything at all, but it is *my* secret, not ours.

I can tell that you are becoming suspicious of me. The fact that you asked me outright if I set the fire is all the confirmation I would ever need, but I just didn't want to tell you. Even with you being so sweet about it, holding me tightly in your arms while kissing me with all the love and sentiment a woman could ever want. I couldn't do it. I didn't want to. I love you, Evan, and I hope this secret won't cause problems, but I can't tell you this.

You were still asleep when I left the house this morning, snoring peacefully in bed as I walked out with a heart that weighed more today than usual. I don't feel good about lying to you. I know you wouldn't appreciate it if you were to ever find out, but I swallowed my guilt and made my way to the precinct, forcing myself to think about anything other than the fact that I'm harboring a new secret that is meant for only me.

When I walk into the office, everything looks as it usually does. Uniformed officers move about like ants next to the detectives dressed in suits and tailored button-ups. The clerk operates from her corner of the bullpen, while Captain Saunders sits in his office talking loudly on the phone with the door wide open. Everything is as it usually is, including the sight of Detective Summers sitting at his desk right next to mine, his chair turned toward the entrance as if he's waiting for me to walk in just so he can flash that irritating smile. Sure enough, when I come through the door, there's the smile.

"Dude, how long have you been facing the door?" I ask when I reach my desk, annoyance already dripping from my words.

"Not long," Summers replies. "How was your night?"

I sit at my desk and turn on my computer. It's already a dreadful morning, and I get the feeling it'll be a dreadful day. *I lied to you last night, Sir, and it's going to weigh me down for every waking minute.*

"My night sucked. How about yours?" I ask, facing the screen even though it's still black.

"My night was interesting," Summers replies. "I

learned some things. Do you want to grab a cup of coffee first, or would you like to hear about it now?"

"What difference does it make?"

"Well, I'm not sure. Are you interested in information about Chad Swanson's alibi?"

My breath catches in my throat as my lungs freeze. My computer lights up and I don't even bother to look at it. I turn around to face Summers and there's something in his eyes that makes me frown.

"You got info about Chad's alibi? How?" I ask, my heart revving with each passing second.

"You know the Shell station he mentioned outside of Center City? I found it."

I swallow hard, wishing your arms were still around me to offer comfort.

"You went there without me?" I inquire, but it's a stupid question. He clearly did.

"I did, and you know what I found?" he asks rhetorically. "Proof."

My jaw tightens. Sir, something feels off.

"Proof of what?" I ask.

"Proof that he was there," Summers answers. "Turns out, the kid was telling the truth. Shell has video of Chad and his girlfriend pulling in to fill up her Jeep at about three-thirty in the morning, which is about ninety seconds before the call came in about the fire at the diner. I checked the route, and there's no way they got from Andrea's to the Shell station in ninety seconds. Unless the kid has the ability to be in two places at once, there's no way he set that diner on fire."

I don't know how to respond. My jaw flexes and I bite my lip as my mind goes berserk to think of something to say, but nothing comes. While I'm still working out answers in my head, Summers starts again, his newfound confidence beaming from his eyes like starlight.

"You want to know something else?" he asks without waiting for a response. "I also talked to the manager of the diner, Robert Clark."

What the fuck?

"I didn't like how there was so much back and forth about whether or not Chad was fired from his job or if he quit. I figured I'd get the information from the man himself. Turns out, Chad was *not* fired. According to the manager, he quit ... right in front of you and Evan. He claims he even mentioned to you that he was upset about losing Chad. Isn't that strange? Did you just forget that part of the conversation? Or did you leave it out on purpose?"

Evan, I need you here. There is something going on with Summers that I don't like, and he is starting to look a lot like someone in need of an "accident."

"Why would I leave it out on purpose, Summers?" I ask, still maintaining my calm on the outside while in a frenzy internally. "Are you actually trying to accuse me of something? Because strangely enough, that's what it sounds like."

"Of course not," he replies quickly. "It's not a big deal to get that information twisted. You were there when the drama went down. You saw the kid storm out and you drew a conclusion. It doesn't change what happened for the most part. The diner was burned down and you used the information you had to form a lead about a possible suspect. If anything, I'd say it was a good hunch to act on. No need to get defensive, Detective."

I lean back in my chair with squinted eyes that stare a hole into Summers' face, unsure of what else I'm supposed to do. I want to call you, Sir. I want your guidance, but you don't know that I burned down the diner so I can't lean on you for help. I got myself into this strange situation with Summers, and I'm going to have to figure my way out.

"Journey," Summers continues. "It's no big deal. We just need to do our jobs and investigate. We'll get to the bottom of who really burned down Andrea's, and when we do, we'll put them where they belong. Don't look so upset about taking one guy off the suspect list. It happens."

The furrow in my brow is deep enough for cars to fall into.

"Umm," I say, shaking my head. "Yeah, that's fine, I guess. I was just hoping we could prove it was Chad and close the case quickly. A little investigative work never bothered me. But why did you go without me?"

Summers shrugs nonchalantly. "Was feeling restless after work so I decided to make a couple of stops before heading home. I knew you were spending time with Evan and I didn't want to bother you. No biggie."

"Right," I say, but absolutely nothing feels right about it.

"Speaking of Evan, can I ask you something?"

Why the fuck would he want to ask me something about you?

"Sure."

"How did Winter react when he found out you were dating a suspect?"

My eyes widen as I lean forward, my world spinning as shock hits me right in the chest. My vision blurs everything around Summers, making him the only thing I can see clearly. Ringing starts in my ears and gets louder ... louder ... louder, until I can't hear anything at all. I have to shake my head, trying to steady myself, forcing my lungs to keep breathing and reducing the pressure building in my body, making me feel like I'm about to explode.

"What the fuck did you just say?" I snap, my normal detective facade slipping away as the ringing in my ears finally starts to fade away.

"Evan Godric. He was a suspect in a missing persons case, right? Sierra Cross?"

Summers sits back in his seat with an emotionless face, his eyes watching me closely. Now, there is no hint of a smile.

"What the fuck?" I snip, scowling at him, ready to risk it all right here in the precinct. "Why are you asking me that as if I wouldn't get offended? The Sierra Cross case is closed."

Summers raises an eyebrow. "Well, it went cold ... and my god you are wound tight this morning. I wasn't accusing your boyfriend of being guilty of anything. I just heard that you met him during the investigation that eventually fell apart, and I was curious if Winter had anything to say about it. It's not every day that a detective falls for a guy that used to be a suspect in a disappearance she was investigating."

"Evan and I didn't start dating until *after* the investigation ... *after* Sam killed himself. So he never knew we were dating, alright. I'm getting pretty fucking tired of you asking me questions about Winter. If you have something you want to say to me, Summers, just fucking say it and stop bringing up shit every other day. He killed himself, alright? He chose to end his life over a multitude of reasons, not just the Sierra Cross case, *which is practically fucking closed*. You're my partner now, but I swear I will go to Saunders and request for a new one if you keep this shit up. Sam was my friend, and I don't like you constantly mentioning him and making me relive his death. Now you're bringing my boyfriend into it. So what is it, Summers? What's your fucking problem?"

Shit. I didn't mean to lose it, but I couldn't help it. He's asking about you now, Evan. He's investigating without me and constantly bringing up Winter. What was I supposed to do? How am I supposed to react when every cell in my body wants to take him out back and put two in his fucking chest? One way or another, I'm going to have to put a stop to this, and I hope it isn't another secret I have to keep from you.

"Wow," Summers says with raised eyebrows. His face softens and takes on an apologetic expression. "I'm really sorry. I had no idea asking that question would set you off like that. I was just curious, Journey, that's all. I know you love Evan and you two are happy and living together. It was insensitive of me to ask that. I truly apologize for being offensive. You're right. I'm letting my weird, morbid curiosity get the best of me. I need to stop and I will. I won't mention Winter again. I'm sorry."

I glare at my partner as thoughts of placing a hand over his mouth and slashing his throat come to mind, playing out in gruesome detail. I can practically feel the blood spraying against my face as I sit back and focus on unclenching my jaw.

"I crossed the line," Summers says, rising from his seat. "I can tell I've pissed you off. I'm sorry, Journey. I know we've got work to do on this diner case, but I'm going to take a few minutes to grab some food so you can have some space. I'll understand if you request another partner or if you just need the day away from me. Take all the time you need. Again, I apologize."

Without waiting for a response, Summers walks away, still shaking his head as he leaves as if kicking himself for going too far. I watch him go, wishing I could shoot fucking lasers from my eyes so I can drop him midstride.

I feel like a thread is starting to unravel, Sir. Something is happening and it's making me anxious. When I get anxious, things start to happen. Buildings burn down. People die. I have no idea how I could possibly get away with killing my partner, but Summers is doing too much. He's making himself look suspicious with all of this, and while I know that having two partners drop dead would put me in the crosshairs, I've always managed to avoid being caught in the past.

Maybe the target on my back would be worth it if it means getting rid of a nosy partner. Maybe instead of killing himself like Sam, Summers just vanishes into thin air. Maybe he gets buried in your abandoned backyard right next to Sierra. Maybe this has gone on long enough. Maybe I'm going to have to add another secret to all the rest.

calm

chapter
twenty-one

WHEN JOURNEY GETS home from work, the dance we've been doing the past few days continues. Tension swelters the room as she walks by, glancing at me out of the corner of her eye, and I let her go without saying a word after our initial greeting. She showers while I watch TV with a cold beer in my hand, and when she comes out, she sits on the couch after merely patting me on the knee. This is what a seed of distrust does when it grows into a towering tree, taking up all of the space in every room we enter.

There she is; the liar. And you are am; the pussy who is letting her.

Journey denied setting the fire that burned down Andrea's Diner, and even though I accepted it outwardly, I think we both know that I have reservations. She can see it on my face just as much as I feel it in my gut. Maybe I could have let it go if Journey acted like she meant what she said. Instead, she walks around like she's on thin ice, afraid her body weight will make the foundation crumble and plunge her into her sea of lies. I fucking hate that there is a river of doubt streaming between us now, but I don't know how to act. Until she delivers evidence that proves someone else did it, I'll continue struggling with feeling like I've been lied to.

You're a fucking Dom. Grab her by the face and shake her until she confesses. Tell her that you will know if she is lying even if you don't. Just get the truth out of her!

Stop it! Journey is not like other women. She's not even like other subs. Sure, I can demand that she tell me the truth, but will she? I have no other means to acquire information. I only have her words.

Don't let love distract you from the truth.

Clenching my teeth, I exit out of a show on Netflix and move onto something I know we'll both be interested in. After pressing play, I set down the remote and let the show begin. Still, no words have been spoken between us. It's not until Journey turns to face me that I realize we might not go the entire night without speaking.

"I have to tell you something," she says.

I can see it in her face that whatever she's about to say is important to her. No matter how frustrated I become with my Little Devil, she's still all I truly care about. I'm still her protector, her savior, and her Dom. When I see the look on her face, I forget it all and sit up.

"What's the matter?" I ask.

Journey hesitates like she doesn't really want to tell me. Is this it? Is there where she admits that she destroyed the diner? Maybe keeping the secret became too much for her and she's ready to let it out. If so, I won't be upset. I won't hold it against her or make her feel bad about it. I know she must have had a reason, and I trust her to make the right decisions for herself, even if I disagree with them.

"I wasn't going to say anything," she starts. "But I don't like the way it feels holding this inside. I thought to deal with it on my own but decided that I wanted you with me. I need you with me, Evan."

"Journey, you can tell me anything, and you know I'll be there to support you however I can. Whatever it is, we can and will deal with it together. You don't have to hide anything from me."

She lets another few seconds pass, seemingly still contemplating divulging the information. When did she start feeling the need to keep parts of her life hidden from me? What else has she tucked away in the dark?

"Something strange happened at work today," she says. "Summers said something that has me thinking we may need to pay him a visit."

Summers. Fucking Summers. With the history I have with the Seventh Precinct, I have always done my best to stay away from that building. The one time I decide to surprise Journey, I'm met by Summers and have to keep myself from stabbing him in the neck with a fork. He's arrogant, with a know-it-all attitude that rubs me the wrong way, and I can only imagine what it must be like for Journey to have him as a partner. The smile he plasters on his face is off-putting. There is something about it that I don't like. That smile is Summers' mask, and there is something devious peeking out from behind it.

"What did he say?" I inquire, placing my elbows on my knees as I listen intently.

"He asked a question," Journey explains. "It's not abnormal for him to ask me questions. He has been asking weird questions since he arrived. But today he asked one that he shouldn't have—one that felt like more than just general nosiness. He asked me how Sam reacted when he found out I was dating a former suspect."

Acid sizzles my veins as my eyebrows rocket upward. "Is that right?"

"Yeah, and I'm not sure what to do about it."

"What else did he say?"

"Well, when I got pissed off about him for constantly bringing up Sam, he seemed genuinely apologetic. He said he was sorry multiple times, and even left to give me space because he could tell I was ready to break his fucking neck. He said it was his morbid curiosity or some shit, but I don't care. I don't like that he's so interested in Sam, and now that he has pulled you into it, I'm fucking done. I don't know how you feel about it, but I'm ready to start planning how to make him disappear. But, like I said, I don't want to act on this without your input."

Still leaning forward, I put my head down and try to think. This wasn't the information I thought I'd be getting. Journey and I still have the issue of the diner fire to deal with, but this new thing with Summers is concerning, to say the least. What the fuck would prompt him to ask her a question like that? Is this guy looking into me? Is he looking into Sam's death? If so, why? As much as I understand Journey's desire to get rid of him, we need more information first.

"Okay, so there are only two scenarios here," I say, my eyes still on the floor while I think aloud. "One— your new partner is really just a curious asshole who doesn't understand the boundaries he crosses. He's immature, and when he found out that he was replacing a man who *killed himself*, he really did become morbidly curious, and now he's asking a bunch of questions that he shouldn't. Or it's two—his interest in

Detective Winter is driven by something else; a need to find out what really happened. In which case you would be right; we'd need to rip his tongue from his mouth so that he can't talk to anyone."

Journey abruptly stands up, her body suddenly filled with excitement. "Alright, so when should we go? I can find out where he lives and if he lives alone. I don't think he's married—at least he hasn't mentioned it—so we could get him the same way we got Cain. We wait until it's late, I'll handle the lock on the door, we bind and gag him so we can carry him out without leaving any evidence behind, and we kill him somewhere offsite—maybe one of the many wooded areas in Delaware. We make sure his house isn't disrupted in any way—no signs of a struggle, no damage, and no stolen property. We make it seem like he just evaporated into thin air."

I smile, falling in love with how animated she gets when talking about killing someone. I fucking love it, and I love how willing she is to go all out to keep us both safe. However, there is more to it than my Little One is realizing.

"I hear you," I say, leaning back in my chair and lifting my beer. "And what happens when you start getting questioned? There's no way we do this without you becoming the focal point of an investigation. Losing two partners so close together will not fly under the radar."

Journey's beautiful brown eyes dance around the room in search of answers.

"Well, that's part of the problem," she admits. "But I can handle that. No matter how many questions I get, there won't be any evidence leading to me. They can ask whatever they want but they can't prove anything."

What an ironic thing to say considering the circumstances.

"Okay, let's say you're right about that. Even if they can't prove that you did anything to either of those fucking losers, the investigation will almost certainly lead them to me. We've dodged scrutiny by keeping our relationship off the radar of anyone in your department. We made the mistake of going out to lunch with your partner *one* time, and he has already recognized my name. What would your captain do if he found out you and I were together?"

Realization slaps Journey across the face, forcing her to sit back down.

"It wouldn't be good," she agrees, nodding with disappointment hanging from her face.

"No, it wouldn't. We have to keep in mind that Winter got approval from a judge to conduct a search on my house. The only reason it didn't go any further is because of your statement saying that you didn't find anything. Sierra's body is still buried there, so we don't need to do anything that could remind them about my connection to her. Investigating you will lead them to investigating me, which would surely lead them back to my house in Strawberry Mansion. That's the last thing we need, so we have to play this smart."

"Okay, so then what do you suggest?"

"We have to wait," I answer.

Journey sits back in her seat, clearly annoyed.

"We don't have enough information," I go on. "Until we know whether the guy is looking into you or is just weird, we can't act. Little One, I know how we handle things like this, and I know you enjoy it. I do too, but we are not serial killers. We don't bury people indiscriminately. We got rid of Winter because he caught us trying to move Sierra's body. We ended Cain because he was talking to Winter about how we attacked him. We had reasons, and until Summers finds out something he isn't supposed to know, or shows that he's looking in places that are off limits to him, we shouldn't risk it all."

Journey twists her lips together, genuinely let down by the fact that we can't kill her partner ... yet.

"Listen," I say, even though she's staring into space instead of looking at me. "I love you, and I love this life that we have together—the toys we have in the basement, The Black Collar, the lifestyle. I love it all, and I'm so glad that we found each other. I would strangle Sierra Cross a thousand times if I knew it would lead me to you all over again. I don't want to risk what we have unless we absolutely have to. Sometimes shit happens and we can react on impulse, like with the guy at the club. With this situation, we can take our time and find things out before making a move too soon.

"So now it's your turn, Little One. You're worried that Summers might be looking into you, well now it's time for you to start looking into him. Start paying attention to what he's doing. Start checking for him, seeing who he's talking to, watching where he goes when he leaves you by yourself, reading his emails if he leaves his computer open. See who he's talking to when he texts. If he wants to wiggle his way into your life, start cutting your way into his. It's no different than when we were worried about Winter and what he might do. We had to wait, and the second you found out he got a search warrant for my place, you called and we acted."

Journey nods, her eyes slowly finding me again. "You're right. I need to slow down and see where this goes. But if I find out that he's checking us out, we're going to have to handle it quickly. I won't want to waste time and risk whatever he learns getting to Saunders or anybody else."

"We won't hesitate for a second," I reply. "If he gives us reason to be suspicious, I promise I will slit his fucking throat myself. Okay?"

Journey nods as a smile slowly takes shape on her face. "Yes, Sir."

chapter
twenty-two

I CAN STILL PICTURE Detective Winter hanging from his ceiling fan like it happened yesterday. His eyes were closed, neck bent at an awkward angle, and his body swayed ever so gently while Journey and I fucked beneath his corpse. Yeah, that's not the kind of memory that fades quickly. I hope it never does. I want those details as fresh in my mind as possible as a reminder of how far Journey and I have come, and how far we're willing to go when we feel threatened.

I wonder if the same fate awaits her new partner. Detective Summers doesn't have to undergo any suffering. He doesn't *have* to die. Since Journey and I moved in together, I've been actively trying *not* to kill people. Sure, I have urges that I give into. The wrong words could easily result in a knife in your cheek or a blade through your tongue, but dead bodies are hard to hide. Hell, my first one is still buried in my backyard. I own the deed and the house isn't up for sale so I'm not worried about it, but Sierra is still there, resting eternally in her permanent grave. The last thing I want is to have to figure out how to hide more corpses.

Eh, maybe it wouldn't be so bad.

What does it mean for us if I end up having to drain this man of all his blood? There's no question that they would look at Journey, and who knows where that could lead their investigation. It's such a huge risk to our life together that I feel as though I have no choice but to wait and see what happens. On the other hand, if Summers really is looking into our past, his existence is just as much a threat as his dead body would be.

"How's it going over here, Evan?"

I swing around to find Trey standing behind me. Shit. For a moment, I forgot I was actually at work. The loud noises of the job site come screaming back to life as a truck filled with concrete raises its chute to pour another wall only a few feet away. Shawn and the rest of my team standby, hands on shovels and concrete rakes, ready to shift the falling 'crete into its proper position in the forms. Two walls have been poured, each of them surrounded by men on their hands and knees, working the mixture with trowels to make sure the finish is level and smooth. We'll be at this for most of the day, yet I can't keep my mind off of what I will probably end up having to do to *another* detective. One day these people are going to have to learn how to stop dying.

"Hey, what's up, Trey?" I say, coming back to reality. "Everything is good over here. Two walls down, a fucking billion to go."

Trey chuckles. "Yeah, it's gonna be a long day, that's for sure. We've been so busy with this shit lately, I feel like I haven't had time to slow down and process it all."

"We've been on the grind for this one," I add as Shawn positions himself next to the chute to guide it when the concrete starts to slide out.

"Just trying to keep us on or ahead of schedule."

"We understand, man. The crew loves you. That's why we all work so hard for you. Once it's all finished, we'll go celebrate like we always do before we move on to the next one. Luckily, we have a good group of people working with us."

"Which I'm thankful for," says Trey. "After that whole Robin situation, I wasn't sure how this would turn out."

"Oh, that's right. I had forgotten about that. Whatever happened to her?" I inquire.

"I guess she went back to where she was before she transferred here. I never heard from her again after the day she came into my office all bruised up and anxious. Luckily, everything is working out for the best."

"Definitely," I agree, but my brows are still stitched together as the details come back to me. "I don't like not knowing why she was acting the way she was, though. Especially when you mentioned my name."

"Man, I can still see the look on her face to this day, even with those dumb-ass glasses she had on. I said the name Evan, and that girl looked like she was ready to run for cover. Unless my eyes were deceiving me, I'd swear she was terrified of you. But who knows? Either way, she's gone and the crew is still rolling right along."

I nod my head as concrete pours out of the chute, splattering at the feet of the men inside the forms as they rake it into place. I see them, but my mind wanders, wondering why Robin would act that way after we had a cordial, friendly day prior to her leaving. I know I didn't do anything to her, so what would make her act frightenend when Trey mentioned my name? It just doesn't make sense.

Unless ...

"So, how's Journey, bro?" Trey asks, cutting off my

thoughts. "You moved in together a while back. How does it feel to be domesticated?"

The two of us laugh together before I answer, "Surprisingly, I like being domesticated. Journey and I are ... we're good. Living with her is a dream come true. To be honest, we're learning a lot about each other."

"I hear moving in together can be tough. It's like realizing the person you've been in love with is actually a disgusting slob who throws their dirty drawers in the bathtub to let them soak instead of using the washing machine."

"Bro, what?" I exclaim, laughing hard. "Is that your situation you're talking about? Because my Little One isn't leaving her panties in the bathtub."

Trey pushes me on the arm as he laughs. "That hasn't happened to me, I'm just using it as an example. People are different when they're at home. It's a lot harder to keep secrets when you have to look at the person you're sharing your space with every single day. You start seeing them for who they truly are and it's like you have to fall in love all over again, but this time with the added information of what they're like in their private life."

"What are you, a couples therapist in your spare time?" I joke.

"Nah, man. I watch TV and shit. Plus, me and Theresa are heating up, and I'm trying to learn as much about her as I can before I pop the question."

"You're going to ask her to marry you?" I ask with saucer-sized eyes.

"Don't look so shocked, Evan," Trey says, his smile as wide as the whole job site. "I'm thirty-one years old, man. Even an old player like myself has to settle down sometime. Plus, I'm just following your lead."

"My lead?"

"Yeah. You committed to your girl, moved in with her, and look at you now—the happiest guy on the job site. I saw the look on your face when I approached you just now. You looked like you were daydreaming about getting your hands on your girl."

I laugh as I say, "I was definitely thinking about getting my hands on *somebody*."

"See, there you go," Trey says, nodding along, completely unaware of how wrong he is. "Alright, I'll let you get back to work. But how about I treat you and your girl to dinner sometime soon? I mean, I was the one who brought you two together, remember?"

"Oh really? How do you figure that?"

"You told me. That night you and I went to the bar and she was jocking you from afar. I got up to go to the bathroom and that's when she came over, remember? You didn't even want to talk to her, but I insisted. Hell, I could've peed at home, but because I left you at the bar all alone, she approached you and you two hit it off. You're welcome."

We share another laugh. "Well, since you're *solely* responsible for us being together, I guess we can let you take us out to dinner. It's the least we can do."

"Cool. Okay, we'll set something up. Now let me get back to work before all of this falls apart. Talk to you later, bro."

"Alright, Trey."

The only person I've ever considered a friend walks away, and I prepare to move into the concrete to help my crew. As easy as it is to talk to Trey and forget about my life's current status, the truth is that everything isn't as peachy as he believes it is. I wish Journey and I were at our best right now, living blissfully in our world of kink, swimming in nightly multiple orgasms. Maybe by the time we have dinner with Trey, we'll be a better example of what a happy couple looks like. For now, the only thing I'm swimming is in a sea of questions, and I feel like I'm drowning.

This is bordering on pathetic. Either get the answers you seek, or leave it alone. All of this back and forth is fucking annoying.

I want to get back to where we were when we first moved in together. Before Journey's partner started asking questions. Before Andrea's burned down and Journey struggled to keep herself from looking guilty. I want less nights like the one we had yesterday, and more like the night we sliced off a man's tongue for disrespecting us—a night that ended in Shibari and great sex.

I want our pitch black version of happiness, and in order to get it, I may have to let go of my distrust. My seed of doubt has sprouted and is growing too much. I need to pull it out by the root and burn it so that Journey and I can be happy. At the end of the day, that's all I really want. Yes, I'm a beast who will squeeze someone's throat until they turn fifty shades of blue and never breathe again, but my beast wants its devil more than anything else. I simply desire a kink-filled life of pain and bliss with Journey, but God help anyone who tries to keep me from having it, and that includes Detective Summers.

chapter
twenty-three

AFTER FAR TOO MANY hours of pouring concrete at the job site, I finally make it back to my world. It doesn't matter how long I'm gone, I miss home every time I leave it. It's the same with Journey. Concerned about the diner fire or not, I miss her every time she's not in my presence. While I'm running around construction equipment and heavy machinery, my mind always finds its way back to her—to wishing my fingers could grip her throat and squeeze until it changes colors. My eyes see work being done and check-boxes being marked as complete, while my mind imagines my Little Devil bent over in front of me, her entire body being squeezed by ropes so that she can't move. Sometimes I think about it so much that the sound of whirring machines is drowned out by the screaming orgasms I hear in my head. The compilation of sounds and images always gives me something exciting to look forward to.

I spent the rest of the day thinking about what my next move will be. On one hand, I fucking hate *Marty* Summers. Looking down on his immobile body while he bleeds out would bring me nothing but pure joy, and I battle the temptation of slicing his jugular. On the other hand, my hatred toward him can't cost us what we've gained by eliminating Journey's last partner. So, as I told Journey when we last talked about it, we'll wait until something else develops. Outside of Summers, the other problem lies with me.

No, it lies ... in her lies.

It's deeper than that. The diner fire is bothering me more than it should. In my gut, I believe that Journey probably set the fire, but in reality I have no proof and never will. All I have to go on is Journey's word, and she says she didn't do it. So that's it. What's the point of dwelling on it? It only tears us apart, and I fucking hate feeling like Journey and I aren't on the same page. With that in mind, I walk into the house making sure that my Little One and I are back where we should be—in our own dark and twisted world.

When I walk in through the garage door, I'm greeted by an unfamiliar sight. Journey is sitting in the living room in black sweats and a tight white T-shirt. Her black hair is tied into a ponytail and her face is devoid of all makeup, which has never mattered for Journey—she's spectacular whether bare-faced or not. Her dark brown eyes find me and hypnotize me in an instant, washing away all remnants of the tiring work day. She's so fucking beautiful.

"Hey," I say as I step into the house.

"Hey, Sir," she replies, her voice softer than usual.

"Is everything okay? How was work?" I ask, making my way over to the coffee table and standing next to it.

Journey clears her throat. "I'm fine. I'm glad you're home. I was hoping we could talk."

The second the words hit my ears, my heart thuds

like a beat drop. Blood rushes through my veins, super-charged by the idea that this is it—Summers has said or done something that is equivalent to suicide. He threatened my queen. He put his hands on her. He did *something*, and whatever it is, I hope he enjoyed it because he won't live to see the sunlight again.

Stone-faced, I sit down next to Journey, one hundred percent prepared for what's to come. I hoped it wouldn't come to this, but Journey is a line that shall not be crossed, and the world will turn to ash for disrespecting her.

I place my hand on her knee and look her in the eye. "Tell me."

Journey hesitates, building up the tension until I'm ready to burst out the door without even hearing what happened.

"Are we okay?" she finally asks.

My brow furrows with a tilt of my head. "What?"

"You and me," she goes on. "Are we okay? I feel like there has been a void between us lately. We're not ourselves and it's not sitting right with me. I can't quite put my finger on it, but it feels like you're holding something against me. You don't touch me as often as you used to. We don't carry constant conversations anymore. We spend our time on the couches in this living room instead of using the toys we filled our basement with. The past week or so has just felt off, and I want to make sure that we're okay. I don't know ... I guess I just miss you."

My heart rate slows as her words sink in. So it's not Summers crossing a red line. Instead, it's me being told I have been cold and distant because of my suspicions. I haven't been treating my Little One the way she deserves to be treated because I've been too preoccupied with my suspicion. I haven't been a good boyfriend or a good Dom since the fire, and now she misses the man I was before the morning I heard about Andrea's.

So this is it. You're letting it go.

I feel like my decision has been made for me. Journey means so much more to me than that fucking diner, and knowing I'll never have any facts other than the ones Journey gives me makes my constant skepticism that much more pointless. It's like I'm trying to grab a fistful of thin air.

When I see the look in Journey's eyes, I know I've been doing far too much. She doesn't even have to say that she misses me. I see it in the depths of her brown eyes.

"Wow," I start, guilt rising up my throat like bile. "I didn't realize I was acting so indifferent toward you. The truth is … it doesn't matter. The only thing that has ever mattered to me is you. All I care about is your happiness and satisfaction, and if I've made you feel anything other than those two things, then I haven't been doing my job for you. I apologize if I made you feel abandoned." I reach out and take Journey's hand, choosing this moment to let go of the bullshit I've been clinging to. "So, to answer your question, yes, Little One, we're good."

The wounded look on Journey's face slowly melts away as she smiles at me. I see relief in her eyes now and it makes me feel instantly better knowing I gave that to her. I desire nothing more than to watch her expression switch between this one and beautiful agony.

"Okay," she says, beaming. "I just wanted to make sure. I know you were concerned about the fire, and you asked if I started it."

"Forget that I ever asked that. It doesn't matter," I

state again, forcing myself to believe it because it's the right thing to do for us. "You and I are good, and my only other concern is your partner. Did he have anything else to say today?"

She shakes her head. "No. I didn't really see him much. We did some digging into Andrea's but didn't come away with anything. He seems bruised by the conversation in which he brought you up. Since the moment he realized I was pissed, he has backed away from anything of the sort."

"Good. Smart man. Maybe he values his life after all. If he ever decides it's worth it to cross that line again, it's over for him. I promise you that. I'll handle it."

Journey smiles as she scoots closer to me and wraps her arms around my neck. "I know you will, Sir."

"But for now, the only thing I want to handle is you."

I turn my head and gently press my lips against hers. For the second time this evening, my blood speeds to life, rushing through me and warming me up from the inside, but this time for a different reason. Our tongues caress each other, slithering together in a sensual dance that arouses my cock along with devilish thoughts and desires.

"I'm going to go take a shower," I say when we manage to pull away. "When I'm done, I'm going downstairs. You'll be on the bed on all fours, and you'll be completely naked while you wait for me. Do you understand?"

Journey licks her lips, making my insides quiver. "Yes, Sir."

"Good," I say as I stand. "Tonight, I'm going to remind you just how much you mean to me. Be prepared, Little Devil. When I get down there, I'll have the belt in my hand."

chapter
twenty-four

AS I DESCEND the stairs in nothing but black pants, my fist grips tightly around a prized possession. The black belt dangles at my side as I step down feeling like a god walking the Earth. This belt is much more than a tool used to keep pants up. For most men, that's all it is and all it will ever be. For me, this belt—this one in particular—is my most cherished toy. This is the belt that changed my life forever. This belt ended Sierra Cross's life. It ended Detective Winter's life, and it is also responsible for bringing Journey into mine. If it wasn't for this long piece of leather, I never would've met her. I never would have been this satisfied with life. Out of all the toys we own, this black belt is by far the one that means the most. It unlocks us like no other, and tonight it's exactly what we need.

The basement is nearly pitch black when I reach the bottom of the steps. The only light shining is the one above the bed, where Journey waits on all fours just as she was instructed, completely naked. From here, I can see her perfect body bent over for me. I can smell the lotion she applied, but even more than that I smell her lust for me. I smell her desire. I feel the heat emanating from her body as I get closer and closer, my cock hardening with each measured step. By the time I reach the bed I'm nearly frothing at the mouth, a rabid animal ready to devour its prey.

"Fuck," I growl, using my free hand to caress Journey's perfect ass. "I love seeing you this way. You're so fucking perfect, Little One. Flawless in every way. Even more than that, you're my soulmate. You're my perfect match—the only one who could ever bring out the best in me ... the worst in me. In a world full of light, you are the darkness I will always crave. Look at you. How could you ever think that I'd want distance from you? From this? From perfection? Fucking never, Little Devil. Lift your head up for me."

Journey lets out a long exhale. "Yes, Sir."

She raises her head, giving me plenty of space to step forward and strap the belt around her neck. When it touches her skin, she sucks in a breath, affected by the belt the same way I am. We know what this toy means, and it has us both ready to dive into our sickest desires.

Once the belt is in place with the loose end pulled through the buckle, I grab the long end and hold it, using it as a leash to keep Journey in place while I walk behind her and drop to my knees. The smell of her pussy is kindling for the fire inside me. I want to eat her until I'm full. My god, I can barely stand it. I breathe in the scent of her and my body fills with hot, untamable lust. She could set a million fires and I would never want to be far from *this*. I fucking need *this*.

"How could I ever say no to this pussy?" I ask, gripping her ass while tugging the leash, removing all slack. "Tell me it's mine, Journey."

She moans. "Yes, Sir. It's all yours."

"Again."

"Sir, my pussy is all yours."

I dive forward, my tongue whipping out as I suck her into my mouth. I devour all of her, swallowing her wetness to quench my thirst but never being satisfied enough to stop. I eat her pussy disrespectfully, slurping and sucking her clit while my tongue performs acrobatics. I refuse to stop until she detonates in my mouth. I'm desperate for it, and I pull the belt to tighten the grip around her throat while I focus on her clit. I suck it into my mouth while flattening my tongue and licking rhythmically. Over and over again, my tongue strokes against the hardened nub until I sense her muscles tightening. Her legs lock in place as I pull the belt harder so that she can't get away from me, and I hear the sound of her labored breathing—a symphony of gasps and short breaths that tell me exactly what is about to happen.

"Give it to me, Journey," I command. "Don't ask for my permission. Just fucking drown me in it."

"Yes, S ... Sir ... Oh, god!" Journey screams in response before clutching the bedsheets in her fists, curving her back, and giving me exactly what I've been dying to have.

She bursts, her entire body set ablaze with tremors and spasms that rock her to the point of muscle failure and she falls flat on her stomach, my grip on the belt bet damned. While she unravels, I keep my mouth glued to her pussy, prolonging her bliss for as long as I can, swallowing her every drop until she finally stops trembling and is nothing more than a sweaty mass of exhaustion.

"Good fucking girl," I say as I stand up, wiping my mouth.

I look down on the woman who has taught me how to love, and my mind stays dark. I don't want to cuddle.

I don't want to caress her skin or make her feel comfortable. Right now, I crave her destruction, because giving her pain is how I show her just how much I love her.

While Journey pants beneath me, I climb on the bed and straddle her backside. With a leg on each side of her, I lean forward and plant kisses up her spine until I reach her neck. I take in the sight of her feebleness and let it run through me. I love seeing her shattered. The sight of her ruin and the sound of ragged breaths plunges me straight into Dom Space. The nerves in my arms are on heightened sensitivity as my blood rushes and my fingers tingle. My entire being feels entombed in a god-like aura. I can do no wrong. The damage I cause is pure beauty. I am a deity brought to Earth for this very moment, and my will shall be done.

"Fuck, I need to be inside you," I whisper in Journey's ear while she's still struggling to regain life in her body. She lies prone in front of me as I sit up, positioning myself just below her ass with my cock at her soaking wet entrance. I tighten my grip around the loose end of the belt and push myself inside until I can enter her no further. "Fuck yes."

Journey gasps, her head finally lifting off the bed as she comes back to life like a zombie. Her fists grip the covers as I pull back on the belt and lean forward again.

"You won't be able to speak soon," I inform her so that she's prepared for what is about to come. "So, it won't be possible to use your safe word. In place of it, you will tap the bed three times, then you'll pause and do it again, repeating the process until I catch on and stop. Per usual, the second I see it everything ends. Do you understand?"

She nods. "I understand, Sir. Tap the bed three times and repeat until you stop. But I'm not worried about it. I am yours to use. Abuse me, Sir. Please. I need it."

"With fucking pleasure."

Without another word, I lean back, yank the belt upward, and begin pounding Journey's pussy viciously. I fuck her as hard as I can, ravaging her insides with my cock, trying to make her scream when I know she can't. The belt cuts off both her oxygen and her ability to utter a single sound. She will have to tap out in order for me to stop, and if she doesn't, she will lose consciousness. Fine with me.

I keep going, rocking the entire bed frame back and forth over and over again, still pulling the belt back until my body exhausts itself and I'm forced to stop. Breathing heavily, I release the tension on the belt and see Journey's head fall forward. I loosen the buckle from her neck and see that she is passed out.

"Journey," I say, patting her on her cheek until I see movement in her eyelids. "Hey, hey. You okay?"

Journey's eyes flutter like moth wings taking flight until she regains consciousness completely and looks at me.

"I'm fine," she says. "Keep going."

I smile like the devil himself. "That's my fucking girl."

Re-tightening the belt, I go back to work, fucking her hard and fast while choking her. I use her body relentlessly, but I never take my eyes off her hands. I see the way they fist the covers, her skin turning red from how hard she clutches for dear life, but she never snaps. Instead of asking me to relent, I see her grip loosen and her neck lose strength. I stop fucking her again and release the belt. Again, she's out cold.

"Journey," I call to her, gently smacking her cheek again.

She wakes up quicker this time, less groggy.

"Keep going," she demands almost angrily. "I was so close to coming."

My eyes bulge as excitement threatens to explode from me.

"Holy fuck," I say, shaking my head in total awe of her. "You're so fucking unbelievable, Little Devil. Do it then. Come for me before you pass out or we'll never stop. It'll be the worst edging of your life. Control yourself before you lose consciousness. I want your cum. Right fucking now."

"Yes, S—"

Her words are cut off by the cinching of the belt around her throat. I lean back and remove all barriers. I will not hold back in the slightest. I begin again, heartlessly slamming into Journey's pussy while pulling the belt back. Each stroke is long and powerful, sending echoes through the house and the need to come ripping through my veins. I watch Journey fist the covers again, waiting for her to snap. My own orgasm builds up and threatens to wash over me like a tsunami wave, and just before I'm overtaken, Journey's body begins to convulse.

She can't scream because of the asphyxiation, so her body caves in on itself instead. She rocks back and forth, the muscles in her limbs cramping as she orgasms and begins to lose consciousness at the same time. Her skin flushes red as her head turns to the side, giving me a bird's eye view of her glorious face being overcome with agonizing pleasure. Then, her entire body relaxes and I know she has passed out again.

I let go of the belt completely, making sure to loosen

it at the buckle so Journey can breathe, but I don't stop fucking. I pound in and out again, and again, and again, until the wave finally crushes me and I am swallowed whole. I come so hard my vision turns white, letting out a monstrous howl that burns my throat and locks my body in place until the bliss is finished with me. Then it's my turn to collapse.

I fall forward, my chest landing on Journey's back, and as much as I want to lie there and take my time recovering, I have to make sure Journey is okay. I remove the belt completely and tap her on the face.

"Journey. Journey, wake up," I plead, my heart racing from coming and the fear that I may have gone too far ... again. "Journey!"

Her eyes flicker before opening, followed by a gasping breath as life re-enters her body.

"Oh, my god," she exclaims between heaving breaths. "That was unreal. It may have been the most terrifying, intense, magnificent orgasm I've ever had."

"You were incredible," I say as I roll off of her so that she can take full breaths without the weight of my body on her back.

"That's the kind of breath play that people don't know about," she says. "They think it's all hand neck-laces and tight collars. No, this ... *this* was breath play."

"And you were so fucking good," I say, now lying on my back. "I thought you were going to snap."

"Never," she replies with a scoff. "I trust that you won't kill me, but if you did, it'd be worth it."

We both laugh as we settle down, our sweat rolling off our skin and soaking into the covers below. The conversation stops as we just try to regain our energy. After five minutes, tears begin to glide down Journey's face, followed by heavy sobs that rock her body.

I don't even ask what's wrong. I know sub drop when I see it. The heavy dose of endorphins released from a traumatic scene like the one we just did is almost always followed by sub drop. The chemicals in her body are in a frenzy trying to recover from the intensity of what just happened, and asking her what is wrong always gets the same answer. *I don't know.* It's fine. I don't need her to know. I'll know for her, and I'll be the comfort she doesn't even know she needs.

I turn on my side and pull Journey into my arms until she's lying on top of me. There, straddling my naked body, she cries into my neck. I caress her back and hair with both hands, simply giving her quiet support until she gets control of her emotions again. No matter how long it takes, I'll be here for her, because putting her back together is even more important than tearing her apart.

chapter
twenty-five

"WOW, YOU GUYS LOOK INCREDIBLE."

"What are you talking about, bro? This is how I always look. *She* looks incredible," I reply as I take my seat next to Journey and across from Trey.

Alpen Rose is an upscale restaurant in Philly, but I never knew just how upscale until tonight. When Trey texted that he had made reservations for the three of us, I had to look the establishment up just to see what it was like. I was pleasantly surprised that he had chosen a steakhouse instead of a place that serves hors d'oeuvres and caviar, because Journey and I are not "fancy" people. While the setting is romantic dim lighting, vibrant chandeliers, and even a fireplace, I don't feel out of place when we're escorted to our table. The waiter who takes our order is dressed in a tuxedo, but he doesn't have his nose in the air as he memorizes what each of us want, and I don't have the sudden urge to meet him out back to stick a fork through his chin.

Journey sits next to me in a sequin black dress that she tones down with a black leather choker that's wide enough to cover the slight bruising on her neck from last night. Her hair crashes down her back in beautiful black waves, and the look in her eyes tells me she can't wait to return home and watch me take off the all-black outfit I'm wearing. The top three buttons of my shirt are undone, giving her a subtle peek at my chiseled upper chest, and I keep catching her glancing at it before sucking her bottom lip into her mouth.

After last night, Journey and I are back on track—the way we always should have been. Her suspicious activity steered us off course, but I chose to re-center us. The scene we pulled off with the belt last night was precisely what we needed, the perfect shade of black to make us feel at home again. Now that we are on solid ground, my thoughts are no longer weighed down by doubt or distrust. All I can think about now is when I'll make her scream for me again.

"Nah, you both look good," Trey says, smiling in a white button-up. His beard is freshly trimmed and he is well put together tonight. "I've never seen you so done up before, Evan. Journey really brings it out of you, huh?"

We all share a laugh.

"That she most definitely does," I agree, but the look Journey and I share is much more devious than Trey knows.

Yes, she brings out the murderer in me. My Little Devil.

"It's nice to see you again, Journey," Trey says, reaching for his glass of water. "How have things been going with you, besides putting up with Evan's shit?"

Journey giggles lightheartedly. "I can't complain. Just doing the same old stuff, really. Work all day, play with Evan all night."

Trey smiles but I can see the apprehension on his

face. "Umm, yeah that's cool. Any interesting cases you can tell me about? I heard a diner around here was burned down."

I keep my eyes on my glass of red wine while Journey speaks on the now taboo topic.

"I can't really get into an ongoing investigation, but yes, Andrea's was burned down recently. That's actually my case and we're looking into it."

"Any leads?" Trey asks.

I laugh mockingly. "Leads?"

"What? That's what they call it on TV," Trey shoots back. "Evan is always hating."

"No, not really," Journey answers. "We haven't had much luck with this one."

"That's too bad," says Trey. "Well, at least the two of you are going strong. I hope I can have what you guys have one day. Love is hard to find."

"It most definitely is," I chime in. "Especially finding someone who's into the same kind of things as you. People say opposites attract, but I think that's not the way to go for the long term."

The waiter interrupts our conversation by bringing out our food and positioning each plate neatly in front of its owner. Journey's beef wellington is a sight to behold, while Trey's lamb looks delectable. My T-bone steak is so mouth-watering that I forget what I'm even talking about.

We spend the next fifteen minutes eating instead of talking. The sound of forks and knives scraping against ceramic plates fills the air, mixed with wine being gulped and glasses clinking back to the table.

In no time at all, all of our plates are nearly empty and our bellies are full of wine. When the waiter returns to ask if we'd like dessert, we shoo him away as if the question is offensive.

"I couldn't possibly eat another bite," Journey says as the waiter walks off.

"I will literally explode if I have one more forkful," Trey agrees. He leans back in his chair and rubs his belly. "Now I'm ready for my Santa Claus audition."

"Santa Claus? You think your future fiancée will be into that?" I ask before bringing my wine glass to my lips and looking at Trey over the top edge.

"Oh, you got jokes?" he quips. "I don't know, but if she is, I'm down for it. Hell, I see that collar on Journey's neck. I might need you two to teach me a little something about getting my girl to be kinky."

Journey laughs as she habitually rubs her day collar. "If she's open-minded, you might be able to introduce her to some stuff. It takes a lot of love and trust to explore kinks, though."

"We've got plenty of love and trust, that's why I'm considering popping the question."

"Just be careful," I join in. "Ease her into the idea of you being kinky. You don't need her snapping on you for doing too much. The last thing we need is you ending up dead over a kink."

We laugh together as the waiter brings the bill to the table and sets it next to Trey, who snatches it up quickly. When I reach for my wallet, he holds out his hand.

"Don't even think about it," he says, shaking his head. "I told you this was on me, so I got this. Plus, I'm your boss. I'm supposed to pay."

"You're my boss on the job site," I correct him jokingly. "See, that's something else you better fix before asking your girlfriend to marry you. You have to earn the right to be a woman's boss."

"I'm not afraid to earn it," Trey says. "Or I'll die trying."

I chuckle. "Good luck. Maybe that's what happened to Cain."

I laugh at my own joke, but Trey doesn't laugh with me. Maybe it's the wine swirling around in my system, but my tongue is certainly looser than it should be, and the look on Trey's face suggests that he isn't amused.

"What?" he asks, his forehead riddled with wrinkles.

Realizing what I just said, I shake my head and try to backtrack. "Ah, nothing. Never mind."

"Don't fucking joke about that, man," Trey snips with a deep furrow in his brow as if he's truly disgusted.

Journey's head snaps over to him so fast I can practically feel the wind on my face from the speed of it. Her eyes widen to twice their size, and she doesn't have to say a word. This is the exact look she had when she met Cain for the first time.

"Yeah, that was ... I shouldn't have said that," I say to Trey while keeping my eyes on Journey who hasn't blinked once.

"Dude, I know Cain was an asshole who picked on you a lot," Trey says, clearly in his feelings. "But he died, bro. He was murdered. Someone broke into his house and killed him in his own bed. They haven't even found the fucking asshole who did it. He and I weren't the best of friends, but he was an associate of mine ... of *ours*. He was a part of our crew for a long time, and while he had some issues that he needed to fix, I can't sit back and let you shit on a dead man's name. That wasn't cool, man."

I nod, knowing it was a bad idea to bring up a man I killed, but I'm not the real issue. Journey isn't happy at all, and that's always a problem.

"Who do you think you're talking to?" Journey suddenly dives in head-first. The fire in her eyes could melt steel as she stares daggers into Trey, totally unafraid.

Journey is not the kind of woman who is scared of getting into it with a man. In fact, I think she relishes it. She's a woman with a tough upbringing who became a police officer and then promoted to detective. She fears no one.

"Okay, we're good," I say quickly, trying to extinguish the fire before it can engulf everything around us. "No need to say anything else or go any further. Trey, you're right. Journey ... Little One ... it's fine."

Journey's eyes slowly shift over to me, and I immediately know that it is *not* fine to her. If there is one thing Journey can't stand, it's the idea that someone is disrespecting me. It lights a fire in her that burns brighter than the sun, and dousing it has proven to be nearly impossible.

"Excuse me?" Trey says to Journey. He swallows hard and straightens out his back, readying himself for an argument if it comes to that. Checking a construction worker is harder than most people realize.

"Oh, you didn't hear me?" Journey says, barreling over my attempt at calming things down. "I asked who you think you're talking to. Don't tell Evan what to do."

"With all due respect, Journey, I tell Evan what to do every single day," Trey replies.

Oh, is that fucking right, Trey?

Tension creeps into the muscles in my face, making it tight as I glare at Trey. He's a friend, but there are lines. There's only so much I'll take, and while I do give him leeway because I like him, the rope can only stretch so far before it snags.

"Trey," I begin, cutting my eyes over to him. "I like you, but let's not get it twisted."

"Get *what* twisted?" he replies with a puzzled expression. "I *do* tell you what to do every day."

"At work," I say a little more aggressively than intended. "We're at dinner just having a good time, so let's not act like that extends outside of the job site."

Or I may have to rescind the pass you've gotten because you're a "friend."

"Okay, I don't know what the hell just happened here," he says, "but the mood has definitely shifted. All I know is that making fun of a dead man isn't cool, and I'd appreciate it if you didn't do that. If y'all want to make it about something other than that, then that's not my issue, it's yours."

"Really?" Journey interjects, her tone dropping to something devious. "Well, I want to make it your issue, since you insist on disrespecting Evan."

"How am I disrespecting Evan?"

"Journey," I cut in before she can answer. "Let it go."

Yes, rein her in before I'm forced to hide another corpse.

"Why tell me to let it go and not him?" she says, now pointing her hostility at me.

"Because he's not my sub," I snip.

I don't mean to aim any aggression toward her, but the sudden change of mood has me quickly irked.

"No, he's just your boss who tells you what to do every day."

Fire blazes inside of me, fueled by Journey's attitude and how fast this night went south. At this point, I'm ready to flip the table and go off on anybody within earshot.

How about a fire?

But I can't do that. My only option is to end it here before it goes any further.

"Journey, get up right now. We're leaving," I announce, standing up to speed along the process. "Trey, thanks for dinner. Have a good night."

"Seriously, Evan?" Trey questions.

"Yes ... seriously. I'll see you at work. Journey, get the fuck up. Let's go. Now."

Journey stares at Trey as I place my hand on her arm and pull her up. It takes everything in me not to place a hand around her throat and force her to obey, which is exactly why I hate being in public. She continues looking back at Trey even as I lead her out the door.

Once we're outside and walking back to the truck, anger and frustration wafts off both of us. Neither of us speaks, but I know that once we're back behind closed doors, we're going to have plenty to discuss.

chapter
twenty-six

"HE'S MY FRIEND, JOURNEY."

"Okay, so that means you let him talk to you however he pleases?"

"No, and I didn't," I reply as I slam the door behind us. We step into the living room and face each other, two opponents arming themselves for battle. "Trey let the alcohol get to him, which is why I told him to relax with how he was talking to me. But I was the one who fucked up, alright? I shouldn't have said anything about Cain at all. It's my fault."

"Now you're defending him?" Journey says, frowning hard. "I don't understand what's wrong with you, Evan. He spoke to you like you were a child. He chastised you for speaking ill of the man who used to verbally abuse you at work every day before you met me. Then he followed that by acting as though he is now your bully, because he tells you what to do all the time. He's your boss every day, all day. Is that it?"

"Journey, I love you so much it fucking hurts, but you're pushing it. I want you to have a voice and be as strong-minded as I know you are even though you are my submissive, but don't forget who you're talking to."

"You're my Dom, right?"

"You're goddamn right."

"So you'll put me in check? Punish me if I go too far? If I disrespect you?"

"Of course I fucking will, and don't ever forget it."

"But you have nothing more for Trey than a few words? Put me in my place but let him walk all over you? How does that work?"

"I didn't let him walk all over me," I yell, taking two steps closer to Journey. "You don't know what you're talking about. Now sit the fuck down and listen." Journey stands there, truly pushing her luck by acting like a brat, but I am in no mood for bratty fucking behavior. "Sit. Down. Now. I've told you a million times, Journey, *you* belong to *me*. You do as I tell you, and I have been as patient with you as I can possibly be, but you are pissing me the fuck off. Sit down or there will be consequences unlike anything in your worst nightmares. Sit!"

Sit your ass down before I grab you by the throat and force you down. You'll turn every shade of blue before I let you go, because that is what you deserve. That is what you have earned.

Journey swallows hard, defiant despite herself. But she sits.

I take a deep breath and try to calm the voice inside my head. I see the mist in her eyes, but I don't let it deter me.

"I know how you feel about me," I begin again, calmer now. "I know you love me, and I know that you and I are not like the people we are surrounded by every day. We don't stand for disrespect. I'd liquify someone in a vat of acid before I stand by and watch you be treated poorly, and I know you'd do the same for me. But Trey is a friend, and friends have disagreements from time to time. He, out of all the people in this world that I can't stand, gets a bit of a longer leash. I'll try to talk it out with him, and you're going to have to accept that. In fact, you don't have a fucking choice. Do you understand me? Let it fucking go. I'll deal with it myself."

The room goes silent as we look at each other. Journey tries to maintain eye contact, but eventually her eyes fall to the floor.

Exactly where they should be when dealing with her Dom.

"Okay," she says quietly.

"What was that?" I ask with raised brows. "Say it louder so I can hear you, Little One."

"Okay," she repeats.

"Okay *what?*"

"I'll let it go. I apologize for being disrespectful."

"Say that part again, too."

"Sir," she says, finally looking up at me. "I apologize for being disrespectful. I'll let it go."

I stare down at her, my anger not dissipating in the least. "Good."

After a sigh, I turn around and walk into the kitchen, leaving Journey silent on the couch while I go to the fridge and grab a bottle of wine and a glass for myself. This was supposed to be a fun night with Trey. I never thought it was going to come to this, but now that it has, I could really use a glass of wine. But as I fill the crystal with the dark red liquid, Journey's cell phone rings.

"Fuck. It's Summers," she gripes before answering the call and placing the phone on her ear.

As she begins talking, Journey gets up from the couch and walks into the hall just as I return to the living room. As I place my wine glass on the coffee table, I hear Journey speaking.

"And it has to be now? Fine. I'll meet you there."

When she comes back to the living room, a fresh layer of annoyance coats her face.

"I have to go," she announces.

"What?" I ask. "Why?"

She lets out a long, tired sigh. "Summers says he got permission to speak to Chad Swanson. He wants to go over the timeline of his alibi one last time before we remove him as a suspect."

"And that has to happen at nine o'clock in the evening?"

"Yeah, I guess so. He says the captain wants us to do it now so we can start fresh on the case in the morning. I'm sorry. I'll do everything I can to try and hurry it along, but I have to go."

My brows furrow, a strong sensation stinging in my stomach without a single sip of the wine on the table. I bite my bottom lip as a million questions fire up in my head, but I don't stop her. In fact, I'm mad enough at her that I almost want her to go.

"Alright then," I say, then I sit down and grab the glass and bring it to my lips.

Yes, give me space before I do something I regret.

As Journey grabs her keys, she stops at the door and turns to face me.

"Sir," she says, all the aggression in her voice now abandoned. "Never forget that I love you."

Then she's gone.

> Hey, I just wanted to reach out and make sure everything was cool. I think we all let the wine get to us a little bit. We were all doing too much. Are we good?

AFTER HALF AN HOUR GOES BY, I realize that I'm not going to get a response from Trey. Understandably, he's probably pissed. I am, too. But like I told Journey, friends can have disagreements and still be friends afterward. I've known Trey for a while now, and it would annoy the shit out of me for our friendship to end over a night we were supposed to be having a good time. Journey and I were supposed to show him what a happy couple looks like. Instead, we gave him a sneak peek at a side of us he wasn't supposed to see.

After another five minutes goes by without hearing from neither Trey nor Journey, I decide to force the issue. If he won't answer my texts, I'll do this the old fashioned way.

I get up from the couch and go into the kitchen, where I open the fridge and pull out a six-pack of canned beer. Trey is more of a liquor guy, but alcohol is alcohol, and I know he won't turn it down once he realizes it is my peace offering.

With my olive branch in hand, I hop in my truck and head to Trey's house.

I'VE BEEN to Trey's place three other times. In the past, he would invite the crew over after we'd finish a project, and we would all celebrate our accomplishment here. Trey, always the gracious host, would be sure to have a keg on-hand to go along with some perfectly seasoned barbeque and tons of alcohol. The last one we had was right after Cain was killed, so it took on a more somber tone, but Trey still pulled it off. His personality was infectious as usual, and by the time the party was done, it almost felt like we were celebrating Cain's life. Only Trey could do that.

As I approach his ranch style house from down the road, headlights shine from the opposite direction. I'm surprised when they turn into his driveway just as I step on the brakes and come to a stop in front of the house across the street. I see Trey get out of his car just before I reach down and grab the six-pack of beer in my passenger seat, but when I turn to wrap my fingers around the handle to get out, I see movement out of the corner of my eye that makes me pause.

Trey, who clearly ignored my text, slowly makes his way up the driveway with a plastic bag from Walmart in his hand. He angles his body toward a door that is centered beneath the small carport in front of him, and doesn't hear or see the shadowed person moving quickly behind him.

I tilt my head and squint, trying to get a better view of the cat-like person progressing up the driveway with something in their hand. They close the distance in no time, and I am knocked backwards by pure shock as realization hits me like a gunshot blast.

"What the fuck?" I say aloud to myself. "Journey?"

twenty-seven
~ journey ~

I SHOULDN'T BE DOING this, but it almost feels like I can't help myself. I know you told me to let it go and that you would handle it, but I can't. I just fucking can't.

I know that Trey is your friend, and losing him will undoubtedly cause you pain, but sometimes certain things must be done. Some pain is healing.

What I'm about to do is disrespectful to you, but as I drive, I feel nothing but the resentment that sat with me at the dinner table tonight. I know that it is wrong, but is it more wrong than allowing Trey to speak to you that way? To act as though he is the new Cain? You may disagree, but I think Trey's treatment of you is far worse. He crossed a line when he talked to you that way about Cain. It's not his place or his business, and if we let him get away with it once, there is no question that he would continue to do it.

In time, I think you'll understand—maybe even thank me. At least that is what I hope. But for now, I'll deal with it, and I'll be there to offer you comfort when you hear about what happens tonight. You'll ask me to investigate the case and find the people who did this to your friend, and I'll do it for you. I'll even go as far as arresting people who had nothing to do with it if it means making you happy and feeding you the justice you'll be starved for. I'll take care of all of it for you, because I love you, Sir. There has never been a person in this world who has loved you the way I do—as much as I do. Love is what is driving this car tonight.

Lying to you doesn't make me feel good. Never has. Never will. But I have to. When I realized that you were dead set on letting Trey get away with talking to you that way, it dawned on me mid-conversation that this was my cross to bear. I could tell that you weren't willing to go as far as me, so when you went into the kitchen, I pulled my phone out and tapped my way to my settings. As you poured your wine, I found my ringer and adjusted the volume so that the ringer would play aloud. I walked away so you wouldn't catch on to the fact that there was no voice on the other end, and then I made up the story about Summers getting permission to talk to Chad. A weak fabrication, admittedly, but it was enough to get out of the house long enough to come here. Luckily, I remembered where Trey lived from the time you brought me for a little shindig he threw after a completed project. If not for that, I wouldn't be here right now. You see, Sir. It's fate.

I really do appreciate that you trust me so much, Evan. Truly. I know I shouldn't abuse it. As your submissive and the love of your life, I shouldn't take for granted that you trust me enough to let me leave the house at this hour for what you think is work. After tonight, I promise to do better. Once Trey is gone, I won't have any more reasons to produce fake scenarios. I'll be perfect for you, Sir.

After tonight.

Initially, I didn't know what my plan was when I left the house. I guess I intended to knock on Trey's door and attack him with the hammer I brought from the garage as soon as he opened up, because if I hesitated or tried to make small talk, he would text or call you about it. However, when I arrived, I realized that he wasn't home. As a result, I'm waiting, and I really hope he doesn't take too long, because the longer he takes, the longer I'm away from you.

I sit in my car by the mailbox of Trey's neighbor and contemplate my life. The investigation into Andrea's hasn't gone anywhere, which makes sense considering the truth, but I need it to move. I have to find a way to either pin it on Chad Swanson, or make the case go cold. There were no cameras in the area—thank goodness—and no evidence left behind, so now that Chad has an alibi, there's no way the investigation can move forward. If I want it over, I'll have to be the one to suggest that we've run out of leads, but I'm having a hard time trusting that my partner will fucking let it go.

To his credit, Summers has backed off since our little dustup in the office. He hasn't mentioned Detective Winter at all, and there hasn't been one instance where he brought you up, Sir. Good thing, too, because I was all but convinced that my new partner would have to suffer the same fate as my old one. Now, Summers spends a lot of his time quietly researching things on his computer, or going through old case files with the clerk. He doesn't involve me unless he absolutely has to, and I'm grateful. I'm clearly not the kind of detective who needs to be best friends with my partner. You're my best friend, Sir. All I need is you.

When headlights approach from the rear, I stare out

of my sideview mirror until they get close. I can tell from the way the car is slowing down and its squealing brakes that they're about to make a turn, so I slide down in my seat to duck beneath the shadows in the car. Sure enough, the car turns into Trey's driveway. He's here. This is it.

I grip the handle of the hammer in my passenger seat and get out of the car as quietly as I can, doing my best to only move when I hear him moving. His sounds mask mine as he climbs out of his car and closes the door just as I round the corner. I crouch down low and put to use everything I know about surveillance and being imperceptible. Trey is carrying a plastic bag that rustles loudly as it blows in the breeze, giving me even more freedom to move without being heard. As Trey approaches the carport, I quickly close the distance between us. I'm at his back in a flash, face-to-face with the moment I've committed to. I can't turn around now. He'll hear me. I have to do this.

Forgive me, Sir.

I raise my hand, squeezing the handle of the hammer as tightly as I can. I take a deep breath.

"Trey!" a voice shouts from somewhere in the darkness.

I'm sent reeling as Trey's head snaps over, searching the area from whence the voice came as I lower the hammer and shove it behind my back.

Trey hears me moving and spins around with a startled expression just as you emerge from across the street, a six-pack of canned beer in your hands.

"Evan? What the—Journey? Man, what the fuck is going on?" Trey stammers, totally taken aback at our sudden arrival.

"I tried to text you," you say, your face devoid of all

emotion. "But when you didn't respond, I told Journey that we needed to just come by and try to ease the tension from earlier."

Trey's face remains twisted into a frown as he eyes us both, and it doesn't move when he pulls his phone from his pocket, checking for your text. While he stares at his screen, you glare at me, the purest form of venom pouring from your eyes.

"I hadn't even noticed your text," Trey says. "My bad."

"It's cool," you say, relaxing the muscles in your face as you speak to your friend. "I didn't mean to sneak up on you, but I just thought we should smooth things over. You and I are friends, man. In fact, you're the only person I think I've ever called that. So I don't want there to be any drama between us. You're a good guy, you're about to propose, and you've never been rude to me. You're my guy, and I want to be there at your wedding to see you get all domesticated. But I can't do that if we're pissed off over a misunderstanding, because that's all tonight was—a misunderstanding. Isn't that right, Journey?"

I angle my body to make sure Trey can't see the hammer, making myself look like an ass while I keep my hand behind my back.

"Umm, yes that is correct," I say, sounding as dumb as I look. "I was out of line earlier, and I never should've come at you that way. So, yes ... big misunderstanding ... sorry."

Trey eyes me wearily. "Yeah, it's cool," he says before turning to you. "You didn't have to do all of this. I honestly figured we would've talked it out and squashed it when we saw each other at work. You didn't have to come by, and you damn sure didn't have to bring me beer that you know I'm not about to drink."

You let out a forced laugh. "Shut up, it was all we had. Well, we had some wine, but I love that too much to give it to you. It was a misunderstanding, but not *that big* of a misunderstanding."

Trey chuckles, and when he turns to look at me, I force myself to giggle. I look at you as the annoying sound leaves my body and your smile vanishes in an instant.

"Anyway," you say, seemingly to shut me up. "This is already awkward as fuck, so we're going to let you go inside and have a good night. I'll see you on the job site."

"Yeah, okay," Trey says, still looking puzzled. "Take that gross ass beer with you. If I didn't like you so much I'd be offended that you even brought that over here."

You laugh as you turn away. "Shut up."

Trey chuckles to himself as he gives me a quick nod of his head and continues up the driveway. I begin to backpedal toward my car just as he enters the house and closes the door. Once he's gone, I think to run to you. I know you must have a million thoughts in your head, and we need to talk. I have no idea how I'll explain myself, but I have to talk to you.

But by the time I look in your direction, your truck has already started and you're driving away.

storm

chapter
twenty-eight

WHEN I GET HOME, my mind is still in a tailspin. I caught her red-handed, a hammer grasped tightly in her hand and raised above his head. If not for me calling his name at the last second, Trey would be dead. Journey would have killed him. My friend. She would have killed my fucking friend.

My wine glass rests on the coffee table in the same place it was when I left. When I sit down, I grab it and chug half, then I throw the entire glass across the room. It makes an impact with the TV, ruining the screen and sending red liquid splattering everywhere.

"What the fuck?" I scream to myself as I stand up and begin pacing in complete disbelief. She faked that phone call while I was in the kitchen. Her partner never called her, and if she lied about that, what else has she been keeping from me?

The fucking diner.

I stop pacing and stare at the wall. Is it true? After I let it go and tried to keep my mind on Summers and keeping us safe; could I have been right about the diner the entire time? Why not question it now? She was going to kill Trey, and probably had a plan to lie to me about it. I bet she would have made up some story about a robbery gone wrong or some fucking bullshit like that. I never would have known what happened to my friend. How fucking could she?

As my thoughts fill me with both grief and rage, the sound of the garage raising freezes me. My thoughts focus solely on what I will say to her when I see her. Why is she even getting back so much later than me? You see what happens when you fucking lie? Now I have to question *everything*.

When she walks in, I see the panic in her face when we make eye contact. She steps over the threshold, lets the door close behind her, and stands in front of it. She waits for me to start, which somehow makes me even more livid.

"What's the matter?" I start, seething. "Have you run out of lies to tell?"

"Sir," she starts, but I snap.

"Don't fucking call me that!" I bark. "All I want to hear from you is *why*. Why were you going to kill him, Journey? I've told you that Trey is the only person I've called my friend, and you disregarded that completely. You didn't even care how much it might hurt me to lose *my only friend*? You felt that slighted over him asking me to not make fun of Cain?"

"He didn't ask, S ... Evan. He told you. He demanded. He disrespected you."

"No he fucking did not. What the hell is wrong with you? You think a grown man isn't allowed to voice his opinion as long as you're around, and doing so should result in death? Being a grown up and communicating should result in blunt force fucking trauma to the back of the head? You can't be serious."

"I didn't know what else to do," she says, her eyes filling with tears that gain her no sympathy from me.

"Bullshit," I say. "I told you what to do. I demanded that you leave it alone and let me handle it. I'm your Dom, and I fucking told you. You just didn't listen. You made a decision on my behalf and chose to end Trey's life regardless of how I felt about it. Plus, you made up that bullshit story about your partner calling you, and even put on a fucking skit to carry it out. You made up all that bullshit right in front of me so that you could go kill my friend."

"I'm sorry," she cries.

"No you're fucking not. You're only saying that because you got caught, just like every other liar and cheater in the world. Even now, you're still lying and unapologetic about it."

"What?"

"Don't play fucking stupid with me, Journey."

"What are you talking about?"

"The diner!" I bellow, my voice like thunder. "You burned that diner down."

"No, I didn't."

"Yes, you fucking did. I know you did it, so don't you stand there and keep lying just for the sake of lying. Tell me the truth."

"Evan, I didn't burn the diner down."

"I swear to fucking—" I close the gap between us and stand directly in front of Journey so that she can see my eyes and know I'm not bluffing. "Listen to me carefully. If you don't tell me the fucking truth right now, and I mean about every lie you have ever told me, I swear I'm walking out of here and never looking back. I have killed for you—risked my life to make sure you were safe and protected. I hung a man from his own ceiling fan to make sure we were both good—to keep *us* out of prison—and now you can't even look me in the eye and be honest. Fine. Fucking fine! Say you didn't burn down the diner one more time. Lie to me about one more thing and watch how fast you're right back to living by yourself. Go ahead. Tell me you didn't burn it down."

Journey's eyes bounce around the room, looking at everything but me. I hear it when she swallows hard, and see it when she decides to keep the lie up.

"I didn't burn down—"

Before she can even finish, I walk away.

"Evan," she says as I walk over to the coffee table and grab my keys.

"Evan," she repeats as I approach the door and try to move her out of the way.

"Evan!" she yells when I gently push her aside and walk through the door she was blocking.

"Evan, please!" she begs as I open the door to my truck and place one foot inside.

"Okay!"

I stop.

"Okay, I'll tell you everything. Please don't leave. I'll tell you."

I pause, one foot on the ground, the other in the truck. "I'm listening."

Journey lets out a long exhale as her tears finally fall from her eyes. I can see how much she doesn't want to do it, but she has no choice now. If she lies, we're done, and she knows it.

"Okay," she repeats. "I burned down the diner. That kid pissed me off, and it was made worse when the manager came out and was upset that the kid quit. He made it sound like I'd cost him a good worker, when Chad was actually an asshole and his business was better off without him. When I felt like he was defending the kid, that was it. I didn't want to hurt a teenager, so I took it out on the diner."

Shaking my head, I say, "And you thought framing him for arson wouldn't hurt him?"

"He's a minor. He wouldn't do much time."

"That's fucking ridiculous, Journey. You hear me? Ridiculous, just like the fact that you decided to lie to me about it when you and I have committed worse crimes together. Why did you continue to lie when I gave you so many outs?"

"I don't—" she tries to say, but her words are cut off by sobs. "I don't know. You asked me to let it go and I knew I couldn't. Once I lied about it, I just kept it up. I just ... kept lying."

I nod my head, feeling like this is only the beginning. She just kept lying, huh? There isn't a chance in hell that this is the only thing she has kept from me.

"What else?" I ask.

"Huh?"

"What else have you lied about?"

"Nothi—"

I face the truck and start to sit down.

"I'm the reason Robin quit."

I freeze again, my eyes wide. "What?"

"It was me. I attacked her," she continues, her head dropping as she accepts defeat. "I lost it when you told me you had a new girl on your crew. I became enraged the moment I saw her from across the street. She shook your hand and sauntered away like she was begging for you to look at her ass, and I knew I had to get her out of there. So I followed her back to her hotel that night and I attacked her. The marks on my knuckles and arms were from her. I'm so sorry, Sir."

My head spins, struggling to remain sane as the information hits me.

"Journey, I didn't even know that girl."

"I know. I just ... lost it."

My eyes fall to the floor. "That's why she was afraid when Trey mentioned my name."

"I told her not to mention you or ever think of you again."

"Jesus fucking Christ. You connected yourself to me while attacking her? Journey what the fuck?"

"I don't know," she bellows, practically bawling now. "I know it was fucking stupid, but I lost it when I saw her, and I thought I was helping."

"Helping with what?"

"I don't know. Helping to protect us from people like her. People who swoop into your life and do damage with their flirting. I thought you might be into her."

"Journey, I couldn't have possibly given two shits about that girl!"

"I know, but I thought that maybe you could if you continued to spend time with her every day at work. So, to me, I was helping. Just like how I helped with that asshole from the bar. I was taking control of the situation before it could get out of hand. The same way I controlled the Sierra Cross case when it began, even though I already knew she was buried in your backyard."

The world completely stops spinning as I stare at

Journey. Her eyes bulge, like she can't believe the words that just came out of her mouth. There's silence for a moment before I'm able to speak.

"What did you just say?"

Journey places a hand over her mouth. "I ... you ... nothing. I—"

I remove my foot from inside the truck and close the door, walking slowly until I'm only inches from Journey. "You knew?"

Panic floods Journey's face. "Evan, I—"

"You just said that you already knew she was buried in my backyard *when the case began*?" I ask, ready to completely implode. "What the fuck are you talking about?"

Journey shakes her head like she's in disbelief. "I'm sorry, Evan. I knew."

"How?" I shout. "How is that possible?"

Journey raises her head, looking up at the ceiling as she begins to explain.

"This might be hard to hear," she says. "But at least when I'm finished telling it, there will be no more lies between us. This is everything."

"Just fucking tell me."

More tears fall as she lowers her head and locks eyes with me.

"I saw you in the club," she says, her eyes never leaving mine. "I saw you at The Black Collar long before you saw me, and I was instantly drawn to you. You were a bright, red hot flame and I was your moth. I think I loved you before I ever knew you, and the same way you had a voice in your head telling you to do things, mine told me that you were meant for me. So, one night I followed you out of the club as you were leaving with some skank. I parked behind your house as you went inside, and I fucked myself to the images playing in my head. I imagined what you were doing to the girl you brought home, and I put myself in her place. Thoughts of you fucking me sent me into the stratosphere, and I came like never before. I was hooked on you.

"Once it happened once, it was like I couldn't stop. I returned to The Black Collar every weekend looking for you. Sometimes you showed up, sometimes you didn't, but when you did, I followed you home. I couldn't get enough of it. The next thing I knew, a year and a half had gone by and I was still following you home after you left the club nearly every weekend.

"One night, the process repeated exactly the same. You left The Black Collar with Sierra and I was right behind you, ready to do what I'd been doing for so long. But this time, the girl didn't leave, and in all the times I saw you have one night stands, never once did it turn into a sleepover. I knew something was wrong, and it was confirmed when you came out the back door with a large footlocker, dragging it through the yard like it was extremely heavy. I watched you dig the hole, nervously looking around to make sure you were alone. I watched you drop the footlocker inside, and I watched you bury it. When the call came in about a missing person who was last sighted at The Black Collar, I jumped at the case because I knew it was you. It was my chance to stop watching and actually meet you, so I took it. That's how we met."

By the time she's done talking, my jaw is on the floor. A million thoughts form and die in my head, filling my brain with everything and nothing at the same time. I can't even speak. A year and a half. She was following me to my house for a year and a half. She watched me bury the footlocker and knew about it the entire time. I can't fathom her meeting me, knocking on my door as a detective, and already knowing I was guilty. From the very beginning, she was lying to me. Journey has been lying to me from the very first moment we met.

"Sir?" she calls to me, her head tilted, surely wondering what I'm thinking right now.

"You knew the entire time," I say as a statement, not a question. I don't have any more questions now. The truth to everything has finally been revealed.

"I should've told you," Journey says, but it doesn't land with me. I don't even fucking care.

When I look at her again, all I see is her lies. They're scrawled all over her face and I can't see past them. Her face is obscured and I can no longer tell who I am looking at. For the first time since we met the day she and Detective Winter arrived on my doorstep, the sight of her sickens me. I can't stand being in her presence knowing she has been carrying this around the entire time we've known each other.

"I have to leave," I suddenly say.

"What?" she says, having the nerve to sound shocked.

"Don't touch me," I bellow when she reaches out to grab my arm. "I don't even fucking know you, and I think I might do something I'll regret if I'm in the same house as you. So I'm leaving. Don't call me. Don't text me. Just leave me the fuck alone, Journey. I'm not interested in sleeping next to the biggest liar I have ever fucking met."

"Evan," she says as I turn around and go back to my

truck. She screams it again when I press the button to raise the garage door. "Evan! Please!"

I hear her, but I couldn't fucking care less. The tires screech when I stomp on the gas, and I keep stepping on it, hoping the roar of the engine will drown out the sound of my own tear-inducing screams.

twenty-nine
~ **journey** ~

YOU DIDN'T COME HOME last night, Sir. Where are you? My heart can't take your absence although I understand why you are upset. I'm sure I deserve for you to leave me standing in the garage screaming, begging you to come back so we can talk about this. I've earned the heartache, but it's weighing on me so heavily I can barely stand up straight. Sir, I'm sorry. Please come back. Please fucking come back.

My morning routine feels like a slow crawl through a field of barbed wire. The things I usually do, the steps I normally take are lethargic as I try to get ready for work. I have no desire to put on makeup, nor the energy, so I don't. I tie my hair up in a loose, carefree ponytail with untamed strands sticking out in different directions. The agony I feel pulls the skin on my face down, giving me bags under my eyes from the lack of sleep and depression. Your leaving did this to me. I'm not the same person without you. I am lifeless in your absence.

I don't think I did a good job of explaining anything last night. I was too shocked to put my thoughts into any sort of order, and you were so persistent. Being faced with the idea of you leaving forced me to let it all out, and once it started there was no stopping it. I spilled it all, including the fact that I knew about Sierra the entire time. As much as I didn't mean to say that, I'm glad I'm free of it. I have no more secrets from you now ... but you're gone. Honesty cost me everything. Or maybe I'm reading it wrong. Lying cost me everything.

The sun is out, but I feel like my morning drive is shrouded in pitch black. I barely notice the other vehicles on the road. My mind shifts to auto pilot the entire drive to the precinct, and I'm parking before I even know where I am. If I ran over ten people on the commute, I wouldn't have known. All I can think about is you. I don't even know where you are, but I've done as you told me. I haven't called or texted, fighting the urge every minute. But you are my Dom and I'm your submissive. I've broken your rules enough, and breaking them now will do nothing to get me back on your good side. So I'll wait for you to speak to me. I'll wait for you to come back. You are coming back, right Sir?

I get out of the car with misery still making me fifty pounds heavier. Slow, dragging steps carry me inside where the hustle and bustle of the bullpen is still happening as if you haven't left, as if I didn't spend my night alone, blanketed by agony. The officers and detectives I've known for so long say my name in greeting, but it doesn't even register. I keep my eyes on my desk until I reach it and plop down, all motivation stripped from my body.

"Jesus, Monroe, you look terrible. Rough night?"

I shake my head, already irked by Summers' jovial

mood and questions. I'm ready to tell him to leave me the fuck alone, but when I turn around, I'm surprised by a different person. Captain Saunders towers above me, his chubby, pockmarked face glaring down at me with curiosity in his eyes. Usually I would sit up straight and try to keep a positive relationship with the captain, but today I don't care. Nothing will matter until you and I are speaking again.

I clear my throat but don't bother to sit up. "Umm, yeah. Rough night, but I'm here."

"I see. Maybe you should get yourself some coffee or something," Saunders suggests, but I don't budge. "You could've called in sick if you're not feeling well. Then again, I would've been surprised if you did, considering the warrant. How come you didn't tell me you were back on the Sierra Cross case?"

Ugh. This is exactly the kind of thing I don't have patience for today. Even when Summers isn't here, the topics he usually brings up are still hovering over my head like a fucking rain cloud.

I sigh hard and loud. "Captain ... what? Warrant? Sierra Cross case? I have no idea what you're talking about."

Saunders' eyebrows slowly knit together. "What do you mean?"

"Just what I said. Summers and I are not on the Sierra Cross case."

"Then why did your partner spend the morning in front of a judge getting a search warrant?"

I frown. "A search warrant for what?"

"To dig in Evan Godric's backyard?"

I instantly shoot up in my chair, eyes as big as flying saucers. "He did *what*?"

"Jeez, why are you acting so surprised by this?"

Saunders asks. "Are you two not communicating or something? I got word that Summers had an appointment scheduled with Judge Palmer this morning, trying to get a search warrant for Evan Godric's property. Palmer granted the warrant. Based on what evidence, I don't know. But Summers must've had something convincing if he got the warrant from Palmer. He didn't tell you?"

Panic ignites in my body like napalm, sending hot pinpricks flowing through my veins at a million degrees. I don't even think to answer the captain. Instead, I jump out of my seat and run through the bullpen, colliding with two uniformed officers before I finally reach the door. I bolt around the corner and into the parking lot, fumbling for both my keys and my phone.

Once I'm in the car, I start it and slam on the gas, sending my vehicle tearing through the lot and onto the busy road. Morning traffic stops me almost immediately, and I try to use the extra time to bring up your name on the phone, but my fingers are too shaky to do it correctly.

Summers has a warrant to search your house. Is that where you spent the night last night? I assume it was, and if I'm right, I have to get in touch with you immediately. Otherwise, unless you've already left for work, you're about to get a terrible wake up call.

thirty
~ journey ~

"ANSWER THE FUCKING PHONE!" I scream as your voicemail comes on for what seems like the millionth time. I know you're upset, Sir, but you have to see the difference. I went from not calling to absolutely blowing up your phone, and now you're sending me straight to voicemail. Can't you see that something is wrong? Can't you feel the urgency? Are you on the job site, or have you already been arrested?

Turn your phone back on and fucking answer it!

I slam my cell onto the seat next to me as I take the exit for Strawberry Mansion, hoping that when I get there the scene is calm and quiet. No flashing lights. No units surrounding the property. No Summers. Fucking Summers.

Why the fuck is he doing this? He has been obsessed with Winter, Sierra Cross, and you since he became my partner, and I just don't understand it. There's no reason I can think of for someone to keep pulling at the same thread like this. I have no answers to his reasons for doing things, but I do know something for sure—I should have fucking killed him after the first time he asked about us.

Since we hung Winter from his ceiling, you and I have gone out of our way to make sure no one in the precinct knows we're together. Yes, we moved in together, but we did it quietly. No one knew. I don't know why we made the mistake of telling Summers, thinking he would just be the cool partner meeting my boyfriend. That was a mistake I wish I could take back. No one should have ever known about us. Look where trying to be nice and friendly has gotten us.

I turn onto the street that I haven't been on since you moved out of this neighborhood, my heart pounding uncontrollably. Beads of sweat form on my forehead as the house you grew up in starts to come into view. From down the road, I can already see unmarked cars parked in front of your place.

"Oh, god," I whisper as I get closer, approaching slowly so I don't draw attention to myself. Once I reach your house, I quickly realize that no one is in the front. Summers isn't standing at your front door. You're not on the porch with your hands cuffed behind your back. No one is at the front because everyone is in the back.

I bring my car to stop in front of your mailbox, then put it in reverse so that I can get a better view of the back-yard. From here, I see Summers in gray pants and a white button-up, and a small group of men in gray and black suits standing in the exact spot where we reburied the footlocker containing Sierra Cross's body. Two men have removed their blazers and tossed them aside, and they're holding shovels, plunging them into the ground over and over, pulling out copious amounts of dirt at a time.

"Fuck," I whisper in astonishment, because I know

what this means. Whatever hunch Summers had about Sierra Cross was right, and unless you came back and moved the body without me knowing, they're about to discover the corpse of the woman who started all of this.

I'm horrified watching it, but the fact that I don't see you makes me feel a bit better. You are nowhere to be found in the backyard, so I search the empty cars parked in front of your house. You aren't seated in the back of any of them, which means you haven't been detained. You're not here.

Just as I'm about to breathe a sigh of relief, I hear commotion in the backyard. I glue my eyes to the group of unknown men and watch as the two with shovels quickly drop them next to the large hole, and reach down. They struggle a bit, but eventually they pull out the black footlocker, its padlocks rusted and dangling but still intact.

I can't do anything to stop it. I have no choice but to sit here and watch as they use a shovel to break off the rusted padlocks and slowly open the box. I see the moment the smell hits them and they step back. I never saw how you put Sierra into the case, so I don't know exactly what they're looking at, but I see when Summers steps forward. He kneels next to the box, reaches inside, and looks to tear something open. I assume it's plastic, and when he gets it open, I know that he has exactly what he has been looking for. He steps back and pulls out his cell phone.

Game over.

I quietly put the car in gear and drive away, knowing that my entire life just changed. I'm stunned into silence because words won't fix this. Nothing will. I worked so hard to keep Winter from finding out anything about Sierra Cross, and to see it all being pulled up out of a shallow grave and presented to my new partner is beyond heartbreaking. Everything I worked for has been ruined, and I don't know how I'm supposed to protect you now, Sir. What am I supposed to do?

I try to call you again, but it's all the same. You don't answer, and I'm mocked by the outgoing message to your voicemail. It's unbearable hearing your voice but not being able to speak to you. I have no idea where you are or what you're doing, and there's nothing I can do. I have no control over this situation, and I fear that everything is about to come to a screeching halt.

As I lift my phone to call you again, it rings in my hand before I can dial. For a half second I think it's you, but Captain Saunders name quickly pops up. Against my better judgment, I answer on speaker.

"Yeah?" I say, all need for respect gone completely out the window.

"Monroe, where are you?" Saunders immediately asks.

"I'm ... uhh ... checking out a lead for the diner fire. What's up?"

"Are you driving right now?"

"What difference does it make, Captain? What's going on?"

Saunders exhales into the phone, preparing himself to say something big that even he can't believe. I grip my steering wheel, holding onto it to brace for impact.

"I just got a phone call," Saunders says, sounding completely defeated. "A call that knocked me back into my seat in my office. I mean that literally. I couldn't hold myself up while I was on this call. So if you're driving, you may want to stop."

"Captain, can you get to the point?" I say, anxious for the hammer to drop.

The captain sighs again. "Your partner ... Detective fucking Summers ... is Internal Affairs."

In the middle of a residential street in Strawberry Mansion, I slam on my brakes and come to a stop just like the captain said I would need to. The cars behind me begin to honk for me to move, but I don't fucking care. I stay there, no hazard lights, no eye contact with the people giving me the finger as they drive around me. My entire world skids to a stop as I listen to Captain Saunders tell me that my life has just been set on fire.

"The call came from the commanding officer of the Professional Standards Bureau , whose name I didn't even bother to remember," Saunders goes on. "He informed me that they sent Detective Summers to the Seventh Precinct to investigate you for misconduct pertaining to your handling of the Sierra Cross missing persons case. They're claiming that they now have evidence that you falsified findings in the Evan Godric investigation and subsequent search warrant obtained by Detective Sam Winter."

I don't respond. I can't. My throat is closed off to any words. All I can do is sit in the road, my fingers squeezing the steering wheel so hard my hands shake.

"Journey," Captain Saunders continues. "They're also claiming that Summers has found evidence that suggests you are now cohabitating with the suspect of an ongoing investigation. They say you're living with Evan Godric, the one and only suspect in that missing persons case. Journey, is any of this true?"

I don't answer as tears sting my eyes.

"I guess it doesn't matter," Saunders says. "They

want you to come in for questioning, Journey. Right now."

I still don't answer as the tears begin to flow.

"Oh, and one more thing," says Saunders, tearing my existence apart brick by brick. "They've issued a warrant for Evan Godric's arrest, for the murder of Sierra Cross."

chapter
thirty-one

I'VE GONE an entire day without talking to Journey. I don't say that with pride, because I don't really know how it makes me feel. On one hand, I'm so fucking mad at her that I could slit a stranger's throat just to let it out. Anger churns in my stomach, filling me with untamed emotion every time I think about what she has done. The image of her sneaking up behind Trey, hammer in hand, ready to take his life, is all I can think about. I see the look of shock on her face when I call Trey's name and walk up from the street, catching her in the act. The moment is on a loop in my mind, and it pisses me off with every replay.

On the other hand, I miss her so much I feel it in the marrow of my bones every time I move. She has become so vital to my existence that it feels like I can't do it without her. I can't breathe with her being absent from my life, and it's like I'm wheezing now, gasping for air and struggling just to maintain consciousness. I crave her skin, her scent, the touch of her hair brushing against me, the heat emanating from her body and warming me up. I'm desperate to have her near me again ... but the anger is overwhelming.

How can I love her so much, when she lied about everything? Better yet, how could she fucking lie to me about so much while claiming to love me?

After I left the house, I drove around with nowhere to go. All I could feel was rage over my inability to control the situation, and betrayal for all of the lies Journey told me. I kept my foot firmly on the gas, lucky that I didn't run into any cops on my way toward the highway, and I didn't stop until I was in Wilmington. I just needed to be out of Philadelphia altogether, and decided to get a hotel instead of going back to my childhood home in Strawberry Mansion. There were just too many memories there. Thoughts of my mother would've crept in, and flashbacks of my time spent with Journey would have been overwhelming. That was the last thing I needed, so I stayed far away.

After checking into the Hyatt, I immediately laid down and got some rest. I was satisfied that Journey had respected my wishes and didn't call or text the entire night. Although it didn't help me sleep, I was glad to not hear from her. I was struggling enough on my own and didn't need her fucked up version of assistance with that. This morning, however, is a completely different story.

I called in sick to work as soon as I woke up, which Trey found odd after he just saw me standing in his driveway last night. I told him I was sick, and while the thought of lying disgusts me right now, at least I didn't lie to Journey. That's the way this is supposed to be. We lie to the world, but never each other. I hung up the phone feeling glad that I had arrived in time to save

Trey, and before I could get out of the bathroom after my shower, Journey was calling.

I let it go the first few times, figuring she woke up in a mood and just wanted to talk to me after the short break. We're not accustomed to sleeping apart now. Funny how that happens after you've gone your entire life sleeping alone, and then you meet someone and can't stand to sleep away from them ever again. But after what seemed like the tenth call in a row, I had to turn the phone off. There wasn't anyone I wanted to talk to anyway.

I spent the day in the bed, scarfing down food ordered from DoorDash and sipping wine from the liquor cabinet that will undoubtedly raise the cost of my stay to the fucking moon. I didn't care, and I enjoyed the silence of the day, but as day turned to night, the urge to check on Journey became too much to keep my phone off.

As soon as my cell awakes from its slumber, I'm inundated by missed call alerts and voicemail messages. I frown, wondering if Journey is just being ridiculous or if there is really something wrong. When I sit on the edge of the bed and begin listening to the voicemails, I get the answer, and my heart sinks.

"Evan, answer your fucking phone!" she screams at the top of her lungs. "I know you're mad, but something has happened. The fucking unthinkable. Please answer!"

"Goddamn it, turn your phone back on! Sir, we have to talk right now!"

"What has happened is bigger than you know, Evan. You have to check your messages and call me back. If you don't, our world will fall apart while your eyes are closed, and by the time you open them there won't be a world left."

What the fuck? I don't even bother listening to any more messages although there are *many* more. It's clear that this isn't Journey being upset over me cutting off communication. She needs me, and when my Little Devil needs me, I don't hesitate.

It doesn't matter if I'm pissed off about her lies; if anyone has laid a finger on her, they will suffer a slow, agonizing death.

The phone rings once before Journey answers, her voice still as emotional as it was in the voicemails.

"Evan, why haven't you been answering your phone?" she blares.

"That is not the way you want to start the conversation with me, Journey. You fucking knowing why I haven't been answering," I reply. "But you've called dozens of times and left numerous messages that I didn't even get through because you sounded so upset. What the fuck is going on?"

She sighs, a sound of defeat I'm not used to hearing from her.

"I fucked up, Sir," she says with a trembling voice. Is she crying? "I fucked up big time, and everything is crumbling. It's over. Everything is over."

Yeah, that's what lying gets you.

"Is this about last night? You have to give me details because I have no idea what you're talking about."

"Summers ... Summers is IA," she says.

I shake my head. "IA? I don't know what that means."

"He's Internal Affairs!" she blares, her voice a mixture of hatred and sadness. "Internal Affairs investigates police departments, Evan. They use their own internal investigation procedures to determine the culpability of its officers for misconduct, and make sure employees follow agency standards of professionalism. They fucking sneak in and snoop around, asking questions and trying to get answers about shit that doesn't even pertain to them."

I don't say anything, but my heart sinks. I know what this means.

That beady-eyed little fucker.

"Summers has been investigating me from the moment he arrived," she goes on, still wound up tightly and crying through the phone. "That's why he has been asking all of these questions and looking into our relationship. We practically sealed the deal for him when we took him to lunch that day. He heard your name and immediately began digging, and as soon as he found out that your name was on a search warrant with Winter's, he latched on and never let go. Sir, he got another warrant to search your house ... and they dug up Sierra Cross's body this morning. IA is asking me to come in for questioning, and they've put a warrant out for your arrest. I'm so sorry, Sir. I'm sorry."

Journey begins wailing, which makes my heart ache because I've never heard her cry before. She's always so strong, confident, and brutal. This has broken her, and while I should be shattered and afraid myself, hearing her cry only stiffens my spine. It only makes me more defiant. I have to protect her, but I'm so fucking upset that I'm not sure exactly what to do. If I don't make a move, I'll witness my entire life come crashing down right in front of me. I can't just stand still and watch it happen. I have to do something with this anger.

"Journey," I say before taking a deep breath and settling myself. "Stop crying. I know you're upset, but it won't do us any good. This was bound to happen. If I would've moved Sierra's body a long time ago, then Summers would've found nothing and we wouldn't be in this place. So it's on me, not you."

"But I should've recognized the signs. I should've known he wasn't a normal detective."

"No," I say, cutting her off. "If he's Internal Affairs, then I'm sure he's trained to make sure you don't catch on too quickly. That's why he backed off when you started questioning him. He knew he was showing his hand and you were onto him. You have nothing to be sorry for.

"Now, you need to listen to me. If they've issued a warrant for me, it's going to get hot. Luckily, I'm not in the city. I'm in Wilmington. I want you to meet me here at the Hyatt. I'm in room 2307. Bring as much as you need to live on the road for a while, because there's a chance we may never sleep in our own house again. When you get here, come straight up to the room. Text me when you're close and I'll let you in"

Journey sniffs before saying, "Okay. What are you going to do in the meantime?"

"Just come here, Journey. We'll talk more once we're together. Okay?"

"Okay, Sir. I'm on my way. I'll see you soon. I love you, Evan."

I try to hesitate because I'm pissed, but the truth comes out. "I love you."

We hang up and I set the phone next to me. I can't believe it. One simple mistake has cost us everything in one swoop. The entire time I was dating Journey before I told her about accidentally killing Sierra, I contemplated moving the body. Over and over again the idea kept coming to me, and I continued to ignore it. Even after we killed Winter, we decided to keep Sierra in my backyard as her case went cold without any leads. I should've known that secrets don't stay buried forever. It's my fault. Now I have to do something about it.

Since the warrant for my arrest is brand new, I assume I have some time to move around here in Wilmington without having to worry about being caught. So, I get up and finish getting dressed. I'm going to need to make a couple of stops before Journey gets here. It's time to prepare for what's to come.

chapter
thirty-two

WHEN THERE'S a knock on my hotel door, I don't even feel like the person I was before I spoke to Journey earlier. Prior to calling her back, I was furious over what she tried to do to Trey. I was aggravated by the fact that I had been forced to leave the city I love and find refuge in Wilmington, desperate to be anywhere but the place where I was lied to countlessly. I was sick over it, no doubt, but now ... now I'm ready to be everything I was always afraid I would become. Now I'm ready to embrace the beast I've always been.

I sit on the edge of the bed staring at nothing, the room darkened by shadows cast on the walls from the glow of the TV and no other lights on. The darkness matches my mood, to say the least. A second knock raps on the door and I force myself to move, the bag on the bed shifting as I get up. I had to go out with a hoodie, keeping my face low as I perused ailes for things I'll need over the next few weeks. I couldn't even lift my head in case there were cameras above me. What a shitty existence. It reminded me of the way I was before I met

Journey—a coward, too afraid to show the world who he truly is. I hated it then, and I fucking hate it now.

When I open the door, Journey stands before me dressed in all-black, two bags in her hands carrying her belongings because she can't go back home either. She's all packed and ready to run and hide. Now we're *two* cowards prepared to go on the lamb until the end of time.

"Hey," she says, a half smile on her face from being happy to see me while still hesitant. She knows I'm not over what happened so she'll tread lightly, but walking soft enough to traipse over eggshells wouldn't save her from the way I'm feeling right now.

I turn on my heel and walk back into the room, Journey following closely. The door to the room closes, and as Journey sets her bags down next to the mini fridge, I reach into my own bag and grip the new rope I purchased for this moment. I squeeze it hard, taking out my anger on the knotted fabric as I turn around to face Journey. When sees me, she glances down at my hand.

"What are you doing?" she asks.

"What *should* I do?" I reply, nearly foaming at the mouth from how fucking pissed I am at the situation that forced us into this room.

Journey frowns. "What? I don't know. What should you do about *what*, Sir?"

"Oh, *Sir*? Am I your *Sir*, Journey?" I growl, gripping the rope even tighter.

"Of course you are," she answers.

"Do you lie to your Sir? Do you keep your Dom in the dark about everything? Do you avoid communication with the person you belong to? Do you fucking sneak—beating up people, burning down buildings, and fucking planning murders without ever thinking of telling the truth? Is this how a submissive acts with her *Sir*?"

Journey is silent, a look of horror on her face before forcing herself to stutter, "Sir ... Evan ... I—"

"Shut the fuck up," I snap, quickly eliminating the space between us with two large steps. My nose touches Journey's as we stand face to face. "You call me Sir and then treat me like I'm just another random person on the street for you to lie to. We were supposed to be partners. We were a team. We have fucking laid people to rest together, Journey, and you lie to *me*. Me! I may be a savage who has stolen the life from people's lungs, but since each of us has learned the truth about the other, I have never lied to you. You planned to murder my friend and didn't speak a word of it. Had I not shown up to Trey's house to apologize and make sure we were good, I never would've been there to stop you. You would've killed him and I never would've known that it was you, and you *never* would've told me. How the fuck am I supposed to trust you now?"

"Evan, I'm sorry!"

I slam my hand over Journey's mouth, forcing her to walk backwards until she is pinned between me and the door.

"Do not speak again," I say, glaring at her. "Every question I ask is rhetorical until I say otherwise. You are allowed to say *nothing* because I can't believe a word that comes out of your fucking mouth. If you want my trust again, you will have to fucking earn every bit of it." I shift my hand, sliding it down from her mouth to her throat. "Now take off your clothes and drop to your knees before I give you what you *really* deserve, and choke the life out of you."

Wheezing, Journey begins yanking at her clothes.

She quickly tears herself out of her shirt but struggles to remove her pants with my hand around her throat. Once she's naked, I finally relent and allow her to drop to her knees in front of me.

"Do not fucking move," I tell her. "If I see as much as a single muscle fiber twitch, I swear I will walk out of this hotel room and leave you to fend for yourself. Do you understand me?"

I glare at Journey, waiting for the beginning of a word to fall out of her mouth, looking for an excuse to let my anger guide me out of this room and never look back. However, Journey doesn't speak. She doesn't nod her head. She stays still, her eyes on mine, letting me know she understands and will obey.

Satisfied with her submission, I finally put my new rope to use. I tie the rough fabric around her neck and create loose knots that hang down to her stomach before spreading them outward toward her back. I take my time, making as many knots and squares as I can until her body is a checkerboard, her arms bound tightly at her sides and her legs the only limbs she has available to use. It's better than my first attempt but still not perfect.

"Stand up," I command, and I don't offer a hand to assist her. She struggles to lift a knee high enough to balance herself before managing to get to her feet and stand in front of me. "Your fucking face disgusts me, Journey. All I see are the eyes that have lied to no end, disregarding our dynamic and the respect we were supposed to have for each other. Turn around so that I don't have to look at the mouth that has spoken so much bullshit to me."

Journey slowly spins until her back is to me and she's facing the bed. I review my rope work a final time before reaching into my bag again and removing a hunting knife with a wooden handle and a six-inch serrated blade. I'm not sure if Journey sees it, but if she does she doesn't show it.

"I could kill you right now," I tell her, just as I gently run the serrated edge of the knife across the back of her neck. "I could stab you and end your life and there isn't anything you could do to stop me. I couldn't trust you, so what makes you think you can trust that I won't take out my anger on you? What makes you think that your lies haven't made me snap? You've watched me kill people before. It has never bothered me. You thought that because I enjoyed our peaceful, lustful life together that I had gone soft. You convinced yourself that I needed you to defend me, as if you didn't watch me cut a man's tongue out for disrespecting you. You let yourself believe that I was no longer like you, but you have no idea Journey.

"You're not stronger than me or more willing to act on your emotions. You're simply more thoughtless. You're less controlled. That's why I'm a Dom, because control is what I'm best at. But being in control doesn't mean being weak. No, in fact, I think I like the sight of blood more than you do."

Slowly, deliberately, I apply pressure to the tip of the knife and drag it down Journey's shoulder blade. Blood blooms brilliantly in a straight line as she lets out a soft gasp before sucking it back in. I keep going until the vertical line is three inches long.

"You see?" I continue, my eyes widening at the sight of blood streaking down her back and soaking into the rope. "I like that. Seeing your life leak from your body makes my cock harder than it has been in a long time ... and you have the nerve to think I need your protection? No, Little One, it is you who needs mine."

I place my hand on the leaking wound, smearing blood on my palm and biting my lip as the feel and scent of it work their way through my system. I'm overcome with sadistic elation as my cock throbs and I push Journey forward until she falls onto the mattress face-first. Her torso lands with a thud as her legs dangle off the edge of the bed. I drop my pants and mount her quickly, straddling her closed legs and gripping the thick rope for leverage.

"You treated me like I belong to you," I say as I push myself into her, stretching her tight, wet pussy to its limits. "But you are the one who belongs to me, Journey. Now, I'm going to make sure you know it."

As Journey lays silently on the bed, I begin fucking her with no desire to satisfy her. I'm going to fuck her like I hate her because right now I do. I abhor what she has done and feel nothing but hostility in this moment, and I'm going to take it all out on her now. This is not about pleasure. It's about ownership.

"You belong to me," I say, thrusting into her so hard I nearly hurt myself. The bed tries to inch forward but is blocked by the wall. Fuck it. I'll fuck her so hard the mattress will break through the drywall. We'll end up in the adjoining room by the time I'm finished ravishing her.

"Lying to me is against the fucking rules."

Thrust.

"You are my fucking property."

Thrust.

"You do as I say."

Thrust.

"At all fucking times."

Thrust. Thrust. Thrust.

Journey bites back a moan as I lift the knife again and embed the tip into her skin, dragging it horizontally to create a line at the top of the first one.

"You will never disobey me again."

Thrust.

"You will do as your Sir commands."

Thrust. Thrust.

"Or I will never touch you again."

Thrust. Thrust. Thrust. Thrust.

"I own every inch of you," I say, moving the knife down to form another horizontal line in the center of the vertical one.

"You are my whore."

Thrust.

"You are my slut."

Thrust. Thrust.

"You are my property."

Thrust. Thrust. Thrust.

I move the knife lower and press down to dig the blade in again. I slide it across her skin until the tip comes in contact with the rope, but I keep cutting. I push hard and rip it across, slicing through both Journey's skin and the rope, shredding it in two and leaving a deep gash in her flesh. She lets out a yelp that she can't bite back, but I don't fucking care.

"And now you wear my brand," I say, dropping the knife and slamming my hand against the four lines on her back that come together to form the letter E. I love seeing my first initial carved into her skin. It drives me wild and I pound into her, my eyes focused on the rose-colored letter.

I grip the rope with one hand while the other stays on the new E on her back, and I fuck Journey hard. I can tell how much effort she has to put into keeping quiet, and I love that she is obeying her master. My dick is a weapon of destruction and I use it to try and split her just like the rope. I fuck hard and fast until I'm ready to explode, and when it comes, I don't stop. I let the wave wreck me, and just as I'm coming, I pull out and stand up straight. My cum rips from me in ribbons that land on Journey's bare back, most of it splashing on her new brand. Breathing hard, I reach down and smear my cum into the E, mixing her blood with my semen.

"There," I snip. "I'm a permanent part of you now, Little Devil. Now I only have one question, and you're allowed to answer." I grab Journey by the neck and wrench her head over as I lean down so that we're face to face. "Who do you belong to?"

With mist in her eyes from the pain and pleasure she just endured, Journey's agonized face slowly shifts into a smile.

"You," she answers. "My Sir."

chapter
thirty-three

BLOOD STAINS the sheets beneath us from Journey's wound even after I've cleaned it up with peroxide and a bandage from my store run, but we don't care. The person who comes to clean the room after we're gone might be bothered by the sight of crimson on white sheets, but we're not. For Journey and me, we're right at home.

I sit with my back against the headboard while Journey lays with her head against my chest, a finger trailing down my bare stomach until it meets the covers before starting at the top again. Her hair smells of vanilla tonight, and I breathe it in. Now that I've taken my rage out on her, I feel better, more accepting of the fact that she's here. I love having her in my arms, and although our future is as dim as the lights in the room, nothing beats having my Little Devil by my side.

I run my fingers down her shoulder, bypassing the congealed blood on her back from her new mark. The letter E stands out even in the dark, and the sight of it soothes me. She let me carve one of my initials into her. If there was any doubt left that she is committed to me, it's gone now. Her torso still holds the outline of the rope criss-crossing her skin, a patchwork of squares, ropeburn, and bruises that make her look like abstract artwork. Even now, after all that she has done and all that has happened, she is a sight to behold.

"I'm sorry," she says out of nowhere, breaking through the silence. She keeps her head down, watching as her fingers ski down my skin, but her voice is emotional. "I was wrong about everything, and I let my insecurity get to me like a teenager. Your coworker—the one I beat up—didn't deserve that. I should've trusted you to remain faithful to me instead of thinking that her mere existence could potentially cause problems between us down the road. I realize I was being ridiculous and I'm sorry, Sir."

"Is that what it was? Insecurity?" I ask, genuinely curious about Journey's mindset. I need to know what makes her tick so that I can be better prepared for her triggers in the future. I can't be the Dom she needs if I don't know absolutely everything about her.

"I guess so," she answers. "I know it doesn't make any sense. Nothing I've done as of late does. I just saw her and let it wreak havoc in my mind."

"Journey, she didn't flirt with me at all, and even if she had, my love for you would never allow me to do something fucked up like that."

"I know ... I was wrong. I've been wrong a lot lately, including the diner."

"Why didn't you admit to it when it was clear that I knew you did it?"

"Because it was a secret I was keeping, and I've been keeping my little secrets my entire life. I'm not used to sharing them with anyone. You and I have our own secrets that no one else knows about, but I had secrets well before I met you and I've always only had myself to share them with. I can't explain it in a way that makes sense, but it's just who I am. It was something I did that I didn't want anyone else to know about, and it didn't matter if that piece of shit kid went down for it. Unfortunately, he had an alibi anyway and I was stuck with it. The entire situation was fucked up and I should've listened to you when you told me to let it go."

"Yes," I say, "you should've."

"I know, and I'm so sorry, Evan," Journey says, her head still unmoved. "In hindsight, I realize how it all makes me look—the girl, the diner, Sierra's body ... I look psychotic."

"Looking psychotic has never bothered me, Little One. If you haven't noticed, I'm a bit psychotic myself. I don't mind lying to anyone else, and I'm not asking you to be some moral statue on a hill for the world to use as an example. I'm not and don't want to be. But we don't need to lie to one another. I honestly couldn't fucking care less about the act of you burning down the diner. It's the lies that I don't understand. That's what pisses me off. It seems that you haven't realized that we're two peas in a pod. There is no one else like us out there, and no one will love you like I do. There's no need to keep secrets from me. You don't have to do anything alone anymore because you're *not* alone. You have me. Always."

Journey doesn't turn around, but I hear her as quiet sobs escape her mouth against her will. This is the second time I've heard her crying, but it doesn't turn me off to her. It makes me love her more. I like seeing her vulnerable. I love knowing that she has a sensitive side that isn't always as cold as ice. Knowing her is all I care about, but there are a couple more questions I need answers to.

"Why didn't you tell me you watched me bury Sierra?" I ask.

Journey doesn't hesitate, finally ready to tell the truth. "I didn't like how it would make me look in your eyes. I watched you in The Black Collar for a long time but ... I liked *watching* you. I'm not even sure it had anything to do with courage. I just liked seeing you, watching the way you moved and how people reacted to you. I couldn't get enough, and while that made sense to me, I knew that you'd lose it if you had any inkling that I was sitting outside your house after you left the club. There was no way to keep myself from looking like a stalker, so I didn't say anything. By the time the investigation started, I was already so enamored with you that I didn't give a fuck about the missing girl. All I wanted was you. I wanted you to want me too, and knowing I had been watching you isn't something that would make you want me. So I made sure Winter didn't get too close while I got as close as I possibly could."

I nod my head, totally shocked by all of this new information. "Wow. I'm not sure I even know what to say."

"You don't have to say anything," says Journey. "I just want you to know that I'm sorry about all of it, especially me plotting on Trey. I realize how fucked up it is for me to disregard how you feel about him just because he upset me. I wouldn't blame you if you didn't forgive me."

I think about it all, asking myself over and over if I actually do forgive her for what she planned to do to Trey. It'd be easy to say that she crossed a line that there is no coming back from, but saying that would be lying to myself and denying how much I love this woman. She has been through so much and may be the only person on this god-forsaken planet who can relate to me fully. I love Journey, and the truth of the matter is that as much as I like Trey, I could live without him. I can, under absolutely no circumstances whatsoever, live without Journey.

"It's hard to forgive," I admit, still caressing her shoulder as her finger slides between my pecs. "But I never asked you to be perfect. If I did, it would make me a hypocrite. Admittedly, I could kill you for what you've done, but I love you far too much to ever contemplate being without you. So, I guess I'll have to do something else."

"Something else? What do you mean?" Journey asks. "What are you going to do?"

I let out a sigh as I stare straight ahead, a plan taking shape in my mind's eye.

"You're always asking me how you can please me. Well, now it's about how *I* can please *you*," I answer. "I'm going to kill him, Little Devil. I'm going to kill Summers. For you."

endgame

thirty-four
~ journey ~

I **WASN'T** sure if we would get back to this place. I wronged you, Sir, in the worst way. While I know that I'm different from the average girl walking down the street, there's no excuse for lying to you. I realize that now. I hope you understand that I'm not used to this. Love. Real love. It's as foreign to me as kanji characters. I can barely decipher my feelings let alone know what to do with them. You've given me something I never thought I could have, and with your guidance, Sir, I am learning.

I've made multiple mistakes, but you are the best man I've ever known, and you've forgiven me. You forced me to my knees and tested my resolve, carving an uppercase E into my flesh and making me bleed for you. It hurt like hell, but no more than knowing I hurt you with my actions. I'm thankful to you for allowing me to be back in your good graces and giving me a chance to prove my commitment. After all of the drama and wrongdoing, you and I are back on solid ground. My knees no longer quiver with fear of what's coming. Thanks to you, Sir, I'm ready for what's next.

I watch you finish getting dressed in the bathroom —black sweatpants with a black hoodie—and I can tell from your demeanor that you're serious about this. I'm not sure whether to smile or be terrified, because I know that everything is about to change for us.

I never saw it coming. One minute everything is perfectly fine, the next they're digging up a body from your backyard and I'm sick with panic. When I saw them lift that box from the ground, I thought for sure that we were finished. Finding Sierra meant the inevitable arrest warrant. It meant time behind bars for you and probably me, too. It meant our time together coming to an end. At least that's what it was supposed to mean.

"Are you ready?" you ask as you stand at the end of the bed, your bag firmly in hand and a look of focus on your flawless face.

"If you are," I reply.

You smile, nodding. "I am. For what it's worth, I'm sorry we're even in this position. I should've moved the fucking body. It's my fault this is broken, so I'm going to fix it. Okay?"

Now I nod. "Okay."

You place a knee on the mattress and lean in to kiss me. Your soft lips are warm and comforting, and I hate that I have to go back to being away from them. I hate all of this, but I'm ready. It is what has to happen.

After our final kiss, you step back and turn around. I watch you walk to the door and place your hand on the knob before looking back at me.

"I'll see you soon," you tell me. "I love you, Little Devil."

I smile. "I love you, too, Sir."

With a final nod of your head, you turn around and walk out, leaving me in the room all alone.

My thoughts threaten to consume me. Anxiety and fear immediately blossom in my belly and begin to work their way through my veins, threatening to hold me captive, but I don't have time to go still. There is no room for error if I want to make it out of this alive, so I have to stick to my plan.

After waiting twenty minutes and knocking back a few shots from the mini fridge, I swallow hard as my heart races. The alcohol didn't make me any less apprehensive, so instead of getting over it, I'll have to become one with it. I close my eyes and breathe in deeply, pushing the air out with a *whoosh*. Then, I pick up the phone.

It rings twice before he answers.

"Detective Monroe," says Detective Summers. "I didn't expect you to call me. I've been looking for you."

thirty-five
~ journey ~

AS I NAVIGATE my car down the road, my heart beats like a kick drum. I'm more anxious than ever, and I wish so much that you were here with me. I know we have to be apart now, but your arms around me would ease the tension creeping up my neck and settling into my shoulders as I turn onto our street. Part of me didn't think Summers would actually agree to meet me here, but when I told him you ran when I confronted you about the information Captain Saunders gave me, his tone changed. As the house comes into view, so do he and his car. He's here. This is it. It's time.

"Thanks so much for meeting me," I say, my face stricken with a concoction of sadness, anger, and embarrassment. I shake my head as I walk down the driveway from the garage and stand in front of him ... him, the man responsible for our undoing. I hold out my hand for him to shake, but he doesn't take it.

"Listen, Journey," he starts as I lower my hand to my side, abashed. "The only reason I'm here is because you and I were partners for a while. I like you. I think you're a good detective who has made some bad decisions. But that doesn't mean you should go to jail over the choices you've made. I'm here to help clear up your name and place the blame where it belongs—on Evan Godric."

The mention of your name sends shooting stars aflight in my body, but I don't let it show. I see the way he's looking at me, his eyes laser focused, checking my body language and mannerisms. He has been doing it the entire time, but I was too caught up in my own world to recognize the signs. His eyes have always been on me, probably in moments when I didn't even know he was looking, and I hate him for it. I want to slit his throat and smear the blood all over his face, clogging his nose with it so that he chokes from the gash in his neck and the blood in his nostrils at the same time. I know you blame yourself for not moving Sierra's body, and I take some of the blame for not realizing that her case was not closed but cold, but all of this is really *his* fault.

"I truly appreciate it," I reply, letting my eyes drop down to the ground. "I couldn't possibly be more grateful for your understanding and willingness to hear the truth. Not to mention the fact that you agreed to meet me here to discuss this instead of forcing me to come to the precinct or the Professional Standards Bureau. You didn't have to do it this way and I really am appreciative. Thank you, Marty."

Seeing the sincerity written across my face, Summers nods. "It's no problem, Journey. Let's just go inside."

As we enter the house, I lead my ex-partner into the home that you and I share and have to bite my lip while he's behind me. The thought of him stepping foot in the place where we love each other makes me livid. I want him out. I want you here. Better yet, I want him dead on the floor while we fuck next to his cold corpse.

"Have a seat," I say, pulling out one of the dining room chairs.

I sit down across from him, and the second we're settled Summers pulls out a small, silver rectangle and sets it on the table top.

"As we discussed, I'm going to record all of this," he says. "Although we're doing this here, it's still evidence in the IA case against you, Journey. I'm here to help, but I have to do it the right way."

"I understand," I say with a nod.

Summers presses a button and the digital recorder comes to life. "This is Detective Martin Summers of Internal Affairs, conducting a voluntary interrogation of Detective Journey Monroe in regard to Case RW100199. The time is nineteen thirty-seven on May second, twenty twenty-four."

Hearing him say the case number makes it all real. It wasn't a dream. He really is Internal Affairs, sent here to investigate me and my misconduct simply because I'm in love with you. It takes every ounce of my concentration not to jump up and attack him right now.

"Alright, Detective Monroe. Let's get started," Summers continues, sitting back in his seat and eyeing me closely. Motherfucker. "After the death of Detective Sam Winter almost immediately following his successful attempt to obtain a search warrant for the Godric residence pertaining to the Sierra Cross missing persons case, the Professional Standards Bureau became suspicious of the warrant findings, or lack thereof. While not directly stated in the verbiage of the warrant, Detective

Winter had pleaded with the judge to be allowed to dig in Evan Godric's backyard after finding him with a shovel in his hand during a routine check. However, there was no mention of digging in your report. You cleared Evan Godric and even pushed to have his name removed from the suspect list in the Cross case. Not to mention that you were not present when Detective Winter saw the judge to request the warrant. This raised red flags, and led the Bureau to believe that he didn't include you because he was suspicious that you were having an improper relationship with the suspect."

My heart sinks listening to him detail how all of this started. Here I was thinking that everything was good. I was convinced that you and I were in the clear—that no one knew about us until the day we went to lunch with Summers. I was wrong. They were suspicious of me from the moment Winter died because I cleared you too quickly. There was never a moment where you and I were free from watchful eyes. If we had been any less careful, all of this would have happened sooner. They were always watching.

"Detective Monroe," Summers says, leaning forward. "I witnessed you enter the bathroom of a diner with the suspect shortly after I became your partner, but when did your relationship with Evan Godric actually begin?"

I let out a sigh, still in disbelief that I'm about to do this. "Regardless of what any report says about me, and regardless of the fact that Sam obtained the warrant without me, I didn't start seeing Evan until after he was cleared as a suspect."

"Well, technically speaking, he never was cleared, at least not with us."

I glare at him and have to quickly lower my eyes to cover it.

"I understand that," I go on. "But my point stands. I cleared him as far as the Seventh Precinct's investigation was concerned. He was scratched off the list and we began dating after that."

"It didn't bother you that he was a suspect in the case you were assigned to?" Summers asks.

"He was a *former* suspect, so no, it didn't bother me."

"At what point did you move in together?"

"After a few months of dating."

"Did he ever mention Sierra Cross to you?"

"Only to tell me that he had nothing to do with her disappearance, which is why I'm doing this now. He lied to me. He convinced me that he was innocent. I now know that to not be the case."

"How do you feel now that you know Sierra Cross's body was found buried on Evan Godric's property? It was exactly where Detective Winter thought it would be."

"I feel like someone who was lied to. I feel like a cop who's ready to make an arrest."

"Is that so?" Summers asks smugly. "Is there a reason why you didn't dig in Godric's backyard while carrying out the initial search warrant?"

I freeze.

"Your partner, Detective Winter, used the shovel in Godric's hand as justification for the warrant. However, while conducting the search *with you*, he never dug. Why is that?"

I don't reply.

"Did you keep Detective Winter from digging in Evan Godric's backyard?"

Fuck.

"Did you know Sierra Cross was buried there while you were carrying out the search warrant?"

Shit.

"I like you, Journey. But I don't believe that Detective Winter cared so much about this case that he killed himself after coming up empty during a search. In fact, I don't believe he came up empty at all. I believe he was right on the money when he requested the search warrant. I believe you knew about Sierra Cross's body all along ... and I believe you murdered your partner for love."

He actually put it all together. He figured it out. The game is over.

Sir, I hope you're ready.

"That's insane," I say, looking past Summers toward the darkness of the hall behind him.

"Is it?" he asks, clearly happy with himself. "If you want to clear your name, you're going to have to have much more evidence than, 'That's insane,' Detective."

I look past him again, then make direct eye contact.

"When I say it's insane, I don't mean that your story is insane," I tell him as I sit up straight and wipe away all looks and mannerisms of guilt and shame. "I mean that it's insane that you figured it all out. It's also insane that you and your recording will never make it out of this house."

I watch gleefully as Summers' eyes shrink into a squint, his mind asking if I'm bluffing and wondering how he'll escape if I'm not. We have a staring contest, wondering what the other will do, but I don't have to move because I have the answers to the test and he doesn't.

I guess he decides that I'm not bluffing, because his

hand slowly leaves the table and starts to reach for the service weapon holstered on his hip. But the smile that takes over my face makes his muscles stiffen.

"Tsk tsk, Marty," you say coldly as you emerge from the dark hall and place the six-inch hunting knife at Summers' throat. "I wouldn't do that if I were you."

chapter
thirty-six

"THINK about what you're doing, Evan," Summers says to me, raising his hands with his palms out. "I'm a detective who was sent here to investigate you and Journey. If I come up missing, there is no way you two are getting away with it. No matter how badly you want to, you can't kill me. Just put the knife down and let's figure out how to end this the right way."

A laugh crawls up my throat because I can't believe the audacity of this man. To think that I would let him live after everything he just said to my woman is insane. I heard the way he interrogated her, baiting her as if he was really here to look out for her best interest, trying to trap her into a confession about Detective Winter's death. He didn't agree to this to protect Journey. He agreed because he is just like all other cops. He wants to ruin someone's life. He wants to put someone behind bars until they die, and it only makes him feel better if he can do it to two people instead of one. Cops do nothing if not protect their own, and now that this one knows we killed Winter, he's out for blood. Unfortunately for him, so am I, but for me it is literal.

What Summers doesn't know is that his being here was always the plan. Journey knew exactly what to say and how to say it to get this arrogant prick to agree to meet here instead of the precinct. He's just like all other dumb ass men, moved and affected by the tears of a white woman. He heard her sniffling on the phone and dropped his guard. Fucking idiot.

I wish I could've been there to see Journey put on her act over the phone, diving fully into character to make sure this plan worked. Seeing her tear up probably would have made my cock hard, but alas, I had to leave first to make sure I got here before they did. I parked my truck in a vacant lot four blocks away and walked here to make sure my vehicle wasn't seen, then waited in the shower behind the curtain for Journey to lure her partner inside and lower his guard. Now that we're here, it honestly all seemed too easy. But I'm not one to find suspicion in the ease of things. I'll gladly take the easy kill.

Smiling while looking at my beautiful Little Devil, I press the knife to Summers' throat hard enough to slice his first layer of skin. "Marty, you shouldn't talk to me like you know me. There was once a time when you could've. I would've taken it then, but those days are over. You're only recently becoming aware of what I've done, but you have no idea about the beast that I am. The right way ... the *only* way to end this is with your body buried somewhere cold and dark. Coming to the Seventh Precinct was the biggest mistake of your life."

Summers keeps his hands in the air. "Maybe so. Maybe I underestimated you and Journey, but if you kill me, then everything ends here. You have to think about it, Evan. Do you really believe that I came here to speak to a woman under criminal investigation—whose boyfriend has a warrant out for his arrest for murder—without telling someone where I am? I'm Internal Affairs, remember? So ask yourself if you really think I'd be that stupid."

I look to Journey who is stunning in her all-black outfit that nearly matches mine. I shouldn't even be thinking of her in this way in a moment like this, but seeing the sweat slide down Summers' brow while I hold a knife to his throat in front of Journey makes me so goddamn hard. If I knew he wouldn't run or shoot us both, I'd eat her pussy right here in front of him before I slit his throat. She bites her lip as her eyes dance around the room. She would know better than me if this piece of shit would alert the precinct about speaking to her here, but it doesn't take long before her face shows signs of disbelief.

"You didn't tell anyone," she says to Summers. "If you did, they'd be here. You wouldn't have to record our conversation if there were people outside listening. They'd be recording it for you."

"Or maybe it's my job to know how to play people like you," Summers snaps back defiantly. His tone makes me grip the knife tighter as he keeps going. "I've been in law enforcement for a long time, Detective Monroe. With all due respect to the current situation, you're out of your league here. Now tell your boyfriend to put the knife down so we can figure this out together."

"Why are you so fucking stupid?" I ask, placing my free hand on the back of Summers' neck and squeezing. "What is there to figure out? We got you here for a reason, asshole. You think we want to talk it out and surrender now? You find a body in my backyard and you think it makes me want to spend the rest of my life behind bars? You're boasting about not being *that stupid* when clearly you are if you think we're letting you bring us in. You're going to need a fucking army to arrest me, and for Journey I'll gladly go to war with them all. It's clear you have no idea who you're talking to, which means you're the one who's out of their league."

"God I love seeing you this way," Journey says, the look of lust beaming from her eyes like sun rays.

I smile back at her. "I know you do, Little One. I want you so much I can barely stand still right now."

Journey gets up from the table and walks over to me, removing Summers' gun from his holster before kissing me on the cheek. "I love you so much."

"I love you, Baby Girl," I reply.

"You two are insane," Summers exclaims, his face twisted into a look of horror. "Do you think you're the new Bonnie & Clyde? This isn't some old, gangster fairytale. The two of you will not escape this if you go down this road, and no amount of playing cops and robbers will save you. You're treating it like it's a game when it's not. Drop the goddamn knife and let me go.

"I can't believe I thought you were a good person, Monroe. I tried to help you but I can see that you're so much fucking crazier than I ever knew. You wear a mask around the precinct all day, hiding your true identity to the good officers you work with. You're no better than the criminals and thugs we haul in. You're one of *them*, not one of us. I see it now. I can see it in the way you look at him that there is no redeeming you. It's clear that you're just as much of a murderer as he is."

I let Summers finish his speech, listening with a smirk until he finally shuts the fuck up. Then, I lock eyes with Journey and tighten my grip.

"You're right, Summers," I say to him. "There's no redeeming us ... and there's no saving you."

I close my eyes and lean forward, placing my lips on Journey's. We fall into a kiss that heats me up from toe to head, and while my tongue dances with hers, I flex my arm and drag the knife back and forth twice, gruesomely slitting Summer's throat with the serrated blade.

His hands fly up to his neck, but there's no stopping the gushing crimson tide. Blood spills between his fingers as he stands up, spinning around as if he's looking for help in an empty room. Journey and I don't even break stride, but I keep my eyes on him, watching him die as we continue kissing and Summers falls to his knees, his hands still clutching his throat. He gurgles like he's drowning before going still, then the sound of his body hitting the floor plays in our ears like music.

When we pull apart, we look down on the dead body in the middle of our living room. His blood pours out and pools around his head, ruining our carpet. It doesn't matter. This was always the plan. All that matters to me is that I ended the man who lied to Journey and put out a warrant for my arrest. The fucking bitch who made it to where Journey and I can no longer live here is dead and gone.

Journey stares at her deceased partner—the second one who has died by my hands—and she smiles. "You did it."

"For you," I tell her. "Now I don't have to worry about him running out of the house while I do this."

"Do what?"

No longer concerned about Summers, I place my hands on Journey's hips as I step in front of her and lift her onto the dining room table. Once she's on her butt, I place a hand on her chest and force her backwards until she's lying down. I claw at her clothes, pushing her shirt up so I can have access to her skin, and I kiss her stomach while pulling her pants off. The second she's naked from the waist down, I drop to my knees and plunge my mouth onto her pussy.

"Oh my fucking god," she blares as her back arches on the table. Her hands quickly find the back of my head and clamp down.

I suck her luscious clit into my mouth and let my tongue walk all over it at the same time. Journey moans above me and it makes my cock as hard as a rock, leaving me no choice but to pull it out and stroke it while I devour her. I keep going, eating her pussy like a last meal while I fist my cock simultaneously. Journey lifts her head and sees what I'm doing and it sends her reeling.

"Oh god. Evan ... Sir, you're so fucking perfect. Oh god watching you stroke your dick is going to make me come. Keep going. Keep stroking it. Oh fuck I'm close. Oh god. Sir, I'm about to come!"

"Come in my fucking mouth," I say, just before Journey explodes down my throat. When I feel her wetness ignite, I follow her lead, shooting ropes of cum all over the floor in front of me.

Both of us erupt into screams and convulsions as we fall into bliss together. We tremble and cuss as our orgasms slowly subside, and then we fill the room with the sound of heavy breathing. I lean against Journey's leg, panting as she stays on her back, her eyes closed as she sucks in air.

Once I'm settled, I look behind me and see Summers' dead body. The blood seems to have stopped flowing and his eyes have taken on a look of vacancy as he stares eternally into nothingness. I smile at him, wishing he was still conscious enough to know what Journey and I just did to celebrate his death. He deserves to know that we're glad he's gone, and that he did nothing to water down our love. We're unbreakable, and I'm glad he got to see it before he died. My smile is a mile wide, but a faint sound in the distance slowly melts it away.

Journey quickly lifts herself up onto her elbows, and her furrowed brow lets me know she hears it, too. "What is that?"

I scrunch my forehead as I turn to the window as if seeing outside will make me hear better, and tilt my head as both of us go dead quiet. I listen intently, slowly leaning back as the realization consumes my reality and darkens my vision. Panic fires to life in my heart when I turn around and find Journey wide-eyed. The sound is close enough now to be clearly understood by anyone who isn't dead.

Sirens.

thirty-seven
~ journey ~

"SUMMERS WASN'T BLUFFING."

I hear the words as they leave your mouth but I can barely believe them. After everything you've done to get us to this point, Summers has still gotten the upper hand on us. Even in death, with his throat viciously cut open, he is still winning and forcing us to scramble to keep up. He deserved every bit of pain that you inflicted on him, Sir. I love you for it, but thanks to his conniving I don't even have time to bask in it.

You don't have to say anything else for us both to know what we have to do next. The plan was to get Summers here and kill him before vanishing into the night. There was a brief second that I thought he might be smart enough to inform someone else that he was coming here to talk to me, but the warrant wasn't for me. IA wanted to question me, but cops were never out trying to track me down so I thought I was in the clear. I'm angry, frustrated, and panicked as I nearly knock the table over trying to get off of it. I pull up my pants as you yank at yours, and we dart into the bedroom to grab the last pieces of our lives that we want to bring with us. Summers may have thrown a wrench into the plan but it's not over yet. Only *we* know what's next, and if we still want it we have to go now.

By the time we exit the room with a backpack full of necessities in each of our hands and run for the garage, the sirens sound like they're right outside. What the fuck did Summers do? Let the entire precinct listen in on our conversation? Red and blue lights flash through the windows on the garage door as we jump into my car, and when our doors close, we stop. Our eyes meet and I can see the emotion in yours. This isn't how all of this was supposed to happen. There were never supposed to be uniformed officers right outside our house. We were never supposed to have to run. It was supposed to be a quiet departure into the unknown and neither of us is confused about what will happen when we open the door behind us.

I see the worry on your face and it sickens my heart. I know how this could end and so do you. What we do next will forever alter the rest of our lives, and that is not lost upon either of us. In order to make it out of here, we have to hope we don't die. We have to survive, and that is not guaranteed.

"I love you, Journey," you tell me, and I see a look in your eyes that I don't think I've ever seen before. It startles me to the point of silence and I just stare at you. It's not fear, but vulnerability. It's like you're making a choice with me right now, telling me that you know it could all end right here and you're okay with that because it is for me. If I never knew what true love looked like before today, I know that I'm seeing it now. This is you telling me that you love me so much that you're not only willing to kill for me, you are willing to die.

"I love you, Evan," I reply, suddenly immersed in my own emotion as tears fill my eyes.

You lean over the center console and kiss me hard on the lips, and my hands envelope your face. This may be the end, but I don't regret a single thing, and I wouldn't change a second of our time together. If we die tonight, it will all have been worth it because I got to experience love in this life. If you go, I go, and I'm ready.

After a final squeeze of my hand, I watch you sit up straight. The vulnerableness I saw a second ago drains from your face and is replaced by a furious determination. You grip the steering wheel with both hands before taking a deep breath, then you shift the car into reverse and press the button to open the garage.

Flashing lights climb beneath the door like long fingers reaching for us, and before the garage is even open all the way, the force of the car jolting backward nearly slams me into the dash. You step on the gas as hard as you can and send the car crashing into the bottom of the garage door. Metal and debris fly everywhere as we explode out of the house, tires screeching as we barrel over the mailbox just as one officer opens fire. Per usual, when one shoots, the rest of them do, and bullets suddenly begin pelting the car and flying inside. Glass erupts and falls on us like razor sharp rain. We both duck, but you manage to shift into drive and floor it again. The next thing I know, the gunfire comes to a stop and is replaced by the blowing wind.

When I look up, I'm shocked to see that we're on the road. Trees fly by us at a blistering speed and the engine screams as you gun it. The back window is completely shot out and there are bullet holes in the dash, but we're alive. We're still going, which means we still have a chance.

When I look at you, you are already looking at me, your eyes roaming my body like you're searching for clues.

"Are you hit?" you ask, still scanning me as if driving is no longer the most important thing.

"No," I reply, then my own sense of panic crashes into me and I begin searching your body for blood. "Are you?"

"No, I don't think so," you answer.

I'm flooded with relief. Somehow, you managed to get us out of the housing development without either of us taking a single bullet. But when I turn around a second time, I see the flashing lights coming for us once again.

"They're coming," I announce.

Now that you see that I'm not injured, your eyes focus on nothing but the road. "I know."

The car curves hard, barely making it out of the turn before we have nothing in front of us but the highway and the endless flow of traffic inhabiting it. You keep your foot on the gas and send us careening forward. Horns blare as you drive like a professional wheelman, weaving through cars as the police catch up to us and stay on our tail. Wind blows my hair everywhere and to my utter surprise, a smile crawls onto my lips. I look at you and see how focused and serious you are, and for reasons I don't care to understand, I fucking love it. I'm turned on by seeing you locked in for us, zooming past slower vehicles with no regard for anyone's safety but ours, and the fact that we're being pursued by cops—my former colleagues—makes it that much better. We really are like Bonnie & Clyde but new and fucking improved.

"You have no idea how much I fucking love you," I

tell you, and the way your mouth curls on the side while you keep your eyes on the road makes me wish we could pull over right now. All in due time, Sir.

Out of nowhere, a police cruiser with flashing lights pulls up alongside us. He's so close I can see him as clear as day through his window as he looks over at me with a menacing glare.

"I think he's going to try and ram us," I tell you, and just as the officer veers away before turning his wheel hard in our direction, you slam on the brakes.

I nearly fly through the windshield as we screech to almost a complete stop and the cruiser crosses right in front of us, missing by mere inches. The officer crashes into the car next to us, which hits the guardrail before flipping into the air and going into a full barrel roll. You, like a trained stunt driver, slam on the gas and shoot us forward as both the police cruiser and civilian vehicle roll into the middle of the highway and collide with other cars. As we rocket away, I turn in my seat and see fire ignite behind us. Someone's engine has blown up and the damage is so bad that no cars make it through the wreckage.

"Holy fucking shit!" I scream excitedly. "They all got stuck. We're fucking home free. Sir, we're home free!" I lean over and put my head out the window to make sure there are no helicopters hovering above us, and I see nothing but the twinkle of stars.

"Okay," you say after releasing a breath of relief. "We have to get off the highway and find another vehicle before they're back onto us."

"Good idea," I say, still beaming as you take the next exit.

Once we're off the highway, everything calms down. I breathe normally again. I'm in complete disbelief as it dons on me that it is all going to work. We're going to get away just like we planned. You did it, Sir. You made this happen. Once we switch vehicles, there won't be any way for them to track us. We just have to keep going. You are unreal. What would my life have been like if I didn't meet you? I can't even imagine and wouldn't dare to.

I reach across the console and place a hand on yours, feeling the strength in your fingers as you continue to grip the steering wheel like a vice. But when I touch your skin you finally relent. I take your right hand in mine and bring it to my lips, kissing it before placing it in my lap to hold, and I smile as I look out the window, ready for the moment when you stop and we take a vehicle to hit the road again.

As I look out my window with glee still energizing my racing heart, I see headlights in the side view mirror. They approach us so quickly that I don't even have time to frown before they're right on our tail, directly in your blindspot. Realization hits me like a shockwave.

"That's an unmarked car," I say, but I know it's too late. "Watch out—"

My words are cut short as the unmarked police vehicle performs a PIT maneuver. The front of their vehicle connects with the rear end of ours, sending us into a tailspin. Smoke and the smell of burning rubber fills the car as we slide sideways off the road completely and into a ditch, before slamming into a tree headfirst.

The engine stops as ringing in my ears begins, and when I look at you I can tell that you're hurt. You clutch your shoulder with a face full of agony, but the fight is still in you. I follow your lead as you look around, trying to gain a sense of what's happening behind us. Then you go for your seatbelt, removing it quickly before stopping completely, your eyes as large as the shining moon above us.

"What? What's wrong?" I ask as panic grips me by the throat.

Your hands slowly raise into the air, and I lean forward to look out your window to find a man standing next to you in plain clothes. He's holding a black nine millimeter to your temple.

"Move, and I'll blow your goddamn head off," the man says, before leaning down and looking into the car directly at me.

The ringing in my ears fades out and is replaced by the sound of my own blood rushing through my veins. I can't even think, let alone move, as I realize I'm staring directly into the eyes of Captain Saunders.

chapter
thirty-eight

"CAPTAIN SAUNDERS," Journey exclaims from the passenger seat, and I don't have to look over at her to know that she's totally shocked by this big asshole's arrival. I've heard the name before. He's her boss, so it's almost fitting that he would be the person to bring the chase to a close.

As I hold my hands in the air, my heart actually slows down. It's as if the organ knows that it's over and has accepted that there's no need to panic. We've been caught and I know there's nothing we can do about it. We had a good run, but the last thing I need is a trigger happy cop unloading on me in front of Journey. I don't want that as the last image she has of me in her head, so I stay still and listen as this fucker talks to us like we're his children.

"I never thought it would come to this," he says, squatting down next to my door. His gun is now pressed against my cheek, but his eyes are on Journey. "I vouched for you a lot, Monroe. I thought you were one of us, and I didn't believe any of the shit Internal Affairs told me they found in their investigation. I argued that they'd gotten it wrong—that you were a good cop who would never suppress evidence and protect a criminal. But here you are strapped in right beside him."

Journey swallows hard and I want to turn to her, but the second my muscles flinch Saunders shoves my face with the barrel of his gun.

"Don't even think about it, Godric," he tells me before looking at Journey again. "You know, I'm not even supposed to be here. IA told me to stand down. They wouldn't even let me bring you in for questioning or conduct the interrogation because it's their case, and I had to sit out pending my own investigation. Yeah, they're looking into the entire department now, but none more than me. They want to make sure I didn't help you in some way, so they shut me down and told me to watch from the fucking sidelines. But I'm a goddamn captain. No asshole from another agency is going to tell me what to do, especially regarding one of my own detectives.

"So I listened in on my scanner for news of your arrest, and lo and behold, there's a goddamn high speed chase taking place on Highway One. I had to see it for myself, so I jumped in my car and hit the roads adjacent to the highway, following the prompts on the scanner about your location. Then a fucking fireball shot up into the sky and I knew you wouldn't be stupid enough to just keep going straight if you managed to make it out of it. I saw you exit and knew I had to stop you.

"Now that we're here, we're doing this my way. It's almost like it was fate. IA should've never told me to stand down, now they're all locked up on the highway trying to block off traffic and check for casualties from the accident you caused. I should've been the one to bring you in anyways. So as much as it breaks my heart, this is fitting. Now please do me a favor, and don't do anything that is going to make me have to shoot you. I like you, Detective Monroe, but I know what you've done. I know they're accusing you of helping this piece of shit hide a body. I know they're accusing you of killing Detective Winter, and I know they found Summers with his throat slit just a little while ago. I can't imagine you doing those things, but I can imagine *him* doing them, and love will make people act surprisingly awful. You love him, but you shouldn't have to go down for the things he has done. Please don't make me kill you over him. Follow my instructions and this will end peacefully. Now both of you get out of the car with your hands where I can see them."

Saunders keeps his gun trained against my face as he opens my door for me from the outside, and I do as I'm told, keeping my hands in the air. It kills me to know that this is it. I exited the highway at the exact spot that this fucker was driving. He recognized Journey's car and took action. Maybe he's right about it being fate, because if it isn't destiny then I must have the absolute worst luck in the world to have escaped the highway directly in front of a police captain. Sometimes fact is stranger than fiction.

I try my best to think as I plant one foot on the ground to stand, hoping I can come up with some sort of idea to get out of this, but when the cold metal of a gun barrel is pressed firmly against your skin you know a simple twitch of his finger could end things. I have no options right now and it tears me apart. I'd rather go down fighting and get killed than let him humiliate me like this.

I slowly step out of the car one foot after the other, and the only time Saunders takes the gun off my flesh is when he has to reposition it as I stand up. It's also the only time he takes his eyes off Journey, who rustles loudly in the vehicle before stepping out herself. Unlike me, she doesn't put her hands in the air. When we make eye contact, her face is impossible to read. She looks both sad and audacious and I wish I could offer her some comfort.

Is she thinking the same things as me? Would she rather die fighting than go out side by side on our knees? In the garage we shared a look. It was like we were communicating without words, both of us resigned to the fact that tonight might be our last night together. We were ready to die together if it came to that, so when Saunders puts his hand on my back and pushes me toward the trunk of the car, I replay that moment in my mind.

"Put your hands on the trunk. Both of you," Saunders orders, his gun kissing a spot behind my ear.

I walk with my hands up and my eyes still on Journey. Her face pleads with me, begging me to do something. I can't let this happen to us. As much as I don't want her to watch me die, I'd rather that than have her watch me be pushed into the back of a cop car with my hands behind my back, knowing the next time she sees me will be in court or on TV, and after my trial I'll be gone forever. Even worse than that is the thought of her sitting in her own prison cell. She's a detective who would have to walk the same yard as some of the people she has put away. It'll be a fucking nightmare for her. I can't allow this.

"Hey," Saunders says, digging the barrel into my skin. "Don't get any cute fucking ideas Godric. Hands on the trunk and don't fucking move." I place my hands on the trunk. "Legs apart." Saunders kicks my feet to force them apart. "Do you have any weapons on you?"

I look at Journey, who pinches her lips together. Fuck. What is she trying to tell me? "No," I reply, but I remain focused on Journey's expression.

She shakes her head slightly, widening her eyes to let me know that she's speaking to me. I can't decipher it but I'm not an idiot. She doesn't want to go to prison any more than I do. She depends on me to be her protector and savior. It's my job as the love of her life and her Dom, and I am failing her right now. No, I can't let this happen. I can't fail at being what she needs me to be. I'd rather fucking die.

Saunders finishes frisking me and takes a small step back, then I hear the sound of him pulling out hand-cuffs, preparing to lock them onto my wrists. I know that once those cuffs are secure, I'm finished. If I don't act now it'll be too late to ever act again. This is it. It's now or fucking never.

Saunders reaches up and expertly fastens the first cuff to my wrist using only one hand, then pulls my arm behind my back to prepare to cuff the other. As he reaches up for my other arm, I throw myself backward and crash against him, knocking him down. I spin around with the cuff dangling from my right wrist just as Saunders hits the ground, landing on his back. My heart is jolted back into overdrive as I see the gun still in his hand. I know I have to get it away from him but he moves too fast. I take two steps toward him and he has the gun up and aimed at me before I can take a third. The shot echoes into the night air and I am spun around, bouncing against the bumper of Journey's car before hitting the ground next to the back tire.

Journey lets out a gut wrenching scream, but she

doesn't move. Honestly, I'm just glad I'm still alive to hear the sound of her voice. He didn't kill me, at least not yet. But unlike when we blasted out of the garage into a hail of gunfire, this time I am most definitely hit. The right side of my upper chest quickly feels like it has caught fire, and the flames are licking all the way down to my right elbow. When I look down, blood begins pooling out of a hole in my shirt as if on cue.

"No!" Journey screams.

"Don't fucking move, Monroe!" Saunders shouts from his position on the ground, his gun now aimed at an inconsolable Journey. She can't see me because I have fallen down, and she thinks Saunders shot me in the head.

"Little One," I call to her as I place my left hand on the gunshot wound. Journey continues screaming so I have to yell, which somehow makes the pain worse. "Journey, I'm okay. I'm okay, Baby. Everything is okay."

"Goddamn it, Journey, I said don't move!" Saunders shouts.

Journey doesn't listen, leaning over the edge of the car to make sure I'm alive.

"Oh my god," she cries, tears cascading down her face. "I thought you were dead. I thought he killed you."

"No, I'm okay," I reply, doing my best to console her as the pain intensifies. "I don't know for how long, but I'm okay. It's nearly a shoulder shot so I think ... I think I'll be fine. Don't worry, Baby. I'm okay."

Saunder stares at me with hatred in his gaze. "Lucky you," he says menacingly. "I guess I'm a bit out of practice. It's been a while since I was in the field. I was aiming for your heart."

Journey's eyes leave me and find Saunders, and I see the poison in her stare.

"You were trying to kill him?" she asks, her tone dripping with venom.

"You're damn right," Saunders doubles down. "And if you move, I'll do the same to you. Don't even shift an inch." He lifts himself off the ground while keeping the gun on Journey, before stepping forward and aiming it at my face. "From this distance, I've got a feeling it'll be over for you no matter how bad my aim has gotten. Now turn your ass over and put both hands behind your back."

With Saunders' help, I have no choice but to turn over and lay flat on my stomach. With his gun now pressed against the back of my head, all of my resolve leaks out of the open wound in my chest, and I let out a defeated sigh. Saunders has won. I'm completely out of moves and my eyes tear up knowing that Journey is watching as he places the second cuff on my wrist, leaving me completely helpless in front of the love of my life. I lay my face on the cold grass and close my eyes. The game is over.

When he's done with me, I hear Saunders stand up and turn to address Journey.

"Alright, Monroe," he begins. "Put your hands back on the—"

Pow.

A gunshot splits the sky, jolting my eyes back open and filling my chest with hysteria. I hear a body hit the ground behind me but I can't see it. Then, another shot.

Pow.

"What the fuck? Journey!" I scream at the top of

my lungs. "Journey! No! Journey talk to me. Baby, please talk to me."

"I'm fine," Journey says in a perfectly calm voice before squatting down next to me.

Keys rattle, followed by my handcuffs being removed. Journey helps me to lift myself up and turn around, and that's when I see Captain Saunders' lying on his back, his arms outstretched as if he has just been crucified. His eyes are closed, and two wounds in his chest leak profusely. I gawk at the body before looking down and finding a gun in Journey's hand.

"What the fuck?" I whisper as I see Saunders' gun lying in the dirt next to his corpse.

"I brought it in my backpack from home," Journey says. "When you got out of the car, I reached inside my bag and grabbed it before getting out, too. He was so focused on keeping his gun on you that he didn't even notice. I tried to communicate that to you when he was searching you and asked if you had any weapons. I guess I'm not good at speaking with my eyes."

I stare at her for a moment, unsure of what to do or think. She shot him. Her own captain. She shot him *twice* and now he's dead. Journey saved us. She saved *me*.

I want to laugh. I want to pull her into my arms and cry with her because I love her so fucking much, but I do neither. I just look at her.

"You're unbelievable," I say, shaking my head in disbelief. "I would love nothing more than to kiss you all over your body, but we have to go. Right now."

Journey smiles. "Don't worry, you'll get your chance once we're out of here. Let's go."

My violent Little Devil kisses me on the lips before

immediately going into help mode. She helps me off the ground. She helps me take everything from our car and put it into Saunders'. She helps me lift his dead body off the ground and helps me place it in the trunk of the car we're leaving behind, then she helps me climb up the ditch one last time and get into Saunders' car. She helps me clean my wound—which she describes as a through and through—with alcohol she finds in Saunders' trunk, and tells me to apply pressure for the bleeding She puts on my seatbelt for me and closes my door because the pain from the gunshot clearly has no plans of calming down, then she climbs into her captain's driver's seat and calmly steps on the gas.

When we drive away, Journey's old car is left in the darkness by the trees, and all we can do is hope that it's not discovered until morning. Sirens wail in the background as we depart, so we know we probably won't have much luck when it comes to keeping Saunders' body a secret, but hopefully we can get enough distance between us and them that it won't matter.

Driving the speed limit, we find our way to a Walmart parking lot and park in the furthest row from the building, as far away from their cameras as we can get.

"We just have to find one that's unlocked," Journey says. "Once I get one open I'll hotwire it and we're good to go. Just sit tight."

I nod, then marvel at the sight of my Little Devil going from car to car checking for one that's unlocked. On her third attempt, she gets lucky, pulling the door open to an older black Chevy with tinted windows. Perfect. We switch vehicles once again, and we're back on the road in no time.

"I can't believe we made it," Journey says, smiling from ear to ear as she heads toward the highway. "We hit

Wilmington, dump the car, walk to the train station, and take the train from Wilmington to Penn Station in New York. Once we're there, I'll reach out to an old friend I grew up with in Philly who moved to Manhattan who'll be able to loan us a car. Then we hit the road and never look back. We still have time to catch that train out of Wilmington, right?"

I sigh, finally in a comfortable enough position to relax a little. My wound is still killing me, but I'll live. We've had the wildest day of my lifetime, and now that it's over, it feels so good to just breathe. After everything we've been through, we've earned it. We've left bodies in our wake like we're professional killers, and I'm not bothered a bit. That's what you're supposed to do when you love someone the way Journey and I love each other. I've said it before and I'll say it until I take my final breath; our love is worth dying for, living for, and killing for.

I look at the clock on the radio and lay my head back against the headrest.

"Yes, Little One," I say, smiling as I close my eyes. "We have plenty of time."

epilogue

"WELCOME TO ALASKA."

I smile at the random woman standing at the exit as we disembark the ferry that brought us from Bellingham, Washington to Haines, Alaska, and I can barely believe what she just said. Alaska? We actually made it here? After everything we've been through, we're not still running? We're safe? Un-fucking-real.

It has taken us over a week to get here. Once we met with Journey's old friend from high school in New York, we took the used car they loaned us and drove it across the country, stopping only to sleep and refuel. Three days went by with us on the road before we finally made it to Bellingham. We had to wait an additional three days there so that we could procure fake IDs, before boarding the ferry and taking the Alaska Marine Highway System, which took another three days on the water before we made it here in Haines. Through each and every day of our stressful trip, I could feel the tension floating off of Journey like steam. She was anxious the entire time, knowing that we'd burned our lives to the ground before leaving the east coast. I'm sure she feels guilty about her part in all of this, but the truth of it is that we bear equal blame. I should've moved the body I buried months ago, and maybe Journey should have caught on to the fact that Summers was a mole planted by Internal Affairs to bring us down, but neither of us is perfect. If we had all of the information that we have now, we would have made different moves. Everyone knows the saying about hindsight.

As wild as the ride was, we have to focus on what is in front of us now. Somehow we made it all the way to Haines, Alaska from Philadelphia, and now we have to rent a car and drive to our final stop; Seward, which is another sixteen hours on the road. I'm sure Haines is a nice place, but it's too close to the edge of the state and a known stop for travelers using the ferry. We need to be somewhere small, a place that gives us culture shock because of how different it is from Philly. It's going to suck for a while, but that is what's required in order to evade the police that are surely on the hunt, hoping we pop up on their radar by being careless. I'll be damned if we make it this far and get caught now. So, Seward it is.

As we make our way out of the port and into the bright sun, I see mountains for the first time in my life and I know I've made the right decision. There was a moment where I was nervous about what I was doing, anxious about the way Journey had been hoarding lies. I was afraid I would have to ditch her because she couldn't be trusted, but she has proven herself.

It's more than just the E carved into her back. While that was a start for me, the way she shot her own captain sealed the deal, and watching her hotwire a car in a Walmart parking lot gave her extra points. She has shown her commitment, and I'm grateful for her. Now that it's all said and done, I couldn't imagine coming here without her. I would rather die. You don't go through the ups and downs we have, barely making it out the other side, and then just throw it away because one of us may have stalked the other. As crazy as that sounds, I can't deny that I followed Journey to her house and watched her through her window before we were together. She's not the only one who has embraced stalker vibes. I'm a lot of things, but I'm not a hypocrite, so we won't let that deter us. We will not be discarding what we've built. We will nurture it and make it grow from here.

Soon, my dark voice will return and I will be tempted to beat the shit out of someone, or maybe even cut someone open and hide the body. When that time comes, I will not give in. I can't allow myself to let the beast take over here, and for more than just myself. I have to keep it at bay because Journey needs it. She needs me to be her example just as much as she needs me to be her Dom.

In Philly, I told her that I didn't *really* care about her burning down the diner, but I did care about the lies. How could I be upset about her setting fire to an unoccupied diner when I have murdered multiple people? However, I will tolerate no such thing here. In Alaska, we will not burn down buildings, or bury people, or cut out tongues, or strangle anyone and make it look like a suicide. Our violent days have to be behind us, no matter how hard or dark it gets. I will provide the example. I will show her the way, and she will follow, otherwise we're as good as caught.

I hate that I had to leave Trey high and dry. By now, he has learned that I've murdered multiple cops and strangled a girl to death. I'm sure he has already lost his mind and had multiple conversations with the guys about me. I'm sure some of them have even alluded to the possibility of me killing Cain. It doesn't matter now. The last time we saw each other was the night I saved his life, and while he may not look back on our friendship as fondly as me, I'm glad he is still on this side of the ground. I won't get to attend his wedding, but at least he'll get to have one.

As I look back at Journey as she sits in the small waiting area watching me rent our vehicle, I smile at her because I know we're going to be fine. As long as we communicate the way we do when we're in the bedroom in the moments that we're not, we won't have any problems. We left a life behind that was riddled with bullet holes and fabrications, and we get to build a new one with all of our best parts and none of our worst. We get to live our dream here ... as long as we don't kill anybody.

"Where you headed?" the very large man behind the counter says after I hand him my new ID with the name Justin Jenkins typed on it.

"Seward," I say, leaning against the counter.

"Damn. That's a sixteen-hour drive," the man replies. "You sure you don't wanna fly?"

If I could fly without getting flagged for my warrant and arrested on the spot, I would've flown all the way there instead of taking the ferry, asshole.

I clear my throat and plaster on a fake smile.

"I'm sure," I reply, pushing the beast away.

The man shrugs and clicks away on his computer. "Okay then. Let's get you hooked up. You can return the vehicle at our branch in Seward. It's going to be the white Toyota in the third row. Have a safe trip Mr. Jenkins."

"Thank you," I reply, taking the keys.

I smile at Journey and she smiles back as she gets up and helps me with our bags. We exit the store and quickly find the Toyota, and Journey assists me with loading the luggage into the trunk, avoiding further damage to my wounded upper chest. Once we're all set, we climb in and close the doors. I don't waste time starting the engine and hitting the road, because this trip is already long enough. I turn the car onto the street and our new life rolls to a start as Journey and I reach across the center console and interlock our fingers together.

This is it, the beginning of our new life. No more bodies, no more lying, no more running, and no looking back. I don't even want to. I'd rather look at the mountains.

epilogue ii

~ journey ~

(Six Months Later)

I'm still not used to any of this, Sir. I know you said it would take some time, but six months should be enough, right? I guess not, but it's fine. One of these days I'll be used to my hair being this short. I'll get used to wearing clothes that look like I was made to be a hunter, fucking earth tones draped all over me. I'll get used to the old manager named Larry working in the office behind me. I'll get used to hearing customers bicker back and forth as they stand in front of the fishing poles while I watch them silently behind the counter, wearing a name tag that reads Shawna. I'll grow used to the fact that I went from being a detective to a cashier at Willie's Bait & Tackle in Seward, Alaska. I'll come to love it all one day, but it's going to take a miracle for me to get used to the constant smell of fish in this building. For that, I ask for your patience.

Seward is a port town dropped on the edge of the most gorgeous piece of land the world has to offer. It's stunning here, surrounded by water and lush green forest everywhere. The perfect place for two wanted criminals from the east coast to hide out for the rest of their lives. It has been six months now, but the night we arrived here feels like just yesterday—the night we killed two cops and evaded all the rest. They still want us in Philly. Desperately. You don't kill an Internal Affairs detective and a precinct captain without every officer in the area foaming at the mouth, wishing on every star that they could be the one to fill you with hot metal. They'll have to keep wishing, because we are long gone. The smell of fish is worth it.

In the weeks following our submersion into this new life, I continued to check in on the happenings at home. To no one's surprise, Detective Summers' and Captain Saunders' deaths were attributed to us before we even boarded the ferry in Washington. The following month, I found a report saying that the Andrea's Diner fire still hadn't led to any charges and was basically going cold in a hurry. Chad Swanson was never charged, and they never learned that it was me. Captain Saunders' wife and kids looked miserable at his funeral, but I've never been the one to be moved by sad faces. Even now, in my peaceful life up north, I'm unbothered by their tears. Saunders wasn't a bad guy, but he got in our way ... and he shot you. Some lines are never allowed to be crossed.

Over time, our names began to fade away. The Seventh Precinct went from press conferences about us, to articles on the front page, to seventh page stories in online-only magazines. I doubt that they've given up, but the truth that the public doesn't know is that people get away with murder all the time. Killers vanish into the night on a regular basis. We've simply added our names to the list of people who managed to get away with our crimes. Journey and Evan are no more, and will never return.

"I just don't know if I want the red one or not," one of the two men says, arguing with his partner about which fishing pole to buy. The way the two of them try to keep their voices down makes me smirk.

"For the love of god, Kaspian. Just pick one," the other man says.

"Fine. You're lucky I love you, Quin," the man replies, still looking between the two poles.

His partner rolls his eyes. "You pay and I'll wait outside."

Quin storms off, shooting a quick glare my way before pushing through the exit with a huff. Once he's gone, his friend approaches the counter with two rods in hand and a smile on his face.

"Find everything you need?" I ask, forcing the smile that I still haven't mastered.

"Yes, thank you."

I ring up the rods and tell the man I know as Kaspian the price, and he swipes his card without small talk.

"Thanks so much for shopping at Willie's," I say before handing him his new fishing gear. "Would you like to fill out an informational card for a chance to win a free trip to Las Vegas?"

"No thanks," Kaspian replies.

"Are you sure?" I ask, as I am required to do by the owner. "It includes hotel accommodations just a block away from the Luxor hotel."

Kaspian takes his rods but hesitates with a look of interest on his face. "Really?" I nod, still forcing the smile. "Well, in that case, maybe a little vacation would do us some good."

To my surprise, he takes the card and begins to fill it out, jotting down his name, address, and phone before handing it back to me. When I look at the name, I frown.

"Your name's Grayson?"

"Yeah," he answers with a polite nod.

"Oh. When you were by the fishing poles with your friend I thought I heard him call you Kaspian."

The man's eyes suddenly shift. His glare is menacing and I recognize something in it. It's like a mask has slipped just enough to show vibrant colors beneath the dull coat of gray he paints on every morning.

"No," he says, staring without blinking. "It's Grayson."

I quickly go from being caught off guard to being intrigued, and I smile.

"Okay," I say with a smirk. "Don't worry. My name isn't Shawna either."

Grayson gawks at me for a moment longer, his eyes bouncing from my name tag back up to my face. He tilts his head as the gears in his brain go to work, before slipping his mask back on and smiling.

"Have a nice day," he says.

"You, too. Thanks for shopping at Willie's."

Just as Grayson exits, a blonde woman walks in wearing a yellow top with blue jeans. She smiles at me as she enters and I return the favor the best I can. I truly hope that you're having an easier time smiling than I am, Sir. My fucking face is starting to hurt.

"Just this, please," the blonde says as she places a large case of bait on the counter. Her blue eyes glimmer as she maintains eye contact and beams at me.

"Great," I say, grabbing the bait to ring it up. "Would you like to fill out an informational card for a chance to win a free trip to Las Vegas? It includes hotel accommodations for two just walking distance from the Luxor."

"Wow. Okay, sure," the woman says. She jovially jots down her information and hands me the card just as the door opens again.

My heart vibrates with excitement when I look over and see you strut into the shop. You're dressed in your work clothes—a black and red flannel with dirty jeans—and you look incredible. Your beard is thicker than ever, and the muscle you've put on since we moved here makes you a brawny specimen totally worth gawking at. I'm so fucking lucky to call you mine.

As you walk in, the blonde walks out, and I smile as you hold the door open for her. She thanks you as she starts to squeeze past you, and I watch her blue eyes drink you in. She looks you up and down before speaking again.

"Thank you *so* much," she says in a voice much higher pitched than the one she used to speak to me. She keeps her eyes fixed on you, and I see the hope in her gaze. She wants you to notice her the way she has noticed you, but you don't. Your eyes find me and never leave. Your smile is only for me, and you let go of the door before she can even exit completely.

"Hey, Little One," you say as you approach me.

The blonde's eyes fall to the floor before she steps out and lets the door close behind her, and I come from around the counter to wrap my arms around your neck. You lift me up and spin me around like we haven't seen each other in years. Then we kiss, ignoring the fact that Larry is watching us from the office with a grin on his wrinkled face. I ignore the entire world for you, my savior.

"Did you miss me?" you ask when we pull away.

"Always ... Justin," I answer, mocking your new name.

"I missed you, too, *Shawna*. How's everything going today?" you ask as you look through the open manager's door and wave to the old man sitting at the desk.

I shrug. "It's fine. The usual, I guess. How is the house coming along?"

"Same as the last one. The guys on this crew are super laid back. I almost wish I switched from constructing commercial buildings to houses a long time ago. These guys are great."

It makes me so happy to hear you talk about how much you like your new coworkers. I know it's different. You build houses and apartments now with a new contractor, and I know you're comparing them to working with Trey. I'm sure you miss his friendship, and I still regret even thinking of taking him from you. Out of everything I've done, plotting on Trey is the only thing I truly regret. I would take it back if I could, but I'm overjoyed by the fact that you're settling in with your new crew here. Seeing you happy again makes my heart smile.

"That's always good to hear," I admit, to which you nod. "So what brings you by here?"

"I just wanted to stop by and see you on my way back from lunch. Like I said, I missed you."

I take your hand in mine. "You're so sweet, Sir. Here, let's step outside for a bit. I've been sniffing fish all day. Hey Larry, can you watch the front for me?"

Larry waves kindly as you and I exit the store and stand in front of your work truck.

"So, any plans for dinner tonight?" you ask, wrapping your arms around my waist and pulling me in close.

"I hadn't really thought about it, but I know what you could have for dessert," I answer playfully.

"Oh I know, too," you say. "I know we're still slowly building our money up since we left everything behind, but as soon as we're good again, I'm ordering a St. Andrew's Cross for the basement. The little toys are nice, but I miss the big furniture."

I smile wide. "You and me both. Don't worry, Justin, I'm willing to let you tie me up anywhere."

"Let me? What makes you think you have a choice?"

Both of us laugh devilishly before falling into another kiss that darkens the sun. The thing I love most about you and I is that it doesn't matter where we are. We can be in Philly, Alaska, California, or fucking Timbuktu. Our names can change from Evan and Journey to Shawna and Justin. I can cut my hair and even dye it, and you can grow a thick, long beard while gaining weight. None of it matters. We are always us. We always treat each other like our love is brand new. The bodies dropping are worth it for this. For us.

"Alright Shawna, I have to get going," you tell me, your forehead still connected with mine. "I can't wait to come home to you."

"Me either," I reply.

Then you kiss me and turn on your heel. The truck engine fires up and you give me a quick wave before backing out of the space. As you go, I pull out the informational card that I pocketed when you walked in, and I read the info on it while remembering the moment you held the door open.

Kay Knight, 1733 Clarion Loop in Seward, Apartment B.

"Sir!" I call you with a wave. You stop and lower your window with raised brows. "Never forget that I love you."

You smile at me with joy shining from your eyes because you know just like I do that we made it. Our plan worked and now we get to be happy. "I love you, too, Little Devil."

I watch you leave, standing in the same spot until I can no longer see your truck. Then I get in my car and enter an address into Google Maps.

I stare at the display as it works its magic, formulating a route to Kay Knight's address in only a few seconds, and estimating for me to get there in just ten minutes. I don't know if she lives alone or not, but it would probably be so easy to sneak in, or wait for her to come outside to take out the trash or retrieve something from her car. I could teach her not to stare at what is mine, and the thought of it makes my heart race.

I raise my hand and let my thumb hover over the word "Start."

But instead of pressing it, I back out of the app. I open my door and climb out of the car, and I go back inside. I pat Larry on the shoulder and thank him for manning the register for me, and I place Kay Knight's card in the pile with the rest of them, pushing it into the middle so that I don't have to look at it.

I think I've done enough damage with the secrets I've kept from you, Sir. We've run enough. We've killed enough. Here in Alaska, we have a chance to start fresh. There are no buried bodies in our backyard, and no buried secrets in my heart. We are free, and I won't let Journey drag old habits into Shawna's new life. Justin doesn't deserve to be lied to anymore than Evan did. So I'll keep my black thoughts at bay the same way you do, following your example and ignoring the voice in my head telling me to do things I know I shouldn't. Together, you and I will create a new dark and twisted world, just for the two of us. Dominant and submissive. King and queen. God and goddess. Justin and Shawna.

Untouchable.

acknowledgments

If anyone deserves credit for the existence of *How May I Please You*, it's my fans. The way you all showed so much love to *The Darkest Kink* drove me to write the book you just finished, which I hope you thoroughly enjoyed. This level of appreciation and attention is all new to me, so to get the sense that I need to continue a story that I didn't intend to have a sequel is a huge change of pace that I love. So, my first acknowledgement this time around will go to my fans. You made this book happen, and I appreciate you all so much for showing me how much *The Darkest Kink* meant to you. If you didn't, we never would've gotten *How May I Please You*. This one is definitely for you.

So much has happened since the last time I had a book published. *The Darkest Kink* came out in November of 2023, and at that time I was still in the military. I had just started to think about what life would be like outside of the Air Force, and just started really making concrete plans to become a full-time author. Admittedly, I never took this job as seriously as I should have because I always had my military paycheck. I never needed my books to sell enough to pay for my lifestyle, but as the end of my military career drew to a close, I knew I needed to change things up. So, I started treating my books and my life as an author like the business it is instead of the hobby it was, and nothing has been the same since.

As crazy as it is for me to type this out; after twenty years and eleven days on active duty in the United States Air Force, I am now officially retired. I'm also officially a full-time author. The books I've published and the fans I've earned made all of this possible, and it makes the publishing of *How May I Please You* that much more special. It's the first book I'm publishing as a civilian. My next book will be the first one I've written from beginning to end as a civilian. I'm in a world of firsts, and while it's brand new and a little unnerving, I absolutely love it. I've earned this freedom with my hard work, and we're only going up from here. Way up!

As I dive deeper into this life of literature, my circle surprisingly has become smaller. I'm very particular about my writing, and super sensitive when I'm in the creative process, so I don't allow a bunch of people to be involved in what I'm doing. The only person who is a constant and has been all these years, is the love of my life. My wife, Isabel Lucero, has always been the rock that I lean against when I feel like I'm struggling to stand on my own, and I'm eternally grateful for all of her guidance, wisdom, and friendship. Baby, you're the only true friend I have. I'd be nothing without you, and I can't imagine a world where I exist without you in my life. I love you so much. Thank you for always being here.

Thank you to Shauna and Becca at The Author Agency. This is our second project we've worked on together and it certainly won't be our last. Thank you for always being ahead of the game and staying on top of things leading up to this book release. I know for a fact that *The Darkest Kink* would not have been the success it was without your help, and I know the same will be true for *How May I Please You.*

I know I don't make life easy for you, Ena Burnette, but I'm so glad to have you as my agent these past couple of years. The tropes I write make publishers and companies shiver, but you go to bat for me anyway. Thanks so much for your continued efforts and support.

Thank you so much to my beta readers for this book: Sierra, Jasmine, Michelle, and Roxanne. It can't be overstated just how sensitive I am when I'm in the creative process, but you all were such a huge help and I appreciate all of your input. Sorry if I get weird.

Lastly, I'd like to shout out to the organizers and volunteers of every book signing I have attended and will attend. Signings are now a major part of my life as I realize and lean into the fact that writing and selling books is what I do for a living, and I absolutely love getting to meet my fans face to face. Thank you so much to every staff member of Indies Invade Philly, ApollyCon, RomaniConn, Authors in the Bluegrass, BRAE, Book Harvest, and RARE. We're going to have so much fun together!

author's note ii

At the end of *How May I Please You*, we see Evan and Journey now living their new lives in Seward, Alaska. Journey/Shawna is working at Willie's Bait & Tackle, and she sees Kaspian and Quin having a little debate by the fishing rods. When Kaspian comes to the counter, he doesn't write the name Kaspian on the informational card Journey hands him. Instead, he writes the name Grayson.

If that little tidbit of information piqued your interest, here is where you learn the intention of inserting Kaspian and Quin into the story. Those two have quite the backstory of their own, and if you haven't already done so, I'd like to invite you to dive head-first into chapter one of an absolutely unreal M/M dark romance, written by a magnificent author, who just happens to be my wife, Isabel Lucero.

Turn the page to find out so much more about Kaspian and Quin in their story ... Dysfunctional. I hope it inspires you to find the novel and give it a well-deserved read.

dysfunctional by isabel lucero

Chapter One

He doesn't think anybody's watching, because he's used to being the stalker. He's too cocky. Too sure that nobody will notice what he's doing. I see him, though.

In the corner booth of The Perfect Blend—a local coffee house in Soledad Square Vermont, I peer over my newspaper and watch as the man smiles charmingly at the waitress as she delivers his order. It's a plain black coffee, because he thinks anything else would be too memorable. However, almost nobody orders plain coffee, so he stands out more than he thinks he does.

When a woman sits at a table across from him, I know that it's her he has his eye on. She's blonde, pretty in an average way, and young enough to be naive.

He's pretty good, not doing too much to be obvious. He doesn't look up from his sketchbook for almost three minutes, focusing on whatever he's drawing while sporadically running a finger under his bottom lip. When he does look up, his eyes land on her, move to his book, then he does a double-take. The girl's eyes were already on him, so she gives him a shy grin when he locks onto her the second time.

His lips turn up on one side as he runs a hand through his hair in a boyish way before going back to drawing. He plays this game well. Show enough interest, pretend to not be a predator, and get your prey to come to you.

Once the girl's coffee is delivered, she takes a few sips, her eyes constantly dancing toward the handsome man in front of her. With half the drink down, she finally gets up and makes her way to his table.

I should warn her—get up and intervene. Instead, I settle in and watch how this plays out.

She creeps over, like she doesn't want to startle him, but he knows she's coming. He anticipated it. He jolts, though, pretending to be scared, and then they share a laugh before he offers her the free chair at his table. She gestures to his sketchbook, and he hesitantly displays it to her. Her hands go to her lips, her mouth ajar, shocked at his apparent talent. The man closes the book and hugs it to his chest, playing modest and shy. They talk for another thirty minutes before he gets up, glancing at the watch clasped around his tattooed wrist. She watches him, expectantly, waiting for him to ask for her number, maybe a date. He puts money on the counter and leaves, the bell ringing above the door. She looks disappointed until thirty seconds later when he appears right outside the storefront window, scratching his tilted head as he gazes back at her with a crooked smile.

She gets up and meets him outside, and once again they share a laugh before he jerks his thumb over his shoulder. She nods, her grin wide, and they take off together.

I shake my head, sighing as I put down the paper. The waitress left my check several minutes ago, so I leave a ten on the table and get up to follow them.

Unaware, like every other person in this quiet, safe town, they amble down the cobblestone road oblivious to the killer among them. In this case, there's two. Now, I don't have proof of what this man does with these women, but considering I never see them reemerge after he's set his eyes on them, I can only assume he does away with them in a permanent fashion.

It's not like I have much room for judgment. My moral compass is broken beyond repair, but this man seems to solely focus on women, and I can't help but wonder why. Color me intrigued. I have to know more because I've never met another person like me.

I first got wind of this guy a couple months back when I noticed him spending time with a woman who worked at the convenience store I frequent to grab my cigarettes. She'd take her breaks to eat with him in the small food court area, then one day, weeks later, she no longer worked there. After that, I started paying closer attention.

The second woman was someone who went to the community college. He conveniently ran into her in a library, like this crazy motherfucker reads books. Not to say that just because he's covered in tattoos, has a piercing through his nose, and occasionally has black painted nails means he's not capable of reading. But unless it's a how-to on stalking, I don't see this guy spending much time with his nose in a book.

I saw him by chance, through a window as I was working outside, and then I kept coming back. He was there pretending to be consumed by The Handmaid's Tale when she noticed him. I expect it was the book that kept her away. She probably thought he was reading it for tips and ideas on how to abuse women. Not the best choice. So the next time we were all there, he was reading A Vindication of the Rights of Woman, which made my eyes roll to the back of my head. Trying too hard. But it worked. She finally approached him when he took a break to take a sip of his coffee.

They met up a few more times, until they didn't. I tried following them on that last evening, not knowing it would be the final one, but of course, I got pulled away by a phone call from work.

I've made a few more visits to the library, wondering if she'd show back up, but she hasn't. Just like the convenience store girl. Neither have been reported missing, but I still feel the need to keep a close eye on him.

With a soft touch on the small of her back, he directs her into a red brick building. I hang back so as to not be too obvious. Scrutinizing the three story structure that curves around the corner, I wonder why he'd bring a victim to a somewhat busy hotel.

Thirty seconds after they disappear inside, I enter, my eyes roaming the lobby for their figures. I worry briefly when I don't spot them right away, but I recognize the plaid button up stretching across his back as they enter a hallway.

With quick, yet calm steps, I head in their direction. Someone touches my arm, attempting to ask me a question, but I hardly hear what she says and offer a polite, if not tight, smile. "I'm sorry. I'm late for a meeting."

If she's offended, I don't stick around long enough to see the hurt on her face. I dart around the corner and watch the blue and black plaid shirt vanish through a doorway to the right.

Is he killing them in a hotel? How would he get them out?

When I come across the archway he went under, I realize it's not a door to a room as I assumed. I push open the door to the bathroom, curious as to what I may see when I step inside, but I don't get far.

He shoves me against the white subway tiles that cover the wall, his forearm pressing into my throat.

"Why the fuck are you following me?"

Download Here

about the author

WS (Will) Greer is the author of bestselling novels such as The Therapist Series, Kingdom, Interview with a Sadist, and The Darkest Kink. He's also a USAF veteran since enlisting in 2004, and retiring after 20 years of service in 2024.

WS prides himself on being a man who writes spicy romance with the absolute best of them, while also understanding and appreciating that he is a guest in the house of romance that women built.

WS grew up in Clovis, NM, and now resides in Delaware, where he lives with his wife--bestselling author Isabel Lucero--and 3 kids.

more from ws greer

Thank you for purchasing *How May I Please You (The Darkest Kink #2)*! Please leave an honest rating and review wherever you purchased your copy. It would be very much appreciated!

Check out these other titles from WS Greer

Frozen Secrets (A Detective Granger Novel)
Claiming Carter (The Carter Trilogy #1)
Becoming Carter (The Carter Trilogy #2)
Destroying Carter (The Carter Trilogy #3)
Defending Her
Kingpin (An Italian Mafia Romance #1)
Long Live the King (An Italian Mafia Romance #2)
Red Snow (A Detective Granger Novel)
Madman
Boss
The Therapist (The Therapist #1)
Shameless (The Therapist #2)
The Fallout (The Therapist #3)
Toxic (The Therapist #4)

Kingdom
Interview with a Sadist
I Love to Hate You
The Darkest Kink

Want more from WS? Visit WS-GREER.COM for much more!

Made in the USA
Columbia, SC
23 December 2024